# THE MEMORY OF A KISS

He was going to kiss her, he decided as he gently nudged her back until she was pressed against the door. It was something he had been aching to do from the moment he had seen her again after so many years. All he had to do was catch a glimpse of her hair as she walked across the bailey and memories of the times they had been together flooded his mind. If nothing else, he needed to know if his memories were true, if she truly tasted as sweet as he remembered.

"Harcourt," she said, the tone of her voice hinting at the protest she was about to make.

"Hush. I but seek to discover if my memories are true ones."

Before she could ask what he meant by that, his mouth was on hers. The touch of his lips on hers sent heat flaring through her body so quickly, Annys gasped from the shock of it. . . .

# Books by Hannah Howell

## THE MURRAYS

Highland Destiny
Highland Honor
Highland Promise
Highland Vow
Highland Knight
Highland Bride
Highland Angel
Highland Groom
Highland Warrior
Highland Conqueror
Highland Champion
Highland Lover
Highland Barbarian
Highland Savage
Highland Wolf
Highland Sinner
Highland Protector
Highland Avenger
Highland Master
Highland Guard

## THE WHERLOCKES

If He's Wicked
If He's Sinful
If He's Wild
If He's Dangerous
If He's Tempted
If He's Daring

## VAMPIRE ROMANCE

Highland Vampire
The Eternal Highlander
My Immortal Highlander
Highland Thirst
Nature of the Beast
Yours for Eternity
Highland Hunger
Born to Bite

## STAND-ALONE NOVELS

Only for You
My Valiant Knight
Unconquered
Wild Roses
A Taste of Fire
A Stockingful of Joy
Highland Hearts
Reckless
Conqueror's Kiss
Beauty and the Beast
Highland Wedding

Silver Flame
Highland Fire
Highland Captive
My Lady Captor
Wild Conquest
Kentucky Bride
Compromised Hearts
Stolen Ecstasy
Highland Hero
His Bonnie Bride

**Published by Kensington Publishing Corporation**

# HIGHLAND GUARD

## HANNAH HOWELL

## ZEBRA BOOKS
### KENSINGTON PUBLISHING CORP.
http://www.kensingtonbooks.com

ZEBRA BOOKS are published by

Kensington Publishing Corp.
119 West 40th Street
New York, NY 10018

All Kensington titles, imprints, and distributed lines are available at special quantity discounts for bulk purchases for sales
promotion, premiums, fund-raising, educational, or institu-
tional use.

Special book excerpts or customized printings can also be
created to fit specific needs. For details, write or phone the
office of the Kensington Sales Manager: Attn.: Sales Depart-
ment. Kensington Publishing Corp., 119 West 40th Street,
New York, NY 10018. Phone: 1-800-221-2647.

Zebra and the Z logo Reg. U.S. Pat. & TM Off.

First Printing: March 2015
ISBN-13: 978-1-4201-3501-5
ISBN-10: 1-4201-3501-5

First Electronic Edition: March 2015
eISBN-13: 978-1-4201-3502-2
eISBN-10: 1-4201-3502-3

10 9 8 7 6 5 4 3 2 1

Printed in the United States of America

# Prologue

*Scotland, summer*

"She found ye a fine place to rest, David."

Harcourt Murray looked around the hill he stood on. The heather had begun to bloom, waves of soft purple broken here and there by jutting rocks. The rockiness of the hills had surprised him when he had first seen them up close five years ago for the large areas of green had hidden it. There was more than enough grazing land to satisfy a lot of livestock especially as the valley below was so verdant. Things he had paid little heed to when he had been here before.

"Aye, my friend, ye have a verra fine view from here," he said, and looked down at the headstone he stood next to.

He sighed and rubbed the back of his neck. Sir David MacQueen had been only three and thirty, a man in his prime. The fact that he was staring at the gravestone of a man so close to his own age was discomforting. It did not help to remind himself that many people died in their prime every year. David might not have been big and braw, had even once suffered what most men would have considered a debilitating wound, but he had been in fine health when Harcourt had last seen him five years ago. The memory of a smiling, gentle, educated man striding through the halls of Glencullaich would not allow Harcourt to easily accept the grave marker with David's name so precisely carved into it.

The man had saved his life, Harcourt thought and cursed. That should have been worth at least a few more years. The one thing the man had asked of him had been no sacrifice at all, which often only added to the guilt he had carried every moment of every day since he had walked away from the MacQueens.

Harcourt sighed and patted the top of the large stone. "Rest easy, dear friend. I will keep them safe."

"Getting late, Harcourt. They will be shutting those big gates soon, I wager. Do we wait until morning or go now?"

Gazing at Callum MacMillan, Harcourt weighed his options before he answered the man. He looked over the five men riding with him. One Cameron, Callum, two MacFingals, and one Murray, his younger brother who had arrived but a sennight before Harcourt had received the call for aid from Glencullaich. All looked like the strong warriors they were. It was a small force, but one that could easily intimidate those at Glencullaich. Unless things had changed drastically since he had left, he knew that David's people were not ones who would attack without provocation.

"We go in now, Callum," he told the younger man. "It is still light enough for them to see us clearly as we approach. E'en if the mon I sent to watch over David, his wife, and child isnae there, there should be someone who will recognize me."

He nudged his horse into an easy trot and headed toward the keep at the head of the valley, his companions quickly falling into formation around him. It was time to find out exactly what trouble had David's widow calling for his help. It was also time for him to face his past.

# Chapter One

Waiting was pure torture, Lady Annys MacQueen decided. She looked down at the small shirt she was mending, sighed, and began to pull out the appallingly crooked stitching. It was hard to believe Sir Harcourt would ignore her cry for help yet it had been a very long ten days since she had sent him the message. Ten days and not even the young man she had sent out with the message had returned. Annys prayed she had not sent young Ian to his death. She doubted Sir Harcourt would hurt Ian but the journey itself would not have been without its dangers.

"M'lady, mayhaps ye should have a wee rest," said Joan as she sat down beside Annys on the padded bench.

Smiling at her maid, Annys shook her head. "'Tis much too early, Joan. Everyone would wonder if I was ill and that would only add to the unease they all suffer from even now. I must try to be strong, and most certainly must at least always appear to be."

Annys wondered why her words made Joan frown. The woman was only ten years older than her but often acted in a very motherly way. Round of body and face, Joan did not even look her age yet she could lecture one like a grandmother. That frown often warned of a lecture being carefully thought out. Annys was not in a humor to endure one but also knew she loved Joan too much to hurt the woman's feelings by revealing that displeasure with some sharp words. They had been friends and companions, as well as lady and maid, since the day Annys had first come to Glencullaich to meet her betrothed.

"Ye are a lass," Joan began.

"I have come to realize that. I was slow to see it, but the breasts refused to be ignored." Annys was not surprised to receive a scowl from Joan that clearly said her maid was not amused.

"No one expects constant strength from a wee lass who has but recently buried her husband," Joan continued. "Ye are wearing yourself to the bone trying to be the laird and the lady of this keep. Ye dinnae need to be both. All here willingly heed the lady, have always done so, so trying to don Sir David's boots is unnecessary."

"And if I dinnae do it, who will?"

"Nicolas."

Annys thought on that for a moment. The man had arrived almost five years ago. He had claimed that he had spent enough time selling his sword for a living and now wished to settle in one place. David had welcomed the man with open arms, readily training him to lead the other, less well-trained men at Glencullaich. Fortunately, no one had complained or taken offense at how the stranger had so quickly moved into place as David's right-hand man. In truth, they had all welcomed his skills. She even had to admit that he had been immensely helpful since David's death.

"Mayhaps he can," she conceded. "He certainly has been most helpful thus far. Yet, I have always wondered why he ne'er just went home to Wales to settle."

"A long journey for a mon who says there is no one left there for him."

"True enough." Annys shrugged and tossed the little shirt she had yet to finish back into her mending basket. "'Tis nay that I dinnae trust him, for I do. I but puzzle o'er it now and then. I will try to put more of the work into his hands, but nay so much that it hinders his ability to keep the men weel trained. Their training cannae be allowed to lag."

"Nay, ye are right. It cannae." Joan nodded. "It is badly needed, sad to say. E'en weel trained as they are now, 'tis a constant battle to keep that bastard from trying to destroy us. If he sniffed out a weakness he would be on us like carrion birds on a fishermon's catch. Have ye heard anything from that Sir Murray yet?"

"Nay. I begin to fear that I have accomplished naught but to send poor young Ian to his death."

"Och, nay, m'lady, dinnae allow that fear to prey on your mind. Ian kenned the risks and he is a clever lad, one who kens weel how to slip about quietly and hide weel when needed. There are many reasons one can see for why he hasnae returned yet. Many. And a sad fate is but one of them."

"True."

And it was true, Annys thought. It was simply a truth she had a difficult time clinging to. Ian had come to the keep as a young boy, orphaned when the rest of his family had died in a fire, frightened, and painfully shy. It had taken a while, but by the time she had come to live permanently at Glencullaich as its lady, he had blossomed. Still sweet, still quick to blush, but settled and happy. He had fallen into the role of Glencullaich's messenger as if born to it, but he had never been sent on such a long journey before.

"M'lady!"

Annys started as the shout from the door yanked her out of her thoughts and she stared at the tall, too-thin young man who had burst into the solar. "What is it, Gavin? Please dinnae tell me there is more trouble to deal with. It has been so blissfully quiet for days."

"I dinnae think 'tis trouble, m'lady, for Nicolas isnae bothered." Gavin scratched at his cheek and frowned. "But there are six big, armed men at the gate. Nicolas was going to open the gates for them and said I was to come and tell ye that."

"I will be right out then. Thank ye, Gavin." The moment Gavin left, she looked at Joan. "How are six big, armed men nay trouble?"

"If they come in answer to your message?" Joan hastily tidied Annys's thick braid. "There, done. Now ye look presentable. Let us go out and greet our guests."

"Guests dinnae come armed," Annys said as she started out of the room, Joan right at her side.

"They do if they come in reply to a lady's note saying 'help me, help me'."

"I didnae say 'help me, help me'."

"Near enough. No gain in talking on it until we actually see who is here."

"Fine but I did nay say 'help me, help me'."

Annys ignored Joan's soft grunt even though she knew it meant the woman was not going to change her mind. She stepped out through the heavy oak doors and started down the stone steps to the bailey only to stop short before she reached the bottom. The man dismounting from a huge black gelding was painfully familiar.

Tall, strong, and handsome with his thick long black hair and eyes like a wolf, he had been a hard man to forget. She had certainly done her utmost to cast him from her mind. Each time he had slipped into her thoughts she had slapped his memory away. Writing him that message had brought his memory rushing to the fore again, however. Seeing him in the flesh looking as handsome as he had five years ago told her that she had never succeeded in forgetting him. Annys began to regret asking for his aid no matter how badly they needed any help they could get at the moment.

She fought to remind herself of how he had ridden away from Glencullaich all those years ago without even a quick but private farewell to her. It had hurt. Despite knowing it had been wrong to want that private moment to say their good-byes, despite the guilt that wanting had stirred in her then, and now, she had been devastated by his cold leave-taking.

Then, abruptly, his gaze locked with hers and every memory she had fought to banish from her mind came rushing back so clearly and strongly that she had to fight to stand straight and steady. Annys cursed silently. It was still there. The fascination, the wanting, was all reborn beneath the steady look from those rich amber eyes. This could become the biggest mistake she had ever made in her life.

Harcourt looked at Annys and his heart actually skipped a beat. He would have laughed if he was not so filled with conflicting emotions. Such happenings were the stuff of bad poetry, the sort of thing he had always made jest of. Yet, there he stood, rooted to the spot, frantically thinking of what to say and how to hide the tangled mass of emotion that was nearly choking him. He nodded a greeting to her and watched her beautiful moss-green eyes narrow in a look that did not bode well for an amiable talk later. Talking was not what he was thinking about, however. He was recalling how soft that long blood-red hair of hers was, how warm her pale skin felt beneath his hands, and how sweet those full lips tasted. That was a memory he needed to smother and fast.

"Are matters as bad as young Ian indicated?" he asked Nicolas, and inwardly winced when, out of the corner of his eye, he saw Annys cross her arms under her breasts.

"Aye," Nicolas replied. "We can have that talk with her ladyship in attendance as soon as we get all of you sorted."

Harcourt nodded and turned his attention to seeing to the matter. Once the horses were taken care of, their supplies unloaded and carted away, he knew the time had come to actually face Annys. He took a deep breath and started toward her where she still stood on the steps only to come to a halt when a small child rushed by him and ran up to pull at her skirts.

"*Maman!* Ye got us more soldiers."

"I did, Benet. I thought it might help stop all the trouble we have been having."

The moment the child turned to look at him, Harcourt clenched his fists at his side. The boy's eyes were a match for his own. Bright amber eyes watched him closely and Harcourt fought against the urge to shout out his claim to this child. He had given up all rights. It had been the debt owed for his life. He could feel the eyes of his companions fixed upon him though and knew he would be facing a lot of questions.

It took every ounce of strength he had to start walking again. He stepped up until he was standing just below Annys and the boy. It was easy to read the fear in her eyes. Young Benet's eye color was not an exact match with his and could be attributed to the tiny gold specks in her eyes or just a different shade of the brown David's eyes had been. The boy's hair was black but so had David's been. As long as he did not say or do something to give the secret away, all would be fine. Yet, Harcourt knew it was going to be a long hard battle not to reach out and claim his son.

"M'lady," he said and took her hand in his to brush a kiss over her knuckles.

That tiny soft hand trembled slightly in his grasp and his body reacted to the sign that she was not as indifferent to his presence as she appeared to be. Harcourt knew it would be unwise to try to begin an affair with her but he was not sure he was strong enough to resist if she gave him even the smallest hint that she would welcome his attention.

"Sir Harcourt," she said and nodded as she almost yanked her hand out of his grasp. "Where is Ian?"

"He was injured in his travels. Nay badly, but I thought it best if he remained at Gormfeurach for a while. He is being given the best of care."

"Thank you for that. I was most concerned when he did not return." She turned slightly and took Benet by the hand. "Shall we go to the hall where you can quench your thirst and have some food while we talk?"

Annys fought to keep from racing into the keep, putting as much distance between her and Sir Harcourt as she could. The touch of his lips on her hand had nearly undone her hard-won composure. It had been five years since she had felt his touch yet the moment his flesh met hers, even in the innocence of a proper greeting, her mind had gone back to those nights by the burn.

Guilt left a sour taste in her mouth. David was barely cold in his grave and she was allowing herself to weaken at the touch of another man's hand. What had happened between her and Harcourt had been wrong, even if it had been condoned by David. She nearly laughed. Condoned? It had been meticulously arranged. David had been the sweetest, kindest man she had ever known but he had also been a man who would not hesitate to do whatever was needed to get what he wanted. He had wanted a son.

She glanced down at Benet who kept looking back at the men following them into the keep. Until she had seen Harcourt again, she had not allowed herself to even think on how much Benet looked like the man. All she could do was pray no one else noticed, especially since there had been the faintest similarities in coloring between David and Harcourt. She would also have to be very watchful for even the smallest possibility that she or Harcourt were giving the secret away in how they treated the boy.

"M'lady," Joan whispered in her ear as they entered the hall and pulled away from the men who went to wash their hands, "it is not as clear to see as ye think it is."

"I pray ye are right, Joan."

"I am. I only see it because of what I ken and I have ne'er heard a whisper that would tell me anyone else here kens the truth or that those who may would e'er say a word. So, ye just be careful in what ye say and do and all will be weel."

Annys wished she had the confidence in that that Joan had. The looks on the faces of the men who had come with Harcourt, looks the men were doing a pitiful job of hiding, told her that they noticed something already. She prayed Harcourt would have a stern word with them all.

"Allow me to introduce my companions, m'lady," Harcourt said once they were all seated. "This is Sir Callum MacMillan, Sir Tamhas Cameron, Sir Nathan MacFingal, Sir Ned MacFingal, and Sir Gybbon Murray."

Annys nodded a greeting to each man as he was introduced. Two redheads, a brunet, and three raven-haired men. All handsome. All warriors. All tall and fit. It was not going to be easy to stop the maidens of the keep from seeking them out. They were, however, a treasure of skill and strength she could not turn away, no matter how much she worried over the chance that her secret might come out.

"I thank you all for coming," she said. "Please, eat, drink, and we can talk once ye take the edge off your thirst and hunger."

The only conversation that ensued as the men ate concerned the journey they had taken. Gormfeurach was not as far away as Annys had thought, although far enough when one half of the partners in a huge secret were concerned. She ate very little, her stomach tied in knots, as she struggled to push aside all worry about what might or might not be exposed by Sir Harcourt's presence. The people of Glencullaich needed these men. They had to take precedence over all of her fears.

As she sipped her wine she glanced between Harcourt on her left and Nicolas on her right. Both were extraordinarily handsome men yet she experienced not one single twinge of womanly interest when she studied Nicolas. Hair the color of dark wood, gray eyes, and a strong body were all things that could please a woman but, although she did like the look of him, nothing else stirred inside her. Harcourt stirred everything inside of her and not all of it was good. The warmth was side by side with the chilling fear of secrets being uncovered. The need was side by side with the guilt for having given in to it even with the urging of her husband. The pleasure of seeing him again sat side by side with a lingering anger over the way he had left her. Somehow she had to clear her heart and mind of all the confusion.

Annys noticed that her son was chatting merrily with the man called Callum, a handsome man with his green eyes and copper-colored hair. Sir Callum showed no sign of being irritated by her son's chatter even though it kept interrupting his meal. The fact that Benet was so at ease was surprising, however, as he usually took a long time to warm up to someone, especially when that someone was a man so much bigger than he was. There was no doubt in her mind that Sir Callum was a skilled warrior yet it was clear he had a magical way with children.

Sir Gybbon Murray's relationship to Harcourt was clear to see even though his eyes were blue. That man kept looking between Harcourt and little Benet in a way that made her nervous. She also noticed that the looks he gave Harcourt not only demanded an explanation but held the gleam of deep disapproval. Since, from all she had heard, men had no real problem scattering their illegitimate offspring around the world with no thought and few penalties, it puzzled her.

Sir Tamhas Cameron sat between the two Mac-Fingals, the three of them jesting and eating heartily. There was a strong family resemblance between the two MacFingals despite one having light brown hair and the other black. They certainly both had the same smiles, ones touched with a hint of recklessness and wickedness. Sir Tamhas appeared to be the most staid of the three men although his green eyes often shone with laughter. She envied his red hair, the color of a fox pelt. Those three she knew would be the ones to watch most carefully around the maidens of the keep.

Catching Joan's gaze where she sat at the far end of the table, Annys glanced toward the three and then slanted a glance toward the four young women lurking in the doorway to the kitchens. The way Joan's mouth thinned and she glared the girls into retreating back into the kitchens told Annys that she could leave that concern safely in Joan's hands. She just wished it would be as easy to leave the rest of her troubles in other hands.

Annys silently sent an apology up to David. He had

# Chapter Two

"So what is this danger ye fear is stalking Glen-cullaich, m'lady?"

Harcourt relaxed in his seat, his belly pleasantly full of good food, and sipped at the strong wine he had been served. He could see that his abrupt question had startled her, but only for a moment. She recovered her composure with an admirable quickness. There was now a look in her eyes that told him she was very carefully considering her reply as she signaled a young page to take Benet from the hall. He wondered what she wanted to hide. Or why she would bother to hide anything. She had sent for him after all.

"Did Ian nay tell you?" she asked and clasped her hands together in her lap in what she prayed appeared to be a stance of complete calm.

"Not in much detail, nay. Ye have someone troubling you with petty intrusions, thefts, and some threats. Since such things could be seen to weel enough by the men ye have here, I am thinking ye fear the trouble will soon grow far more severe."

Out of the corner of her eye she saw Joan wave away the women who had slipped back inside the hall and was pleased to see them go. Her people were increasingly uneasy. The things she had to discuss with Sir Harcourt would only make them more so.

"Our trouble has a name," Annys said. "Sir Adam MacQueen, cousin to my late husband and a man who would have been the heir to Glencullaich if David had had no son."

"But David did have a son." Harcourt was not surprised at how difficult it was to calmly name David as Benet's father.

"Adam doesnae accept Benet as David's son. He doesnae believe a woman should be acting as laird here, either. It is his loudly stated opinion that the lad needs a mon to tend to his inheritance. That is, if the lad actually has one. Adam believes he should tend Benet even as he tries to prove Benet is nay the heir yet doesnae see why that is ridiculous. I am nay sure his opinion on who should be acting as the laird here would change e'en if he finally has to accept that Benet is David's heir and naught will change that. Naught will change his mind that it is wrong for a lass to act as a laird either."

Harcourt shrugged. "A complaint we have heard before," he said and his men nodded. "'T'will get the mon nowhere. Did David nay name some mon to stand for ye then?"

"He named Nicolas Brys as his second several years ago," she replied and nodded to the man seated on her right. "Then, when David began to grow so ill, an illness he couldnae shake free of, he named Nicolas as the mon he wished to oversee the protection of Glencullaich as weel as Benet. He also stated the wish that it be Nicolas who trained Benet in all a laird must ken to be strong enough to protect his lands and people."

"And Sir Adam disagrees with that as weel?"

Annys nodded. "Quite vehemently. At first he attempted to have Nicolas removed but that did not work. It is verra difficult to get the courts to ignore the stated and witnessed last words of a laird. E'en those in power who leaned to Sir Adam's side didnae want to do that for they wouldnae want anyone to think it could be done to their wishes after they are gone. After that failed, he made the claim that Benet wasnae David's true son. He hasnae succeeded with that, either." Although she hated to reveal Sir Adam's latest game, Annys knew she had to tell Harcourt everything. "He now spreads the tale that I killed David."

The way the men all grew still and stared at her made Annys both angry and embarrassed. It was hurtful enough that not everyone Adam voiced his accusation to had shrugged it aside as nonsense. She did not like to think that these men, ones who had come to help her, might now be suspicious of her. It embarrassed her to repeat Adam's false accusations. It angered her that anyone would even briefly consider that such accusations might be true, and that anger grew stronger every day. Unfortunately, so did her fear that Adam may have finally found a way to be rid of her and take Glencullaich, perhaps even be rid of her son for, as a convicted murderer, she would not live long.

"Is anyone listening to him?" Harcourt asked after glancing at his companions and seeing only a recognition of the threat such accusations carried.

"A few." She hastily took a drink of cider, attempting to ease the dryness of fear from her throat. "David was kenned weel by many in power, and weel liked. He didnae die in battle or"—she smiled just a little, knowing it was mostly bitterness and not humor that curved her lips—"in some monly accident. He died in his bed like a sickly old mon." She shook her head. "In the end, he bore a likeness to one as weel."

"A wasting sickness?"

"Who can say? David was ne'er truly robust yet he was ne'er what ye would call sickly." She pushed aside a sadness that always twisted her heart when she thought of her husband's slow, painful death. "I cannae say what afflicted him nor could any of the others I sent for in the hope of finding some help, some cure, for him."

"But nay one of those fools kenned what ailed the laird or how to help him," said Joan. "Most often they just wanted to purge the poor mon or bleed him. That was the verra last thing our laird needed. He was naught but skin and bone in the end."

Annys reached out to pat Joan's hand, clenched tight on top of the table. Joan had grown up with David, the daughter of his mother's maid. He had been as much a brother to her as he had been her laird and Annys knew the woman grieved for him as deeply as she did.

Harcourt frowned. "It sounds akin to a wasting sickness."

"And so it may have been, yet I remain too uncertain to name it so," Annys said.

"What were the signs of his illness?" asked Sir Callum.

"The one most clearly marked were the pains in his belly," she replied. "He couldnae keep food down. E'en the plainest of broths would have him retching. Then it would pass for a wee while and we would think he was regaining his health, only to have it begin all over again. And, aye, 'tis true that purging and bloodletting were the worst things to do since he was so weak, yet there were times, after a purging, that David recovered for a while."

"Ne'er after a bleeding though," said Joan.

"Nay, that ne'er seemed to help him," agreed Annys.

"What else?" asked Sir Callum. "Was there more?"

The intent way the man watched her as he asked his question made Annys wary even though she could see no hint of condemnation or accusation in his expression. "David would complain about burning pain in his hands and feet, at times e'en in his throat, although all that miserable retching could weel have caused that."

"He began to lose his beautiful hair," Joan murmured.

Annys nodded. "And his skin would be covered in a rash and then it would peel away. The most frightening times were when he couldnae move at all, but that, too, would then pass. In the end he had such fits it would take several of us to hold him down and e'en then it wasnae easy. Ye must see how difficult it is for us to put a name to the disease which ended his life. There are too many things it could have been and, just when one thought one kenned what it was, there would be something that didnae fit."

"There is one ye may nay have considered," said Sir Callum. "Poison."

The blood drained from Annys face so quickly that she became dizzy and welcomed Joan's steadying hand on her arm. "I didnae poison my husband."

"Of course ye didnae," said Sir Harcourt. "That isnae what Callum was saying, is it, my friend," he said to Callum, giving the younger man a hard look.

"Nay," Callum said quickly and smiled faintly. "I didnae say ye did it, m'lady, or e'en considered that ye had, but I do believe the mon may have been poisoned. 'Tis an old poison, if I am right in what I now believe, and one that has been used before at least once within my own family. It was but a few years ago that a distant MacMillan cousin of mine was poisoned by his wife's lover. The signs of his illness sound verra much akin to the ones your husband suffered."

"Did he survive?" Annys asked.

"Aye, though it was a verra long time ere the mon healed. But, with care, he was soon strong enough to see his wife and her lover hanged."

Annys winced at his hard words but understood. Those people had tried to murder one of his kinsmen. She also agreed with the punishment. It was just one that always made her shudder just a little. She had seen one hanging in her life, stumbled upon it by accident while wandering the streets of a village near her home. It had been a spectacle that had held her horrified attention despite how sick it had made her. It was not an easy way to die.

"How did ye ken that was what was wrong?" she asked.

"Caught the one putting it into his drink. He, too,

would seem to become better now and then. Most often after a hard purging. I think that clears out a great deal of the poison thus starting a cure. Then the one with the poison just doses them again."

"Which means it would be someone close enough to dose his food or drink."

It was a horrifying thought. That meant that someone in the keep, one of the people they trusted, had murdered David. It was hard to think that anyone at Glencullaich would do so. David had been well loved by his people, respected and honored. She could think of no one who had ever shown any sign of being angry with him or hating him.

"I have no idea how we would e'er discover who may have done it," she said as she rubbed her forehead. "David was beloved. I cannae e'en think of who could be persuaded by anyone to do it. And, e'er ye ask, Sir Adam was ne'er here in any way that would have given him the opportunity to do it."

"It is just something one should consider, I think."

"Aye," agreed Harcourt. "Sad to say there can be many a reason for someone to turn on their laird, e'en one as weel loved as David. They could simply be someone easily convinced of some lie or given some promise that made them do it e'en if they may have had regrets for their actions afterward."

Annys studied him for a moment, thinking on how careful he had been with his words. "Ye think it may have been some woman."

Harcourt sighed and gave her an apologetic smile. "Poison does tend to be a lass's weapon."

Considering the other ways there were to kill a man, she supposed he was right. There was something less intimate, less violent about poison. Women could be violent but they had the disadvantage of usually being smaller and weaker than a man. Poison required neither strength nor stature. Yet, again, she could think of no one who would do that to poor David.

"Could it not have simply been as we thought? A sickness, some kind of wasting illness we had just ne'er seen before?"

Sir Callum smiled. "It could be. It was just that the signs ye mentioned sounded akin to what my cousin suffered."

"And that means it would be wise to consider the possibility," said Harcourt. "Ye ken weel that there is one who wants what David had, who has always wanted it. He may nay have been close enough to easily do the poisoning himself, but there is always the chance he found someone within these walls who did it for him. Through lies, promises, or threats."

Annys nodded. "Ye are right. It would be wise to consider it. If only so that we keep a keen eye out for any hint that it is happening again."

"And to take some time to watch those who would have had the chance to do it," said Joan.

"Ah, Joan, I dinnae want to do it. I ken it, but it must be done. If that mon has convinced someone in this keep to do his sinful work for him then we need to find them."

"Now that David is gone there remains you and the lad in his way. He could decide to set that ally on either of ye."

That was the fear she had tried to ignore. It was foolish to do so. Ugly though it was, if there was even a small chance that someone inside Glencullaich helped Sir Adam, he could turn that person against her or Benet next. It was only wise to accept that hard truth and act to protect herself and her child.

"Agreed," Annys finally said. "Mayhap we shall be fortunate as someone will be so crushed with guilt they will simply confess. Then we will have them and Sir Adam."

"I will wish ye luck in that," said Harcourt and briefly raised his tankard in a toast before taking a drink. "Howbeit, I would like ye to make up a list of those who would have had the chance to slip some poison into David's drink or food."

Annys nodded and then politely excused herself. It was early to turn in for the night but she needed some time alone. Seeing Sir Harcourt again, realizing he could still stir a fire in her blood, and discovering that someone could have murdered David was all she could bear for now. She needed time to just be alone, to think about it all, and sort through her confused emotions.

It was not until she entered her bedchamber that she realized Joan had followed her. Annys told herself she had no reason to be surprised by that. The woman did act as her maid after all. Yet she had taken no notice of Joan falling into step behind her. She said nothing as Joan helped her prepare for bed. Sitting still before a fire while Joan brushed out her hair worked to ease a lot of the knots in her belly, however, and Annys was soon glad the woman had followed her.

"Dinnae let it prey on you, m'lady," Joan said as she sat down beside Annys.

"I dinnae want it to but I am nay sure I can stop it." Annys stood and moved to her bed, sitting on the edge so that Joan could lightly braid her hair for the night. "So much has happened today. Mayhap it is just that I am unaccustomed to so many disturbances in my life."

Joan laughed softly. "Weel, six verra handsome men coming in answer to your request for aid is certainly disturbing. It would be to any lass with blood in her veins."

"True and it will be verra hard to keep the maids in hand while they are here." She looked at Joan. "But ye ken why I find one of them more disturbing than all the others, aye?"

"He is as handsome as he was all those years ago."

"And looks so verra much like Benet."

"Only if ye ken to look for it." She patted Annys's arm when she saw the woman's look of doubt. "Truly. Our laird had black hair and brown eyes. And ye have that touch of gold in your eyes. Any other features that may match Sir Harcourt's willnae show for many a year yet. But, in truth, there is a strong similarity betwixt him and our poor laird. The mon is just bigger, stronger, than Sir David e'er was."

"Are ye just saying such things to ease my worries?"

"Nay. 'Tis the truth. Only if ye ken what we do can ye look and see it. If ye dinnae ken that he bred the lad, weel, then it isnae so clear to see."

Annys sighed in relief. "Good. That is a trouble I dinnae need."

"Nay, ye have enough to deal with now. I think ye should write to Sir Adam's sire and tell him what that fool son of his is doing."

When Joan stood up, Annys settled herself in her bed as she thought over that suggestion. "And how can I be certain his father isnae the one prodding him to do this?"

"Ye will ken it by what the mon says in reply."

"Ah, there is that. It cannae make matters any worse, I suspect. I will think on what to say. Sleep weel, Joan. I forsee a verra busy time ahead for us."

"If only because we have six big knights to feed and tend to."

Annys laughed softly and made herself more comfortable in her bed as Joan left. She thought on Sir Callum's suggestion that poison may have caused her husband's death, unable to banish the thought as she wished to. Having spent so many years at Glencullaich she found it hard to believe that anyone would hurt David. She did not even understand why Sir Adam would have done such a thing for it was not enough to place Glencullaich in his hands. There was still Benet standing between him and the laird's seat.

That thought chilled her to the bone. If she accepted, or even proved, that David had been murdered, then her child was in terrible danger. If Sir Adam could get to David then he could get to Benet. He could claim his hands were clean if accused of poisoning David for he had not actually done the deed. All he needed was a way to be able to claim the same thing when he struck at Benet.

Her growing fear for her child made it impossible to sleep. Annys got up and pulled on a robe. She moved into the small room where there was a door that let her go up on the battlements. A pang of grief went through her as she opened the door and heard the soft bell ring. David had been so pleased when he had arranged that warning to the men on the walls. It had allowed them some privacy if they chose to go outside at night. She had never appreciated it more than she did now.

Climbing the narrow stone stairs, Annys fought to calm her fears. She could find reasons for someone to betray them all by helping Adam rid Glencullaich of its laird. Yet, try as she would, she could find none for anyone helping him murder a small child. She simply could not believe any of the people she knew would be capable of such a heinous crime. If she did not convince herself to accept that possibility, however, she would be putting her son's life in danger.

Resting her arms on top of the wall, Annys looked out over the moonlit lands of Glencullaich. She had no trouble at all in understanding Sir Adam's greed for the place. It was too far from the border to suffer from raids, and too out of the way of the roads to the cities or the king's court to have to worry overmuch about an enemy force sweeping through. It was good land and well watered. A man would not have to work hard to have a very comfortable life here, a rare thing in Scotland. David had even managed to keep them out of any local feuds.

Sir Adam MacQueen was not a man to appreciate such things, however, she decided. He would settle into Glencullaich and immediately want more. He was also of a temperament to tangle the clan up in feuds with the neighboring clans. Yet, she could think of no way to get him to end his quest to gain hold of the lands.

"Weel, I could just kill the fool," she muttered.

"Kill who?" asked a deep voice from right behind her.

Annys squeaked in alarm and looked behind her.

She was relieved to see that it was Harcourt but also annoyed that he had frightened her. The way he looked at her as she stood there in her nightclothes swept both feelings aside, leaving her struggling to crush the warmth of welcome and womanly interest.

"Who do ye think ye should just kill?" he asked again as he stepped up beside her.

"Sir Adam." She looked back out over the land. "I dinnae think he will e'er stop trying to get his hands on Glencullaich."

"Nay," agreed Harcourt. "He willnae. 'Tis good land." He patted the wall. "With a good strong keep. And that has ye worried?"

"If your friend is right, then he has already killed David. The only one left standing between him and this land is Benet, a little boy. *My son.* Aye, I am worried."

"Good." He smiled at the way she frowned at him. "Then ye will be keeping a verra close watch on the lad and all who draw near him. I ken ye do now, just as any mother does, but ye have always trusted everyone in this keep, probably everyone in the clan."

"Aye, I do." She sighed. "Did." She shook her head. "I try to deny that my husband was murdered with poison yet it answers too many questions about the strange illness that took his life. I have seen most illnesses a mon can get and I had ne'er seen one quite like that. The learned men we brought in to help were uncertain as weel, although they did their best to hide that. I e'en ken most of the things that can poison one and what happens but ne'er that. The way it can be slipped into food or drink by an unseen hand is the most frightening. How does one fight that?"

"Weel, some kings have someone taste their food first."

Annys smiled. "Benet may nay like that. But it does give me something to think about. Mayhap his meals should be prepared only by one I completely trust until the threat to him has passed."

"And who would that be?"

"Joan."

"Of course."

Harcourt was finding it difficult not to touch her, to reach out and stroke the thick braid of hair hanging down her back, touch her soft cheek, or even just hold her small hand in his. He wanted her but knew it could be something that would only add to the troubles she now carried. The whole keep would know as soon as they became lovers. Even if that did not make everyone look more closely at Benet, it could weaken her position as lady of the keep, as the one acting in the stead of the laird.

"Why did I hear a bell?" he asked, trying desperately to get his mind off how sweet she smelled and how badly he wanted to pull her into his arms.

"Ah, David fixed that. I have always liked to come out here if I am too restless to sleep. He wanted me to be comfortable in doing so nay matter what I was clothed in." She blushed as she ran a hand down the side of her robe. "Some nights he would join me and we found it helped us sort out some problem to stand here looking at the stars and talking quietly. He wanted no one to interrupt those moments, either. So the men move away from this small part of the wall when they hear the bell."

"Clever. And have ye been able to sort out the problem that brought ye here tonight?"

"Aye. I must accept that someone in this keep helped kill my husband and may be convinced to try and kill my son." The moment she said those words she knew she had finally accepted that chilling truth and nodded. "I ken it now and so now I will work to keep Benet safe and find out who betrayed us all."

She looked at him standing so close to her that she could feel his warmth. He awoke something inside her that had been sleeping since he had walked away a little over five years ago. Annys was not sure what she should do about that. A part of her insidiously whispered that she should take what she wanted but the practical side of her hesitated, mulled over how complicated that would make her life, and reminded her of how her heart had broken when he had just walked away. It was just another thing she had to think about.

But not tonight, she told herself. Not when he was standing so close her hands itched to reach out and touch him. Not with the night sky bathing them in a soft welcoming light that had her memories of their time together rushing to the fore of her mind. None of those things made a rational, practical decision possible.

"I had best get inside," she said even as she started to move away from him. "It has been a verra long day and it appears there will be many more to come. Adam will make certain of it. Sleep well, Sir Harcourt."

"And you, m'lady," he replied and watched her until she went back into the keep.

The little bell rang as she shut the door and he

could hear the men returning. Nicolas was the first to appear and he waved the man to his side. It was past time to have a long talk with his friend.

"Did ye come up here with Lady Annys?" asked Nicolas as he leaned against the wall next to Harcourt.

"Nay," Harcourt replied. "I came up on the wall from another route and found her here. I was actually hunting ye down. Ye have made a fine place for yourself here."

"I have. It is a fine keep with good lands and it used to have a verra fine mon as its laird." Nicolas cursed under his breath. "He suffered and I will make the one responsible for that pay when we find him."

"It may be a her."

"Doesnae much matter to me. The murder of the laird was the darkest of betrayals, especially when that laird was as good a one as Sir David. I was nay here long before I realized I had found my place and often silently thanked ye for that. I didnae fool the mon for long, either. He soon kenned just where I had come from and who had sent me."

Harcourt smiled and nodded. "I thought he would. A quick-witted mon was David. Since he didnae send ye back, I will assume he wasnae offended that I asked ye to come here."

"Nay. He said he was nay surprised ye would do so, either. He occasionally expressed regret that he had e'er asked ye for that gift. He kenned it wouldnae be easy for ye to turn your back on the lad. By the looks on their faces, I suspicion your companions wonder on it all as weel."

"They do and took the first moment we were all

alone to question me. I told them the truth. They understood yet I still suffered under the lash of their tongues for just walking away from my own child and the woman who bore him. That took longer to explain. Since David was such a good mon, and my companions kenned that soon after entering the keep, it softened the inquiry and what could have been a harsh condemnation. E'en from the Mac-Fingals."

"Weel, for all they are a mad lot and their father breeds more bairns than should be allowed, that mon ne'er walked away from them."

"True enough. There was no other way."

"Nay, there wasnae, nay if David was to have the heir he and Glencullaich so badly needed."

"I am ashamed to admit how long it took me to realize that I wasnae truly comfortable leaving my child in the hands of another mon."

Nicolas studied Harcourt for a moment and then said, "I suspect it wasnae so easy for ye to walk away from the lass, either."

"Nay, it wasnae but it took me a while to admit to that, too." Harcourt gave a laugh that held little humor in it. "Foolish young idiot that I was, it took me a while to accept that I hated nay being able to claim or raise the lad as weel as claim his mother. The beliefs of my kinsmen are obviously rooted more deeply in me than I kenned."

"The lad was weel loved, and treated weel, too. David was a good father to him. Wheesht, he adored the lad. One reason Sir Adam was banished from the hall is because he openly stated his opinion of the lad's legitimacy. In front of the boy. For a moment

I thought David would kill the fool. Now I wish he had."

"And how do the people of this clan feel about Benet?"

"They love him. I have ne'er seen anyone be anything but kind to the boy, even a wee bit too indulgent from time to time. They ken he wasnae David's." Nicolas nodded at the shock on Harcourt's face. "They dinnae care. The laird made his love for that boy so clear, his claim of the boy so loud and unwavering, that they all just joined in with the game. They kenned the mon might ne'er sire his own child and it had worried them. Benet's birth soothed their fears. Most e'en suspect their laird arranged it all for they kenned he could be sly and ruthless when needed. Their acceptance of Benet as their future laird was complete, ne'er a doubt shown or spoken. 'Tis why I find the possibility that someone here murdered David verra hard to accept. I do believe Callum is right about it being poison but it will take a while ere I can think of it without that instinctive denial."

"Annys also found it hard to believe but she does now. She also accepts that Benet is now in danger."

"Good. It will make it easier to keep a watch on the lad. It willnae be easy. He is accustomed to running free here and in the village. I will make certain someone is with him at all times though."

"Just be certain it is one ye trust."

Nicolas nodded. "I will."

"How ready are these men to meet what could become a full fight for these lands?"

Harcourt listened to Nicolas's report and was heartened by it. Work was needed but the men of

Glencullaich were not completely green. He was determined, however, to turn them into a highly skilled fighting force that any king would envy. Every instinct he had told him that Sir Adam MacQueen would soon get weary of playing with Annys and then the real fight would begin.

# Chapter Three

Sir Adam MacQueen's appearance at the gates of Glencullaich the next day did not surprise Harcourt at all. Knowing how fast word could travel about any strangers in an area, he had suspected the man would hear about him and his men arriving and staying with Annys. Harcourt had had his men watch for anyone leaving the keep or village, for anyone acting the spy, but they had found no one slipping away. That, too, was not surprising although he had hoped for a bit of luck there. The talk roused by the appearance of strangers had obviously been enough to alert Sir Adam, however.

It took but one look at how the people of Glencullaich reacted to the arrival of Sir Adam MacQueen and his men for Harcourt to know that the man would never be a welcome choice for their laird. The people in the bailey looked at Sir Adam and his men as one would a pack of feral dogs, worried that one of the animals would leap at someone's throat at any moment. Harcourt looked into the man's cold blue

eyes and decided the people of Glencullaich had
very good instincts. David had used the same judg-
ment as one of the reasons he so desperately needed
an heir. It also better explained how it was these
people could accept as heir a child they were all fairly
certain had not been sired by their laird.

"Greetings, Sir Adam," Annys said as she walked
out of the keep and stood next to Harcourt on the
steps. "We were nay expecting you. Have ye stopped
for a rest in your travels?"

"I have come here to judge for myself if the rumors
I heard were true or nay," he snapped as he dismounted and strode to stand at the base of the steps.
"I now see that they were the truth. Ye have hired
yourself some swords."

"Nay, I havenae. These men are nay hired swords,
Sir Adam. Ye lack courtesy to so quickly name them
so. They are old friends." Seeing the way Sir Adam's
eyes narrowed as he studied the six strong men now
flanking her, Annys hastily performed the introduc-
tions.

Anger had put a hint of color into Adam's cheeks.
Recalling how he could strike out when angry, Annys
desperately tried to think of something else to say
before the man had a chance to spit out his anger in
ill-chosen words. The very last thing she needed was
a battle starting right inside her bailey.

"I have heard of the MacFingals," Sir Adam said,
disdain weighting each word.

"Aye, my clan is weel kenned far and wide," said
Sir Nathan MacFingal, "and our fame and glory grow
with each passing day. 'Tis kind of ye to note it."

Annys looked at the man, struggling to hide her

surprise over such a boast. Sir Nathan was grinning as widely as Harcourt and the others were, apparently oblivious to the insult that had just been delivered. That made no sense for they were not stupid men. Yet, every one of them looked one word away from tumbling into a hearty bout of laughter. She wished she knew what jest they shared. The way Adam clenched his hands into white-knuckled fists told her he knew and this reaction to his attempted insult was infuriating him. When Adam turned his glare upon her, Annys barely stopped herself from stepping back in alarm. To hide her fear, she stood even straighter and idly brushed a stray lock of hair from her cheek.

"My cousin isnae e'en cold in his grave but a few weeks and ye have already collected yourself a new stable," Adam said in a cold, hard voice. "But, mayhap this one isnae so new, aye?" he added with a faint nod toward Harcourt.

Joan's gasp of shock came from behind Annys but she was more interested in the sword point touching Adam's throat. She had not seen Harcourt move yet the man was one short step from ending Adam's life. It was very tempting to let him, but Annys knew she would regret it as soon as the deed was done. She needed proof of Adam's crimes against her. Without it, she and Benet would fight the charge of murder for the rest of their lives. At its weakest it would hurt them in any relationships, truces, or treaties they wished to make to better the lives of the people of Glencullaich. At its worst, it could get her neck into a hangman's noose and leave Benet alone and unprotected. It would cause Sir Harcourt a great deal of trouble as well since it would be his sword that had drawn Adam's blood.

"Since ye appear to have come to Glencullaich to do naught but insult me, Sir Adam," she said, "I believe I would verra much like ye to leave. Now."

"Ye would force me off my own family's lands? Off MacQueen lands?"

"I would demand that ye leave *my* family's lands, sir. Lands still held by a MacQueen whether ye be standing on them or nay. Lands I ken my late husband has already banished ye from once."

For a moment she feared the man would attack her despite the sword point tickling his throat. Annys wondered if she had pushed the man too hard but could see nothing else she could do or say. To ignore such an insult to her honor, one delivered before her people and her guests, would reveal a dangerous weakness. That would cause even more trouble than she was facing now. She lightly tapped Sir Harcourt's sword arm and he slowly pulled back his sword, but only a little.

"Ye go too far, woman," Adam said and moved to remount his horse. "So does this mon ye call friend. Ye will regret it. Ye may trust me on that."

Annys was too slow to shield her face with her hand when Adam and his men kicked their horses into a gallop and rode out through the gates. Dust and grit stung her eyes and made her cough. It gave her some small comfort to hear others doing the same, indicating that she was not the only one too slow to guess that Adam's leave-taking would be as rude as his arrival. When Joan, softly cursing Adam in ways Annys would never have guessed the woman knew, pressed a cool, wet cloth into her hands, she quickly put it to use.

As soon as her eyes were clear, Annys looked at Sir Harcourt. It was irritating to see that he and his companions had obviously anticipated Adam's petty action. All six watched Adam and his men ride away with such intensity it made her belly tighten with unease. She suspected not one of them would accept much of Sir Adam's arrogant disrespect. They would not ignore a threat, either, and there was no question that Sir Adam had just delivered one. And this time Sir Adam had committed his crime in front of a whole bailey full of witnesses.

"His rush to your gates upon hearing of our arrival was the act of a mon who allows his anger to rule him," said Harcourt as, once certain the gates were again well secured, he took Annys by the arm, and began to lead her back inside. "That is a weakness."

"Doomed fools," said Sir Nathan and winked at her before hurrying back into the great hall. "Ah, the angels smile upon me for there is more of that fine ale."

"A mon easily pleased by the simple things in life," Harcourt said, a hint of laughter behind his words.

Annys could not help but smile, although that pleasant touch of amusement only lightened her heart for a moment. Adam's visit had been uncomfortable for many reasons. His anger and threats were something she now anticipated each time she saw him. It was the way he had looked at Harcourt that troubled her now. Annys had seen the glint of recognition in the man's eyes. She just wished she could know if it was because Adam recognized Harcourt from the time he had stayed at Glencullaich or if he saw as much of Benet in the man as she did. Joan had assured her that the resemblance between Harcourt and his son was not that obvious, but Sir Adam had seen it, or thought he had. She could only hope that the man did not start flinging accusations at Harcourt, too.

She sat down, smiled at the young boy who served her some cider, and tried to ignore how pleased she was that Harcourt sat next to her. It was a foolish thing to be pleased about. She was no young maid too inexperienced to deal with a handsome man. Blushes and a flutter deep in her belly were the reactions of a virgin maid and she had not been one of those for a very long time.

Then she thought on the anger Adam had revealed, the hatred she had seen in his gaze as he had glared at her. That hatred had bloomed after Adam had looked at Harcourt. Annys could understand the anger since Adam felt he was being denied something he was entitled to. She could not understand why he would be so twisted with hatred for her, however. He had not looked at her like that before today and Benet was almost five years old, a child Adam had never believed was truly David's despite how loudly and widely David had claimed the boy.

"I think we best keep a close watch on everything," said Harcourt and watched all his companions nod in agreement.

"Because of the threat he made?" Annys asked.

"Aye, although I believe the threat has been there for a while. Mayhap just nay spoken so clearly or openly. There were a lot of witnesses to what he said. The mon has no patience. He wants what he wants right now. Ye have been a thorn in his side for too long."

"David hasnae been dead that long."

"True but we now think Sir Adam may have had a hand in that. Yet, despite that, he still cannae claim what he thinks should be his. And why is that?"

"Ah, because David married me and I gave him an heir."

"Exactly. E'en worse, ye are refusing to cower and let fear move ye to just hand him what he demands, mayhap e'en flee this place. Ye have every intention of holding Glencullaich for your son. Now ye have brought in more men, ones he doesnae ken the strength and skill of." Harcourt slowly shook his head. "That must be feeding his anger as weel."

"Why would he e'er think I would just hand him my child's inheritance and scurry away without complaint?" she asked, certain she had never done anything to give Sir Adam the idea that she was such a coward.

"It may be what he is accustomed to having women do." He shook his head. "It does us little good to try and understand the why of his unreasonable claims and demands. All that matters to us is making verra sure he doesnae get what he wants and that he doesnae hurt anyone before we put an end to his fool game."

"That is something I can stand behind. Joan has suggested that I write to Sir Adam's father and tell him what the man is doing."

Harcourt frowned and slowly tapped his fingers against the table. "Do ye think it will be that easy to solve this? That the mon's father can stop him?"

"Nay, not truly. Yet, what harm would be done to try it?"

"Ye dinnae believe the father is making Sir Adam try and gain hold of this place?"

It was a good question, she thought as she slowly cut up an apple. "I dinnae truly ken the mon but I would think he would be here himself, making his own demands or standing right behind his son. The few times I did meet him, he was a verra forceful mon. Sir William was always demanding, always expecting a lot of favors of David, and someone ye were pleased didnae come verra often."

"Sounds like a mon who would do his own work and nay one to hand it to a younger son. Aye, do write to the father if ye wish to. Now or later. It cannae hurt. I just wouldnae expect much help against his son. He may nay be hand in hand with Sir Adam and his plans, but what ye just said makes me think he wouldnae mind at all if his son got what he was after."

She nodded and inwardly sighed. David had been cursed in his kinsmen. Annys had always believed that she had been but, although unfeeling and stern, her family had ne'er tried to gain any more than the marriage settlement and a connection with the Mac-Queens through marriage. They had come to Benet's christening, congratulated her on doing her duty, and then left. They had come to David's funeral, suggested she make certain she did not lose what was the heir's, and then left. She doubted her fear for her child, and herself, would be enough to bestir them to offer her any help.

David's kin, however, had been persistent in attempting to get all they possibly could from him. One of them showed up at nearly every season claiming poor harvests, cold winters, too many mouths to feed, and all manner of disasters in order to get a donation of some food or stock from David. Cloth was another thing they were often after. She still felt David had always been too generous with those people. Finding some of what they had given his kin for sale at a market near their home had angered her, but David had continued to supply them when they asked. She began to think he had done it to keep any of them from trying to just take what they wanted.

Needing a rest from all the talk of Sir Adam, David, and the threats to her and Benet, Annys excused herself and went to the solar. A letter to Sir Adam's father could wait. She needed to lose herself in the mindless work of mending and sewing. It could be thought cowardly of her but she did not care. For just a little while she wanted to pretend all was as it had been. Quiet, prosperous, and even happy despite the fact that her husband was a friend and not a lover.

"She doesnae like this," murmured Nathan after Annys was gone.

"Who would?" asked Harcourt.

"I mean that she doesnae like the changes. From all I have gathered this was always a peaceful place. They have enough for their needs plus enough to sell and put some coin in their purses. They are out of the way of any army or reiver, have ne'er been in the middle of a feud, and appear to have ne'er drawn the attention of the Crown. The homes and lands are in fine shape, the people content, clean, and nay hungry. 'Tis near unreal it is so, weel, content and quiet. Then comes this fool thinking he has some claim on it all. Little troubles start to enter this wee paradise. Then we all come, weel-armed and ready to fight. Aye, I believe it is hard for her to settle into the fight that will be needed to end this."

"Do ye think she will balk, mayhap e'en try to bargain with the mon?"

"Nay, I just think that she will need a nudge to put an end to it all. She is a clever lass. She kens weel that there really is only one way for this to end. That fool will have to die. He willnae let this go any other way."

"True. Did ye hear if they have any allies that may be of use?"

"Nay. They have allies, but nay ones with that bond. Ne'er needed such a bond, did they. If people dinnae ride right past them, they come to the market and help fill their coffers. I havenae heard one story of any battle or feud or attack. Nay anything that doesnae begin with saying back in my father's father's father's time or even further back. Which explains why the men are trained, but nay like most of us, we who live in places where trouble comes to visit now and then."

"Nor have I heard of any trouble ere this," said Callum. "Most of the anger at Sir Adam, and there is a lot of that, comes from how he has, weel, disturbed their lives." Callum grinned. "'Tis nay something I have e'er confronted before."

Harcourt sipped his wine and considered all they had told him. They were right. Glencullaich was odd in its way. It was as if the whole place had been plucked out of the midst of the world's troubles and tucked in these hills, out of sight and out of mind. David had been well known in court circles as well as those of the learned. Yet he stayed here for most of the year, quiet and out of the way. Harcourt was not sure he would want to be so sheltered.

A tug on his shirt drew him out of his thoughts. He looked down to find Benet next to his seat, an apple in his dirty hand. The boy's golden brown eyes peered at him through black curls that refused to stay in place.

"Can ye cut my apple with your knife, sir?" the boy asked.

Harcourt glanced at the hand Benet pointed to and realized he had been twirling his knife in his fingers as he had been thinking. He almost smiled. His mother had always smacked him on the back of the head for doing that.

"Aye, hand it over."

"I like thin slices," Benet said as Harcourt began to core the apple.

"Those are better for eating," said Harcourt, placing the apple on a small plate to cut it into slices.

"Joan says I cannae run about like a stray dog anymore. She said I have to have someone stay with me all the time."

"Ah, aye, ye do." He nudged the plate toward Benet.

"Why?" the boy asked around a slice of apple.

"Because there is a bit of trouble here now and we dinnae wish ye to get harmed while we work to stop it."

"'Tis just some stealing. I am nay a cow or sheep. No one would steal me."

"They might. Best we make sure ye are nay alone and easy to steal. Aye?"

"Mayhap."

Harcourt did not have to see the slight pout to the boy's lips to know Benet did not like the new restrictions. "It will make your mother happy."

"Why?"

"She willnae worry about ye as much as she is right now. It will only be for a little while and then all will be as it was before."

"Because ye are going to gut the bastard?"

It was not easy but Harcourt ignored the choked laughter of his companions. "Best not to speak so to your mother." When the boy nodded, he added, "We will stop Sir Adam and make him go away. That is our plan."

Benet nodded again, grabbed up the last few slices of apple, and ran out of the hall. Harcourt shook his head. The ones who would have to watch the boy were going to have to be very alert and fast-footed. The boy did not like the idea of being restricted in any way and that would make the job of watching him even harder.

"He will fight against the leash we put on him," said Callum.

Harcourt nodded. "Just as I was thinking. And so says Nicolas. Warn everyone picked to guard him closely. He may nay e'en slip the leash intentionally, merely out of habit. The lad has ne'er been held back because everywhere he went there were ones watching o'er him but only gently as one would do with any wee lad. Now, with someone within the clan giving aid to Sir Adam, that peaceful freedom needs to be reined in."

"We will make certain everyone understands that," said Nathan. "That will mean the one helping Sir

Adam will ken it, too, but that may nay be a bad thing."

Satisfied that the whole of Glencullaich would soon understand that a very close watch needed to be kept on their future laird, Harcourt decided to wander around the keep and make certain there were no weak spots. Sir Adam would not continue simply trying to push Annys into a corner, to make her walk away, for long. The time for an open attack, to take what he coveted by open force, was drawing near. Glencullaich needed to be prepared for that.

David had been a clever man and a good laird but it was soon apparent to Harcourt that the man had been too accustomed to peace. The keep was secure enough for repelling some raid by reivers but would never stand up to a determined attack. The gates were strong but he could see that the men were not well trained in the swift closing of them. The port-cullis was of such fine work that it was a perfect study in the combining of strength and beauty. The works needed to lower it or raise it and secure it in place were in need of repair, however.

Harcourt was making a list in his mind as he rounded the corner of the keep and found Annys. She sat beneath a leafy bower at the far edge of the flower garden, a pleasurable spot that was a rarity in the keeps he had been to. David had boasted of it, having read of it, and even having visited one in France when he had been younger. The practical side of him saw it as a waste of space that could have been taken up with something more useful even as a part of him deeply appreciated the peace and beauty of it. He walked over to where Annys sat, moved by the sadness in her expression.

"Have ye accepted what must be done yet?" he asked when she looked up at him.

Annys sighed. "I have accepted that we must do all that is needed to save this place from falling into Sir Adam's greedy hands."

"I dinnae think ye will be talking him out of trying to take it."

"I ken it. Doesnae mean I like the truth I have to face or willnae try to do this without the spilling of blood. What I also ken is that one cannae stop Sir Adam with strength of arms without a few of the people here suffering for it. I dinnae wish for e'en one of them to spill a single drop of blood."

"But ye must ken they are willing to fight for this place, for ye and wee Benet."

"Och, aye, most certainly. That doesnae mean I wish to have them do so."

She stood up, knowing her quiet time had come to an end. Doing her mending had helped some but she had suddenly needed to be out in the air and come to the garden. She realized it had helped her understand what would need to be done, and what was at risk if she lacked the courage to do it, far better than hiding in the solar. Now that moment was over.

Annys studied Harcourt, fighting to ignore the allure of him, and see him as only a warrior. He had been the right one to call to her side to help her and her people. She knew that. It annoyed her, however, that all those years away from him had not killed her attraction to him. He would be staying at Glencullaich until her troubles were over. Of that she had no doubt. The temptation of that was going to be difficult to fight. That had been yet another matter she had tried to come to some decision on but it was still fraught with confusion, which she was more than content to keep pushing aside.

"But, we will fight if we must," she said. "It is nay something we have done much and that is what worries me."

"We can strengthen the men's skills. I have also just had a good look at your fortifications and seen where they can be strengthened." He took her by the arm and walked back toward the keep with her.

"Is there a lot that must be done?" Annys forced herself to pay heed to the importance of their conversation and not the all-too-welcome warmth of his hand on her arm.

"Nay, but I fear David was nay interested in making certain the keep was fully prepared for an attack. Weel, I doubt there e'er was one in his life here."

"Nay, I dinnae think there was, or, naught of any great consequence. Ye truly believe Sir Adam means to try and take Glencullaich by force, dinnae ye."

"I do. There may be time yet that he tries to just keep picking at ye, causing wee troubles here and there that keep ye busy, but I believe that now any of that will be done to slow your preparations to withstand an attack."

Once inside the keep, Annys stopped and stepped away from him. The loss of the warmth of his touch caused her to feel a pinch of sorrow, but she clasped her hands in front of her to stop from reaching out to him. What she wanted to do was burrow into his strong arms and hide for a while. She would not, could not, give in to that weakness.

"Aye, that makes sense. So, best we prepare as soon as can be. I suspect Nicolas needs no direction from me to heed what ye say and we are nay without funds if they are needed. I hate this and, God forgive me, I loathe Sir Adam for bringing us to this, but I will see it done."

Harcourt nodded. He could see how troubled she was and admired the way she was looking past her own qualms to do what needed to be done. The temptation to pull her into his arms and offer some comfort was strong, but her stiff posture told him such a gesture would not be welcome. Instead he gave her a small bow.

"Then I shall set to it, Lady Annys."

Annys watched as he walked away. She was both lonely and proud. Proud of herself for being strong but finding that being strong made her loneliness sharper.

As she made her way to the kitchens to oversee the preparations for the next meal, she finally admitted to herself that she had been lonely since the day he had ridden away from her. Anger and hurt over the way he had not taken even a moment of his time to exchange some private words before leaving had dimmed that sense of loss for a long time.

It would be all too easy to reach out for Harcourt to ease that loneliness. Annys suspected her people would think nothing of it. There were many small reasons not to do so but the one that truly held her back was the fear of being hurt. The way he had left her without a word after the many times they had been together, the many sweet words he had whispered to her as they had made love, had cut her to the bone. Even knowing he had had no right to claim her, that she could not be with him openly, had not eased her pain. Annys did not think she could survive it a second time.

Shaking such thoughts from her head, she went to work. Hard work had assisted her in keeping Sir Harcourt Murray out of her thoughts before, when he had walked away from her without looking back. It should be able to do so again even though he was now back within reach.

# Chapter Four

Annys sat back on her heels and idly tried to rub away the aching twinge in her lower back. Taking advantage of a rare beautiful summer day, she and Joan were carefully tending to the kitchen garden. She had forgotten just how much hard work that was. There was not one part of her that did not ache or feel very dirty.

"It grows verra warm," said Joan as she moved to sit next to Annys and wiped the sweat from her face with her apron. "I think I am sweating enough to water the plants. Time to leave the work for the younger lassies."

"I prefer to think of myself as one of those younger lassies," murmured Annys.

Joan laughed. "Aye, but at times it serves us weel to be older."

Annys smiled. "True and there are days when I can feel verra old indeed."

A young girl brought them each a tankard of cool cider and Annys thanked her. Since they were at the far edge of the garden, she and Joan moved back a few feet until they were beneath the shade of an old oak tree. It took only moments in the shade, sipping the cool cider, for Annys to begin to feel refreshed. She was just not certain she was refreshed enough to return to working in the garden.

"Ye are the lady of the keep. Ye dinnae need to do this work if ye dinnae wish to," Joan said.

"There are times, Joan, when I think ye can see every thought inside my head."

"Nay, I but saw that ye were looking at the garden in the same way I was and I kenned what I was thinking. Decided ye must be feeling the same."

"I should nay feel so guilty for wanting to quit it. I have worked here for most of the morning."

"Aye, ye ne'er hesitate to get your hands dirty. We all ken it and ye should ne'er feel e'en a pinch of guilt for leaving some of the heavier work to others from time to time. Mayhap ye should wash the dirt and sweat off and go see what your handsome champion is doing. He has been working verra hard these last two days."

One glance at the sly smile on Joan's face was enough to tell Annys what game her maid played. "Ye will nay play the matchmaker, Joan."

"Och, I wasnae doing that."

Annys did not believe that but asked, "So what were ye doing then?"

"Weel, ye are a woman alone . . ."

"A new widow."

"The laird, God bless his kind soul, has been gone from us for a long time."

"Not that long."

"Long enough." Joan scowled at Annys but then quickly smiled again. "They are all strong, bonnie lads."

"Ah, I see. Ye wish me to try them all, aye?" Annys laughed at the look of shock on Joan's face.

"Wretched lass. I saw the way that Sir Harcourt looked at you, lass." Joan lowered her voice to a near whisper. "Remember, I ken who sired our lad and I ken how our laird was ne'er a true husband to you. All I am saying here is that ye might consider finding yourself a wee bit of warmth for once in your life."

"David loved me and he treated me verra weel." Annys hated to hear the hint of defensiveness in her voice.

Joan patted her hand, which Annys suddenly realized was clenched into a tight fist. "I ken it," she said. "The mon loved you. Like a sister. It wouldnae hurt you to be treated like the woman ye are for once, however."

"And give everyone a chance to begin questioning who truly fathered Benet?"

"Ah, weel, we have all kenned the truth of that from the verra beginning." She nodded when Annys stared at her in shock. "We have. I ken ye thought it was just me, and that made ye happy so I let ye think so. But everyone kens it. There were a few weeks where anger at ye ran a wee bit strong in some until we saw how joyful the laird was o'er the coming bairn. Then we began to ken the truth. What afflicted the laird was nay a secret to all of us, ye ken. We just let him think that it was. A secret held by all out of the respect we felt he was due."

Annys was not sure how she felt about all that. A

part of her was deeply relieved for she had carried the weight of that secret for so long. It was also uncomfortable to know that everyone at Glencullaich knew she had been unfaithful to her husband. It did not really matter that the man had asked her to be just as no one could be certain he had done so. It had all been done very privately.

"Annys," Joan said quietly, her lack of formality revealing how concerned she was, "nary a person here has e'er condemned you. It didnae take us long to fully understand what had happened. The laird's utter joy o'er the bairn told us all we really cared to know. He kenned the bairn wasnae his. Had to, didnae he? Yet naught could hide his delight. We decided he had arranged it all. The way he so proudly named the bairn his son was but another confirmation of that. And we had all worried about the fact that there would be no heir so were pleased to claim the child ourselves, as weel. Wee Benet's birth saved us from having Sir Adam, or one of his ilk, step in as our laird. Although we didnae expect to lose our laird as soon as we did."

"Nay, nor did I, and I begin to believe we shouldnae have. Ye heard all that Sir Callum said, and he suspects a poisoning. I didnae want to consider it then but I have been doing so, and now I believe he may be right. Someone at Glencullaich helped Sir Adam kill our laird."

Joan cursed and took a deep drink of cider. "Who?"

"I dinnae ken." Annys sighed. "I still struggle to understand it e'en though I believe that is what happened. What Sir Callum said held the ring of truth and I ken that he has a verra sharp wit, yet I cannae think of any of our people who would e'er help

Adam. And most certainly nary a one who would help him kill David."

"Nor can I." Joan muttered a curse. "If I find one helping that bastard, ye willnae have to fret o'er them betraying us again. I promise ye that."

"So bloodthirsty," Annys murmured, a little amused by Joan's ferocity.

"I feel so when I think on it. The laird was taken from us much too soon. If one of our own sent him off to an early grave then I will be verra pleased to see to it that they rot in hell."

This time Annys was stunned by the fury in Joan's voice. The woman actually trembled from the strength of it. She knew all of the people of Glencullaich had cared for their laird but she now had to wonder if her maid, her dearest friend, had cared far more than most, more than as a sister cares for her sibling.

"Joan? Did ye love David?" she asked, keeping her tone of voice as soft and gentle as she could.

"Of course I did. He was my laird." She looked at Annys and briefly laughed. "Och, nay as ye are now thinking. Nay, there was no lust in my love for David, no fire in the blood. I thought ye kenned my love was that of a friend, e'en of a sister."

"I did but, for just a moment, I thought I may have been wrong."

"Nay. I have a few years on ye, m'lady, and ken weel what a gift Sir David was, what a good mon and good laird. A rare thing, and trust me to ken the truth of that. If some fool nudged that good, kind mon into an early grave to please that bastard Sir Adam or gain a few coins for their purse, they didnae just betray the laird. Or ye. They betrayed every mon, woman, and child in Glencullaich."

Annys nodded slowly as she considered those words. "Aye, that is exactly what they did." She sighed. "Weel, unless someone wishes to come forth and confess all, we shall ne'er ken the truth. Aye, poisoning makes sense to me, explains so much about David's illness that I just couldnae understand, but proving it now that David is dead and buried is impossible. Och, we could only have proven it when he was alive by the way he would have been cured or by catching the one who did it slipping the poison into his food or drink."

"I will still watch closely for the one who may have done it. If that one could kill a good mon for that wretched Sir Adam, who kens what else the bastard is capable of?"

"True. I will watch as weel although I think ye will have better luck because ye are nay the laird's wife. I but appear and whoe'er did this will be fully on his guard."

"I am nay so far from being treated the same, but I ken better who to trust amongst the ones who would have had the chance to do it. I ken better who to watch as weel."

"Do ye have some suspicions, Joan?"

"I cannae think of one amongst the men but there is a lass or two I will be watching. I think that is where the danger is. Some fool lass who believes herself in love or enough so that she heeds every lie told her by Sir Adam or one of his men."

Annys was choked by sadness for a moment. It was not just because David had been murdered by one of his own people, people he had treated well, but it could have been the result of some foolish young woman's seduction. How anyone at Glencullaich could ever believe that David deserved the painful, lingering death he had suffered, no matter what some handsome man promised, she did not know. Nor could she think of any woman at the keep who could be so easily swayed by some man's lies.

"It is too sad to think on," she murmured. "Poor David ne'er did anything that would make anyone here think him so bad that he deserved that death."

"Some lasses can believe anything if the mon they desire tells them it. But, aye, it is unbearably sad that our laird would die because one lass is too witless to ken what are lies and what is truth. Whene'er I think on it, I want to beat the guilty one until they are naught but a pile of shattered bone."

"Find her, Joan. Or him, although I believe ye are right in what ye think concerning the killer."

"I will and I swear I will nay kill her but bring her to face justice."

"Good. I truly need to hear the why nay matter how witless it may prove to be.

"There are times when I dearly wish Nigel didnae die o'er there in France, and nay just because he was also too young to die. But I would have wed with him as I was supposed to, David would still live, and"—she lowered her voice—"I wouldnae be part of a plan to deny a verra good mon his son."

"True enough but ye wouldnae have Benet now, either, would ye?"

Annys softly cursed. "Nay, I wouldnae and I would ne'er wish him gone. Weel, with that thought in my head, I will now go and clean up. Mayhap see what is being done with our defenses," she said as she stood up and brushed off her skirts.

"The men are verra pleased with all the training they are getting for all they like to groan and complain about the work and the bruises. We have been blessed in how peaceful we have had it here but this trouble has let us see that we have let that blessing make us soft. We willnae be any longer."

"That is a comfort. One has to wonder what sorts of life Sir Harcourt and the others have led, however, that has made them so knowledgeable about good fighting and good defenses."

"Just one that was lived in a place which isnae so cleverly out of sight as we are. Go on, I will direct the lasses in finishing the work."

Annys left Joan to order the younger women around, something she knew her maid got a great deal of pleasure out of doing. Although everyone called Annys *my lady,* she was not so vain as to think that meant that she actually held all the power at Glencullaich. Joan held a lot of it in her work-worn hands as well.

Ordering some heated water on her way up to her bedchamber, Annys began to wonder if Joan would be able to find the one who killed David. She was not even certain how one could winnow the guilty out of the herd. The killer had escaped any justice for months, escaped even being caught as she killed her laird. That amount of cleverness did not match with the image of some silly love-stricken lass doing anything her lover asked.

Then again, she mused as she let in the young girl

bringing her the heated water to wash with, just how clever does one have to be to use poison? The moment the girl left, Annys shed her clothes and washed off the sweat and dirt she had collected while working in the garden all the while pondering that question. It was one she should have asked Harcourt, she thought.

Dealing with murder, betrayal, and deceit was not something she felt confident to do. She had never dealt with such things before. The men now training her men and shoring up Glencullaich's defense showed they had lived a harder life, one touched by such darkness as battle. Sir Callum knowing about poisoning as well as the lack of shock on the faces of the other men as he explained to her about his cousin, told her they probably all knew a lot more about murder than she did. Determined to speak to one of them, she quickly dressed and hurried out of her bedchamber only to meet up with Harcourt right outside her door.

Harcourt caught her by the shoulders before she ran into him. He had come to ask her about getting some supplies and if the recommendations her men had given him were of people she wanted to deal with. The questions were now stuck in his mouth as he stood so close to her he could smell her freshly washed skin. It was an achingly familiar scent, despite the years they had been apart, for he had often scented it when his mind had returned to the time they had been lovers. Worse, whenever he had caught a similar scent in the air, he had been taken back to that time by the river and the feel of Annys in his arms.

He was going to kiss her, he decided as he gently

nudged her back until she was pressed against the door. It was something he had been aching to do from the moment he had seen her again after so many years. All he had to do was catch a glimpse of her hair as she walked across the bailey and memories of the times they had been together flooded his mind. If nothing else, he needed to know if his memories were true, if she truly tasted as sweet as he remembered.

"Harcourt," she said, the tone of her voice hinting at the protest she was about to make.

"Hush. I but seek to discover if my memories are true ones."

Before she could ask what he meant by that, his mouth was on hers. The touch of his lips on hers sent heat flaring through her body so quickly, Annys gasped from the shock of it. Harcourt took quick advantage of her parted lips, thrusting his tongue into her mouth. The abrupt increased intimacy of the kiss only added to the fever of need possessing her. Annys flung her arms around his neck, pressing her body close to his, as he stroked the inside of her mouth with his tongue. Each stroke sent heat straight to her loins.

She wanted to wrap her whole body around his. She wanted to feel his skin beneath her hands, rubbing against hers as they clung to each other while naked as the day they were born. She wanted to be surrounded by his heat. She could feel his hardness pressed against her and she wanted him inside her.

It was the strength of that desperation that finally pulled Annys free of the frantic need his kiss inspired. It was so fierce, so sudden, that it frightened her a little. She put her hands against his chest and pushed even as she tore her mouth away from his. The dazed look upon his face both pleased and worried her, especially since she suspected she looked much the same. It was all too much, she thought. Too strong, too overpowering, too mindless. Annys had little doubt that, if she had not come to her senses, they would have ended up coupling against the wall right there, in the hall, where anyone could see them. She certainly had not had the willpower to put a stop to it while caught in the power of his kiss.

"Annys," he said as he struggled to catch his breath.

"Nay." She pushed at him again, moving out of his reach when he stepped back from her. "Nay." She could feel the burn of a deep blush on her cheeks. "Sweet Mary, we are standing right out in the hall."

"Then let us go somewhere more private."

"I think not. I am the lady of this keep. 'Tis best if I act like it."

Harcourt watched her walk away, although she moved so quickly it could fairly be called running away. He resisted the urge to chase after her like some animal but the urge to do so was surprisingly strong. It was undoubtedly for the best that she retreated now. If she had not pushed him away he would have taken her there, up against the wall where anyone in the keep might have seen them.

He was still achingly hard. Shaking his head, he began to make his way back to the stables where he had been carefully examining every harness and saddle. With each step he willed himself to go soft. Harcourt did not want anyone seeing him in such an aroused state, especially since most would know exactly whom he was lusting after.

And all from just one kiss, he thought in amazement. It was as if all the hunger the memory of her had stirred up over the years had simply settled down inside him, just waiting for the moment he had her in his arms again. The need that had rushed over him when he had kissed her had been overwhelming, blinding him to everything but the craving to bury himself deep inside of her. This time there would be no seeking out some willing woman to ease that need, either. He did not want one.

Pausing after he stepped outside, Harcourt mulled over that last thought. He had been as close to celibate as he ever wished to be for over a year and as far from celibate as a man could be before that. Yet all hint of the need to bed a woman faded away at the thought of going to one, one who was not Annys. The hunger gnawing at him was for her and only her.

Harcourt waited for the guilt he had always suffered to pinch at him. It did not come. He still felt a little for bedding a married woman but, at some time over the last five years, he had come to terms with what he had done. What he needed to come to terms with now, to make a firm, clear-headed decision about, was what he wanted from Annys. Harcourt was beginning to suspect the answer to that was everything.

Annys stared at the tapestry she had been working on. It was not helping. She could not shake the memory of that heated kiss. She could still taste

Harcourt on her mouth, still feel the heat he had stirred within her even though it had subsided to a soft glow. Unfortunately, as it had faded, guilt had once again raised its ugly, tormenting head.

It was a senseless guilt, she thought crossly. There had been no betrayal. She and Harcourt had done exactly what David had wanted them to do. Annys did not think she had ever seen anyone as delighted, as joyous, as David had been when she had birthed Benet. She may have broken one rule of the Church by lying with Harcourt while she was married to David, but she had obeyed her husband just as the Church advised all wives to do.

"And I was fruitful and multiplied," she muttered.

"Weel, only the once."

Startled by Joan's voice coming from behind her, Annys turned to glare at her maid. "Ye shouldnae creep up on a person that way."

"Sorry," Joan said, not sounding at all sincere. "Still wrestling with yourself, are ye?"

"Joan, I broke the rules."

"Only one and your husband ordered ye to do so."

"He *asked,* nay ordered."

"We both ken that David was verra good at making orders sound like requests so that ye couldnae say nay. He ordered ye to go with Harcourt because he wanted a bairn. That ye actually gave him a son only delighted him more. Do ye ken, when I could see how much he loved that child, I would begin to fear that he might try to find ye another stud."

Annys gasped. "He wouldnae have done that." The moment she uttered the denial, Annys found herself wondering if it was deserved.

"Aye, I can see that ye are now thinking on it.

David couldnae give ye bairns. Wheesht, he could barely consummate the marriage. That was because of his own guilt or confusion as much as it was from his injury, I think. I dinnae think he was e'er able to forget that ye were intended to be his brother's bride. He had kenned ye as Nigel's promised wife for far too long to shake free of that idea just because Nigel was dead. But, e'en if he could have o'ercome that, he still couldnae have given ye any bairns. That jealous husband's sword took all chance of that away, didnae it. So he came up with the plan to breed ye like some mare. We argued about it, ye ken."

"Oh, Joan, nay, I didnae ken that."

"Aye, but then I saw how ye and Harcourt looked at each other and decided a bairn from a mon ye truly wanted wasnae such a hardship for you."

"I sometimes think that is why I often feel so guilty. It should have been a duty, nay a pleasure. Somehow the fact that there was pleasure made it all seem, weel, sinful."

Joan grinned. "Aye, and I suspect the Church has a few rules about a lass feeling any pleasure in the arms of a mon, at least one who isnae a husband trying to breed his all-important heir." She grew serious again. "And it was the knowledge that ye would enjoy yourself that made me shut my mouth. I believed ye should have that, at least once. David wasnae giving it to ye, couldnae, and at least once a lass should feel the fire. And now that ye are a widow, mayhap ye should be helping yourself to another taste."

"'Tis too strong," Annys said.

"Mayhap that is just because it has been too long with only memory to cling to."

"I am sorely tempted despite the lingering guilt."

"Yet ye hesitate."

"I cannae explain weel. It consumes me and that is frightening. Mayhap it is just as ye said, a matter of having tasted it once and waiting too long to have another taste. Yet, e'en if I can brave that, o'ercome the guilt, and cease worrying so much about sin, there is still one thing that remains."

"What would that be?"

"It hurt so much when he left. I kenned he had to. I kenned there was no future, that what we had was all we could have, but it still hurt."

"And ye think he will ride away from ye again when this trouble ends?"

"He cannae stay, Joan." Annys saw Joan frown and sighed. "He has a keep himself. He has kin close at hand there, people who depend on him to protect and provide. And I must stay here."

Joan sighed. "I suppose ye must. There really isnae anyone else to put in your place, nay who can hold Benet's inheritance safe for him."

"Nay, there isnae. I certainly wouldnae trust a Mac-Queen to do that. So, whate'er I decide to do, in the end, Harcourt must ride away again."

Joan patted her on the shoulder. "Mayhap ye need to just accept that truth and decide whether or not ye have the stomach to take all ye can get before that end comes."

"Ye mean, make some new memories."

"Aye, sometimes that is all one ends up with anyway." Joan sighed and then winked at her. "Then again, mayhap ye could end up with yet another lovely wee bairn."

Annys stared at her maid and closest friend. She knew she should be shocked but she was mostly intrigued. A child. It was so tempting. It was also so very wrong but that did little to end the thoughts dancing in her mind.

"I should be utterly ashamed of myself for e'en thinking of it, but I am thinking." Annys shook her head. "We shall see. Thinking may hasten the death of that last flicker of guilt, if naught else. Yet, as I hate the idea that David might have seen me as much akin to a mare to breed, it would be wrong to look at Harcourt as just some stallion."

"He rode away from the first child he left ye with."

"Aye, he did, and that, too, is in my mind. If he can leave one child behind, why cannae he leave another?" Annys stood and brushed down her skirts. "But, let us go and see what there is to feed these men. After all, if I am contemplating using Sir Harcourt as my stallion, it would be wise to make certain he is fed weel and keeps up his strength."

# Chapter Five

Market day in the village was something Annys had always looked forward to and enjoyed. The people of Glencullaich were skilled in many crafts. People came from miles around to purchase their goods. Every merchant was busy, local and traveling ones alike. Every room available for a traveler was occupied, every place where a horse could be stabled or a carriage sheltered was full, and the alehouse could not hold all the men looking for a drink. The sight of such promise for Glencullaich was one that always lifted Annys's spirits. Today it was not doing so. The blame for that could be placed squarely on the broad shoulders of one Sir Harcourt Murray.

Annys cursed her own foolishness. The man was not the master of her emotions. The confusion she suffered from was one of her own making. She could still taste him, still recall all the heady warmth of his kiss, and was shamed by that lust he stirred within her. Her husband had been dead for only ten weeks. It was wrong for her to want another so soon.

But want him she did. She could not shake him

from her mind. Memories of the times they had visited their hidden bower near the burn kept crowding into her thoughts. Her dreams left her aching and all asweat each morning. Guilt over that was a hard knot in her chest. The realization that, although she had loved David and respected him, she had never desired him added to that guilt. Somehow she had to get past that but she could not think of a way to do so. She had, after all, broken a lot of rules during her time with Harcourt. It was a tiring circular path her mind refused to get off.

She was starting to annoy herself. Such fretting and indecisiveness was not like her. She had been the lady of a busy, prosperous keep for too long. At five and twenty she should be able to cease leaping from one thought to another and just act. She was letting her emotions rule her thoughts, pulling her in every direction. Just decide, Annys, she told herself. Aye or nay. It is that simple.

A noise from deep within a narrow alley to her right drew her attention and she welcomed the distraction. Annys stepped into the mouth of the alley that was little more than a narrow, stony path cut between two houses and running down to the burn. She listened closely, heard nothing over the sounds of the busy market, and was just about to return to wandering through that market, when the sound came again. It sounded very much like an animal in some distress. Annys hurried down the alley, going deeper into the shadows, and silently scolded herself for having a too-soft heart. The stable master had already complained about the number of cast-aside or injured animals she had brought home. He would not be at all pleased to see another.

When she first saw the cat, she cursed and hurried toward it, idly wishing it was a puppy. The stable master liked dogs. Someone had tied the cat to a small stake in the ground, the binding visibly tight around the animal's back leg. It stood there looking utterly exhausted and she knew it had struggled mightily against its tether. She may need to have another talk with the children about how they should treat the animals that shared their homes and lands. Annys did not care if people thought her concern strange, only that they followed her wishes in how they treated their animals.

Speaking softly, she crouched in front of the cat. It hissed but she did not flinch for the warning was not accompanied by a show of claws. Cautiously she edged closer to its trapped leg, pausing to gently scratch the animal's ears, a touch that was slowly accepted. Just as she reached out to see if she could easily untie what imprisoned the cat, someone grabbed her from behind. The cat hissed and tried to leap at something, claws out, only to be pulled back by its tether. Before she finished drawing a breath for a scream a gloved hand was slapped over her mouth. Someone had used her too-well-known softness for animals against her.

"I cannae see her," Harcourt grumbled as he searched the crowded market for some sign of Annys.

"Joan said she was here, that she had seen her near the ribbons," said Nathan, pausing to smile and wink at one of the younger women selling ribbons. "That woman usually kens right where her lady is at all times."

"True. She does keep a verra close watch on the lass. Doesnae trust that fool Adam. Nor do I. Too much anger, e'en hatred, in the mon. Aye, greed and envy as weel. I believe he sees Lady Annys as the reason he isnae sitting in the laird's chair right now. As if David was too witless to ken what he wanted and what would be good for the people of Glencullaich."

"Sir David was a verra learned mon, wasnae he?"

"Aye. And he ne'er stopped trying to learn more. He stirred a greed within me to do the same."

"Your kinsmen prize learning from all I have heard. Did they nay teach ye that?"

Harcourt chuckled. "They did. They still do but young lads are nay always interested in such things. I was too busy learning how to wield a sword and woo the lassies. But, David read to me whilst I was trapped in bed healing from my wounds. Nay only clan histories or bards' tales, either, but learned books, ones that taught ye something aside from who sired whom or who sighed after whom. I discovered I liked it e'en when what he read left me with as many questions as it answered. I gained a hunger to find those answers. It hasnae hurt me none."

"Nay," agreed Nathan, "and that hunger has certainly helped ye at Gormfeurach."

The sound of a brief scuffle from within the dark alley to his left caught Harcourt's attention. He stepped closer to the opening but heard nothing else. Instinct was urging him to go down there, to get a closer look into the shadowed part where it sloped down toward the burn running alongside the village.

"Something wrong?" asked Nathan, stepping up beside Harcourt and peering down the alley.

"Thought I heard something," Harcourt replied, "but 'tis quiet now."

"Yet ye remain as taut as a bowstring."

"Gut is telling me to go and have a look."

"Then let us go and see if your gut is right."

Annys struggled as hard as she could in the grasp of her kidnapper. He cursed her when her heels slammed into his shins. Although it was muffled a little, she was certain she recognized the man's voice. She could not believe Sir Adam could be so utterly witless as to try to drag her out of her own village in the middle of market day. And, if it was not him, it was someone he had sent after her, for there was no one else who would be interested in abducting her.

All her struggling finally succeeded in altering his grip on her just enough to allow her to slam her hip into his groin. It was not as telling a blow as one could make with a fist or a shod foot, but it still served its purpose. He let her go, instinct and blind need causing him to cup his privates. He cursed her for a bitch with a ferocity that was chillingly familiar. Annys did not waste any time looking at her captor, but started to run back toward the mouth of the alley. She glanced back once to see that her captor and his two companions, the lower halves of all their faces covered by cloth, had abruptly halted their pursuit of her, turned, and run. Then she ran into something tall and hard.

She staggered back only to be grabbed by the arms. Annys tensed, preparing herself to fight some more, and looked up into the face of her new captor.

Sir Harcourt stared down at her, anger and concern tightening his fine features. She was so relieved, it was difficult to keep standing. She just wanted to curl herself into his strong body and hold on tight.

"Are you harmed?" he asked.

"Nay," she replied, determined to hide her embarrassment over her brief weakness, and then found herself quickly set aside.

"Stay here."

Before she could object to being ordered about as if she was some soldier under his command, he and Nathan ran after the ones who had attempted to abduct her. Annys sighed and shook her head as the sound of hoofbeats echoed in the distance. There was little chance of catching anyone. Harcourt had no horses near at hand to give chase. Realizing she was right back where she had been caught, she slowly approached the trapped cat.

It was young, she decided as she crouched down in front of it. Weaned but not for very long. She murmured soft, nonsensical words of comfort as she cautiously moved to unbind the animal. Too thin, dirty from its battle to get free, and trembling, the cat was a wretched creature but it had eyes very much like Harcourt's. Dunnie, the stable master, was not going to be very happy to see this one show up at Glencullaich.

For a moment she thought of just letting it go but then, as she slowly ran her hand along its side while reaching for the tether that held it to the stake, she felt its ribs and knew she would be taking it home. Cats and dogs bred too freely, and too often, leaving far too many animals to feed and care for. She could not get everyone to cage the animals they had when they went into season. Neither could she let the unwanted just starve. She certainly could not ignore the pleading in those eyes that matched the ones she saw too often in her dreams.

To her surprise the cat stuck its head under her armpit as she slowly untied the rope holding it trapped. It was not yet wary of people. That could prove to be a good thing.

"What are ye doing?" asked Harcourt as he stepped up on the other side of her, Nathan close behind him.

"Someone has tethered this poor cat to a stake and I mean to set it free," she replied, silently cursing how tightly the knot she worked on was tied.

Harcourt sighed, easily recognizing another so much like his kin, one who could leave no sorrowful looking stray unaided. "This is how they lured ye into their reach, isnae it?"

"Aye," she admitted reluctantly and made a soft sound of triumph when she finally got the knot untied.

The cat just pushed itself deeper into her side, ramming its head more snugly up into her armpit. She resigned herself to the possibility of ruining her gown and getting some fleas as she picked it up in her arms and stood. The way both men looked at the cat burrowed into her armpit almost made her laugh. They both looked sadly resigned to what they clearly saw as foolish womanly softness.

"Are ye certain ye wish to take that with ye?" Harcourt asked.

"Aye," said Nathan, trying to get a good look at the cat. "Dirty, thin, cowardly. Nay a grand find."

"'Tis certain that it belongs to no one so, aye, I will

take it home with me. I do try to get the people to cage any dog or cat that goes into season but they dinnae always do it. 'Tis extra work, isnae it, e'en though I have the cages for them and have e'en had a shelter built to put the cages in. So, at times I find myself with a few that need some shelter. I have almost succeeded in getting the numbers down so that any newly born are usually taken in by others without hesitation."

Harcourt watched as she moved to walk out of the alley, the cat tucked up hard in her arms. He had been at Glencullaich long enough to know that Annys collected the animals tossed aside as avidly as several of the women in his clan did. Glencullaich did not really need yet another stray cluttering its bailey or keep. He knew he had no chance at all of convincing her of that as he listened to her talk soothingly to the still-shaking animal.

"It will need that leg looked at," Harcourt said as he carefully examined the way the tether had scraped the animal's leg raw, ignoring the growling noises the animal made since it did not move from its place in her arms with its face tucked up in her armpit.

"Dunnie is verra good at that. He will ken what to do," she said.

It did not surprise Harcourt when Dunnie took one look at the cat Annys showed him and scowled at her. The man probably saw far too many. It did take some time to detach the cat from Annys, however, before Dunnie could haul it away to fix its injuries.

"Who do ye think tried to grab ye?" Harcourt asked as they slowly walked toward the keep.

Annys had hoped the lack of questions immedi-ately after saving her had meant Harcourt would just accept it all as one of those dangers of market day. She should have known better. Unfortunately, she did not really have all that much she could tell him. Not with any certainty.

"I think it may have been Adam," she replied. "All of them wore cloth tied around their faces, but just the way he spoke when I made him let go of me made me think it was Adam."

"Just how did ye make him let ye go?"

She could not fully repress a blush. "I slammed my hip into his, um, groin."

"Clever. Weakest place on a mon. Instinct most often makes him reach for himself after such a hit as weel."

"Which is what he did. Then I ran. I kenned that if I could just get back to the opening of the alley, I could call for help."

"It was a risky thing for him to do."

"I thought the same."

"Mayhap he grows desperate."

"O'er what? The fact that Benet and I still reside here? Still breathe?"

"Aye, exactly that," replied Harcourt. "The mon didnae appear to be one who had a lot of patience. Nay, nor one who could make any plans that would require it. What he did today is the sort of thing a mon does simply because an opportunity arises and he snatches at it without much thought."

"I did wonder how he could e'er have thought he would succeed. Weel, I shall write to his father now."

"Do ye think that mon will be of any help to you?"

"Nay," she replied as they stopped outside her bedchamber door and she struggled not to think of what had happened the last time they had stood there together. "He was verra angry when David chose to marry me. I was to be Nigel's wife, nay David's, he said, and since Nigel was dead, I should just be sent back home. Me and my dowry, of course. David wouldnae send me home as he kenned it wasnae a good place for me to be, nor could he give up my dowry. Many of the improvements we now enjoy were made with it."

"Then why write to the mon if ye ken that he willnae help?"

"So that I can honestly say that I tried to get the family to help, tried to seek aid from my late husband's kinsmen. It may prove important if Sir Adam gets himself killed." She sighed. "And he hasnae actually hurt us yet so I would like it ended ere that happens."

"He killed David."

"We ken it, but unless we can catch who put the poison in David's food, I can ne'er prove that."

"And ye dinnae think he was planning to hurt you today?"

"What good would that have done him? Benet wasnae with me."

"Because without ye, Benet would be even more vulnerable. Aye, we would still be here to protect him, but Sir Adam may nay believe that. I think he believes we would leave, that 'tis only ye who hold us here." He nodded when she frowned, her expression revealing her doubt of his words. "The mon doesnae think a plan through. That is a belief I have become more certain of each time he tries something."

"I am nay sure any of David's family has the wit to do so," she said. "Nay any of the ones I have met. David was their brightest light once Nigel was gone.

I oftimes felt they all resented him for that, for being such a respected, learned man."

"There is one thing that puzzles me." He hesitated, uncertain of how to ask his questions without risking offense, and then decided to simply ask, "Why, if ye were chosen to marry Nigel, did ye wed David?"

"Ye do ken, dinnae ye, that I was betrothed whilst little more than a bairn?"

"Ah, one of those marriages arranged to make some sort of alliance."

"Exactly. I was just nearing the age to be old enough to marry when I was brought here to learn all about being the lady of this keep. It wasnae long after that when Nigel sailed off to France. He had heard too many tales of men making plenty of coin fighting for the French and how that might e'en give him a verra good chance of fighting the English. I wasnae heartbroken when he left though I had spent enough time with him to think he would be a suitable husband. So I waited. And waited. And waited. David sent out inquiries when we had gone a year without any word from him. Then we got a short visit from a mon who claimed he had fought alongside Nigel and his men and that he was dead."

"With all the men that went with him? I assume he took some men with him?"

"Aye, some. I fear he did take our best-trained men but that was only a half dozen or so. But, this mon had no information to give us on their fate. He said Nigel was alone by the time he met up with him."

"And David accepted the mon's word?"

"Nay, not fully, although he couldnae think of any reason for the mon to travel so far just to tell us a lie. But, he didnae really want it to be true if only because Nigel was the last of his family. His father died ere I came here and his mother died soon after. We have ne'er received any word that would reveal that mon to have been a liar though."

"And so then ye married David. Did ye nay ken the truth about his injury?"

"I did. Joan told me. E'en David tried to stutter through an explanation. It didnae matter. E'en a childless marriage was better than being sent back home." She could see that he now meant to ask her about that last statement so she opened the door to her room. "I must see to getting the letter to Sir Adam's father written now."

Before Harcourt could say another word he found himself staring at a shut door. He was already reaching for the latch, intending to follow her into the room, when he accepted that it would be a mistake. The need to know why she would dread going back home to her own family was strong, but he knew he had to stand back and allow her to tell him when she was ready to. Cursing softly, he turned to leave. There was more than enough work for him to do to stop his mind from preying on what Annys had not told him.

Annys listened to Harcourt walk away and breathed a sigh of relief. She had not meant to say anything about why she had chosen to marry David, at least nothing beyond the fact that he would be a good husband and a kind one. Only David and Joan had known that her acceptance of David had had little to do with betrothal contracts, dowries, or some attempt to still become a laird's wife despite the fact that the laird chosen for her was dead. After the three short visits her parents had made to Glencullaich she suspected the people here fully understood her reasoning. Most had undoubtedly guessed that she had married Glencullaich more than that she had actually married David.

No one had told her parents that she had married a man who could not give her any sons. As far as she knew, no one had ever even confirmed that to the rest of David's kinsmen, either. The men who had gelded David were all dead. Nigel had seen to that before he had departed for France, leaving her with the promise that he would return a rich man in time to marry her.

She shook her head as she walked over to her writing table. Men with their quests for fame, fortune, and land were the bane of women everywhere, she decided. Nigel had been a good man, would undoubtedly have made a good husband, father, and laird. He had been tall, strong, and handsome with his wild black hair and light green eyes. Now he was gone. There was not even a grave site at Glencullaich where one could go to mourn his loss.

"How can such witless oafs rule the world?" she asked aloud as she sat down at her writing desk and began to sharpen her quill point with a small knife.

A soft meow startled her and she looked down to find the cat she had rescued sitting by her chair, watching her with those eyes. She wondered if Harcourt had yet noticed how closely the animal's eyes matched his own. Frowning, she looked at the closed door and then back at the cat. It was clean, its golden fur freshly washed, and it smelled slightly of the herbs used to get rid of fleas. A clean bandage was wrapped around the leg that had kept it cruelly tethered to a stake in the alley. It looked like it would recover nicely from its wound. It also should be in the stables.

Shaking her head again, she patted her lap and the cat immediately leapt up on it, curling itself into a tight ball. "I dinnae ken how ye got in here but ye *will* be returned to the stables. Howbeit, for now I dinnae mind the company."

The cat began to purr, a deep, rumbling noise she found strangely comforting.

"I think ye might weel prove to be some trouble."

Annys laughed when it opened one eye to look at her and then closed it again. She set a sheet of fine French linen paper in front of her and stared at its pristine emptiness for a long time. This was not going to be easy. How did one politely tell a man to rein in his son before they had to kill the man for his crimes?

Harcourt watched the young man ride off to deliver Annys's message to Sir Adam's father. A glance over his shoulder revealed her standing in the doorway to the keep looking worried. He hoped she had not put too much hope behind her letter to the elder MacQueen. No man could be that blind to what his son was doing so he had to be condoning Sir Adam's actions, if only by ignoring them.

The MacQueens outside Glencullaich had to be helping Sir Adam because he came and went from the area too often and left no trail to follow. It would also explain how he had obtained a spy within the

keep itself. Harcourt was now well acquainted with
the deep loyalty of David's people living at the keep
or even in the town. Sir Adam or one of his men
would have had to work hard over a long period of
time to gain an ally, especially one willing to kill
David.

He walked over to Annys, resisting the urge to take
her into his arms and try to ease her obvious concerns. "Ye dinnae think he will help."

"Nay." She sighed. "I cannae make myself believe
he will do anything to stop Sir Adam, nay matter how
much I argue with myself. All I am nay certain of is
how great a part the laird is playing in his son's plans.
The one thing that keeps me uncertain is that I
cannae believe the laird would kill David."

"He didnae, did he. Nor did Sir Adam."

"Someone had to tell someone here what to do."

"Aye, but they could talk their way out of that accusation for they didnae do the deed themselves,
were ne'er here to do it."

"Ye have some opinion about who it was, dinnae ye."

"As has been suggested, I think it is a lass. That
means she was wooed by someone loyal to Sir Adam
and, I believe, that would have taken some time. This
isnae a new plan the mon has. He has been working
on it for quite a while."

Annys nodded. "And I suspicion his plans began
when David loudly proclaimed Benet as his son and
heir. The lack of a child before that undoubtedly
raised his hopes of gaining this place. He may have
e'en kenned about David's injury. Then comes
Benet. Benet needs to be verra closely guarded."

"He is. He will be. That was seen to the moment
we all kenned David was murdered."

She rubbed a hand over her forehead in a vain attempt to dispel a growing ache in her head. "Then I shall start praying my son stays close to his guards."

"That would be helpful." Seeing the pinch of pain on her face, he asked, "The letter was difficult to write?"

"Oh, aye. The hardest part was nay saying what I truly felt."

"Go and rest." He stroked her arm. "Now all ye need do is wait for an answer."

"And find the one who betrayed us."

"'Tis a woman, Annys. Look there first."

"We already are."

He waited until she was back inside the keep before going to look for Callum. That young man was not adored by just the children. All the maids tried very hard to catch his eye. The MacFingals had not been around long enough to gain any information and he had plans for those two that would put them on another trail. However, Callum was not going anywhere. It was time he set a skilled spy of his own amongst the people of Glencullaich.

# Chapter Six

Harcourt did not know whether to laugh or curse when he found the MacFingals. He had been searching for the two men for an hour. Now he realized he should have gone to where the maids were first. Nathan and Ned were very busy trying to charm two bonnie maids into offering them their favors. If the blushes and giggles of the women were any indication, the MacFingals were close to succeeding in their quest. Although he had thought they would be a good choice to gain some information from the maids, something that might lead them to the traitor, Harcourt did not think they were doing that at the moment. They looked far more interested in warming whatever beds they found to sleep in. When Ned suddenly looked his way, Harcourt signaled him to join him and then impatiently waited while the two men took their leave of the maids in a way that left the women still giggling.

"Has something happened?" asked Nathan.

"Nay," Harcourt replied, walking back toward the stables where he had begun his long search for the two men, both of them falling into step at his side. "I but need your reputed skill at finding things."

"What have ye lost?"

"The trail of that bastard causing us all of this trouble."

"Ah, aye, kenning where he is would be helpful. Ye think he must be close at hand, dinnae ye."

"It would explain the ease with which he slipped away yesterday. I also think all these wee attacks, and annoyances, are meant to weaken us. Mayhap distract us just enough to nay see what his true plan is."

Ned frowned. "And that would be?"

"To attack, to take what he wants by force and, I suspect, to make certain that Annys and Benet dinnae survive to continue to argue about his claim for this land." He stopped, leaned against the side of the stables, and frowned. "He may think to just be rid of Annys and Benet to clear his path to the laird's chair here but he has already failed to get hold of her and Benet is verra closely watched at all times."

Nathan nodded. "He has also tried his luck with the courts and the king and gained naught."

"So that leaves war," Harcourt said. "If he cannae take Glencullaich easy, he *will* take it hard."

"Ye think he may be gathering an army." Nathan looked around at the men of Glencullaich working in the bailey. "I dinnae think these men are prepared enough to fight an army."

"Nay," Harcourt agreed, "but they are gaining skill every day. That may be something Adam doesnae ken. He saw us, judged our skill as a threat, but I dinnae think he has the wit to see that we could weel give some of that skill to these men. And he doesnae have enough respect for them to believe they could learn. These men may nay be full ready to repel an assault on this keep but they have the heart and stomach to do their best to try. Dinnae think Sir Adam kens that either. At least that is one weakness we might be able to make use of."

"And ye want as much information on where he is and what he is doing as possible."

"I do. E'en what alehouse he goes to or what maid he is swiving."

"We will get ye what we can."

Harcourt watched the two enter the stables to select their horses and sighed. The MacFingals had a reputation for their ability to spy or steal with a skill none could match. The clan had, more or less, stopped stealing since their laird, Ned and Nathan's eldest brother, Ewan, was trying very hard to shine up the MacFingal name. The skill they had for spying, however, as well as their reputation for being fierce, skilled fighters, had proven very helpful to Ewan in getting some of his far-too-many brothers into good positions with other clans. Harcourt knew the necessity of what he asked of Ned and Nathan but hoped he had not put them in too much danger.

Nathan and Ned had soon selected their horses and packed their supplies. After wishing them a safe journey, Harcourt turned to go back into the keep only to catch sight of Annys. She stood watching the MacFingals leave, her soft, full lips curved into a small frown. Harcourt's gut clenched with want as the memory of her kiss washed over him. It had been two long days since he had kissed her and she had done her best to avoid him since then.

That would stop now, he decided, as he walked toward her. He refused to be ignored. He wanted more than the occasional kiss snatched when he caught her alone at some weak moment. Harcourt decided he was going to seduce her and he smiled when he reached her side, looking forward to the challenge. The way she looked a little wary did not surprise him. He suspected he looked somewhat predatory, the hunter inside him revealing itself in his smile.

"Has something happened?" Annys asked. "Is that why Nathan and Ned are leaving?"

"Nay, nothing has happened." He was not surprised that the question was so often asked around Glencullaich. "I just decided it was past time we kenned where that fool Adam is and just what he may be doing. Kenning where he is could be a great help. He slips in and out of your lands with far too much ease and disappears far too quickly. I want to ken how he does that."

"It is going to get worse, isnae it?"

"Oh, aye. The mon has only two ways to get his greedy hands on this land, doesnae he. He can be rid of you and Benet. Or, he can just take it all away from you, making verra certain that ye and Benet dinnae survive the taking to challenge him later."

She paled and he put his arm around her slim shoulders, pulling her up close against his side. It was a harsh truth but she had to face it. Harcourt suspected she was aware of what the next step in this dance would be, certainly after Sir Adam's attempt to kidnap her, but it was time to face the truth with her eyes wide open and her mind clear of doubt or false hopes. She needed to be fully prepared for the battle he knew was coming.

Annys forced herself to stop enjoying how he held

her close and started thinking again. The man was skilled at muddling her wits. The moment he was near all she could think of was how badly she wanted to kiss him. She inwardly cursed, recognizing how cleverly she could lie to herself. In truth, when he was near, all she could think of was making love. She was failing miserably in shaking free of that weakness.

"I ken it," she said, pulling away from him and ignoring how her whole body protested the loss of his warmth. "I do. I just wish it wasnae so. Worse than that, I think too often on how Sir Adam is actually right to claim that Benet isnae the true heir."

"Oh nay, lass. Benet is indeed the true heir. David claimed that lad as his son and the lad was born within the bounds of your Church-blessed marriage to the mon. That is all the law and the Church require. Lass, trust me to ken this as truth when I tell ye, Benet will nay be the first heir who carried none of his mother's husband's blood."

"That is rather sad."

"At times. At other times 'tis for the best. I dinnae think many do as David did but others ken weel that the son they claim as heir, the lad they raise and train, isnae truly their get. There are many reasons for that, too. Nay begetting a son of his own is the most common of reasons. The moment David held Benet and claimed, 'This is *my* son,' Benet became the true heir to Glencullaich in the eyes of the law and the Church."

"That fact doesnae stop the whispers Sir Adam has stirred up with his talk. Whispers and doubts my son may have to suffer from for the rest of his life."

He sighed as she walked back into the keep. Harcourt knew she was right. And in this matter the truth would not free Benet from that. He inwardly shook his head at his own heedless actions of five years ago.

Then he thought of all David had said to convince him. To his shame it had not been that difficult for the man. Harcourt had wanted Annys from the first moment he had seen her, opening his eyes to find her leaning over him and bathing his feverish brow with a cool damp cloth. There was no disputing what David had said, Sir Adam's actions now proving that the man's fears for Glencullaich had been well justified. Yet, Harcourt could not help but think that it had not been his head doing his thinking for him at the time.

As he stepped into the great hall to see Benet sitting next to Annys, the boy's short legs swinging back and forth as he told her about some snail he had seen in the garden, Harcourt sighed. He could torture himself with guilt, bemoan the way he had allowed lust to lead him, and even suffer the pangs of shame for walking away from her and the child he had bred, but one thing he would never change. Without all that had happened, all that was wrong, there had been one blessed outcome of the past: Benet.

"Och, the snail couldnae have been that large," he teased as he walked up to the table to sit down facing them and noted with amusement that Benet was holding his hands at least a foot apart. "A snail that big could chomp on a wee lad like you."

Benet sat up straight and puffed out his thin chest. "I would fight. I would beat him with my stick." He frowned down at his feet. "I would stomp him with my shoe but then it would get all messy and I like my shoes."

"Ah, aye, they are verra fine shoes. Of course, it isnae good to kill a poor creature that is just trying to find a meal for itself. But it needs to leave the garden before it eats all that we need for our meals."

Benet leapt up and scrambled out of the seat. "I will get Tomas and Robbie to help me put it outside the walls."

And then he was gone and Harcourt shook his head over the speed with which the boy moved. "Who are Tomas and Robbie?"

"Joan's sons. They are older than Benet. Ten and twelve and they work in the stables most days. But they are verra good with him."

"'Tis good for a wee lad to have some older ones willing to play with him. We dinnae oftimes see it, but they can teach a wee lad a lot he needs to ken. But, are there no younger children about the keep?"

"There are a few lassies his age but they dinnae play together much. They have all reached that silly age where they each believe the other sex is dim-witted or worse. Benet complained yestereve that all wee Jenny wants to do is kiss him and he hates it because it makes his face all wet." She grinned when Harcourt laughed but then slowly grew serious again as she looked toward the door Benet had just run out of. "I didnae give it a thought but he just ran off alone."

"Nay, he isnae and willnae be alone until this problem with Sir Adam is settled. Every place he can leave the keep is being watched and a mon will linger close by at all times."

"Ah, a loose rein."

"Too tight a one and he might try to slip free of it."

"True." She finished off the small cup of cider she had poured for herself and stood up. "The Mac-Fingals willnae be in too much danger, will they?"

"I willnae lie and say they are in no danger at all, but they are verra, verra skilled at what I have asked them to do. As their father liked to say, MacFingals could steal the coins off a dead mon's eyes and be gone before the mourners e'en realized they were there."

"Oh. What a verra strange recommendation for a spy," she murmured, then laughed and shook her head. "The MacFingals are a wee bit unusual, arenae they."

"A wee bit." He stood up and walked over to link his arm with hers. "Come. Walk with me and I will tell ye all about them."

Annys knew she should say no and go do some work, but it was a fine day and she decided to allow herself just a little weakness. She nodded and he led her out of the keep. They strolled around the grounds, ending up in the garden, now empty of snail and boys. All the while she listened to him tell her tales of the MacFingals torn between shock, laughter, and pure disbelief.

"So many children," she said and shook her head as he led her to the bower and urged her down to sit on the bench next to him. "Yet, he kept them all."

"Aye, he did. And for all those many, many lads grumble about the mon, they love him. He kens each and every one's name, when they were born, and who the mother was. Not one of them doubts that in his too often outrageous way, their father cares for them all."

"A good thing for a child to ken."

She suddenly felt both sad and angry. She was the legitimate get of her parents, their only daughter and one of a mere three children. Yet not once had she felt cared for in the way all those dozens of Mac-Fingals had. Annys fought the fear that it was her fault even as she wondered what was wrong with her parents that they could not even compare well to a man who bred so many bastards, was proud of his skill for thievery, and made enemies of all his neighbors until his own son had to take his place as laird just to avert war with everyone for miles around them.

"Ye have gone verra quiet," Harcourt said as he slipped his arm around her shoulders.

"I was but thinking that the MacFingals, for all that is wrong there, had a better parent than I e'er did." She cursed softly at what she had just confessed. "Dinnae heed me. I but had a moment of feeling sorry for myself."

"I did hear that your parents were nay here verra often."

"The wedding, the birth, and David's funeral."

"Then what did they think to gain from arranging the marriage? So few visits imply they were nay trying to gain much from David."

"Oh, they got what they wanted. David's father got them into the court circles. They had ne'er been able to get there for my mother's father had angered the wrong people years ago and the whole family was banished. The ruler of the court may change but the ones who dinnae wish to see ye or yours take longer to disappear and the talk of some taint, e'en longer than that. But they are back and from all I hear, they are rarely anywhere else."

"So, they didnae really care which son ye married as they had already gained what they sought."

"Aye. I was brought here to learn to be the wife of the laird of Glencullaich."

"They didnae e'en try to make a new contract when Nigel was cried dead?"

"Nay, although I think they did get a few wagons of goods from David." She looked at him. "I think 'tis more embarrassing than aught else. I would thank them for placing me in such a wonderful keep save that I ken weel they didnae care much about that, or e'en about what sort of mon Nigel was."

"Ye have sisters or brothers?"

"Two brothers. One younger and one older."

"Why did ye nay ask them to come and help ye with Sir Adam?"

"Colin is too busy trying to keep our lands making enough coin to support my mother and father. Ah, and Edward has just wed a lass whose father sees him as his heir to his small holding. I do get word from them now and then but I kenned weel that I could find no aid there. That isnae meaning they wouldnae have offered, just that they cannae. I kenned ye were a warrior. My brothers cannae claim that, either."

"And that is why ye didnae wish to go home. T'was cold there, aye?"

She felt the press of his warm lips against the corner of her eye and answered, "Aye. That and my cousins. Evil boys. Men now, but long gone from there. I complained about them once to my mother and got a beating for it. I was too naïve to realize that it was my uncle and aunt who had the money e'en though my father had the land."

Harcourt had a fair idea of what those "evil boys" had been trying to do with their very young cousin. He gently tugged her closer but it was not just sympathy for the lonely child she must have been. There was nothing he could do to change the past. What he wanted was a kiss and for some odd reason he was approaching the matter with all the skill of an untried boy.

Annys realized she was nearly sitting in Harcourt's lap. The thought made her blush for a large part of her thought that would be a lovely place to be. One look in his amber eyes told her that he was not thinking about comforting her for rousing bad memories at the moment.

"Harcourt," she began, trying to put a warning in her voice, which came out sounding a little too welcoming.

"Just a kiss," he said and brushed his mouth over hers.

It was never just a kiss to her but Annys had no intention of confessing that. She told herself to get up and walk away, perhaps even leave him with a few sharp words of rebuke. But his lips were so soft and warm. Even the light touch of them on hers was enough to make the heat of need flow through her body. As she let him draw her more fully into his embrace a little voice told her that she would pay dearly for giving in to such temptation. Annys ignored it.

Her whole body welcomed his kiss. As his tongue caressed the inside of her mouth her hunger for him grew until she ached. For a moment she tensed when he moved his hands up from her waist. Then he stroked the sides of her breasts with his fingers, making them swell and ache for the feel of his caress, and she trembled.

The strength of her reaction to such a light, not quite intimate, touch startled her and broke the spell his kiss had put her under. Annys became all too aware of their surroundings. The bower might be shaded, but they were not completely hidden away. Anyone, including Benet, could stumble upon their little tryst. Sharing heated kisses in the garden was not the way the lady of Glencullaich should behave.

Harcourt silently cursed when her soft, willing body abruptly grew tense. He wanted to hold her tight and bring back the fire he had tasted in her kiss but he knew that would be a mistake. What he desperately wanted to know was what had happened to douse her fire. He could then make certain it never happened again.

Unless it was some memory of him that turned her cold and cautious. It was an alarming thought. Harcourt could not think of anything he had done. He knew men could be complete lackwits about what would and would not upset a woman, but he prided himself on being more astute than most. The women in his family took pride in making sure their men, especially their sons, had some faint ability to see when they had done something that might offend or upset a woman before they went out into the world. If he did not find out what was turning her cold soon he was going to be useless in the coming fight. He would be too crippled with unsatisfied lust to even walk, he thought, and almost smiled at that nonsense. In truth, he would more likely be eager to kill as many of their enemy as possible.

"Annys? Is something wrong?" he asked when she pulled free of his embrace. "Ye look concerned."

"Of a certain I am concerned. We are in the garden!" The look of confusion that passed over his handsome face made her want to hit him even though she knew most of her growing anger was aimed right at her own weakness. "Anyone could see us."

Harcourt opened his mouth to argue that when a young male voice called out to her. A moment later young Gavin hurried over to them, having spotted them from the moment he had entered the garden. The chances of such a thing happening every time he sought to steal a kiss in the garden were very small, but one look at Annys's face told him it would be wise if he kept that opinion to himself. She looked briefly horrified and embarrassed before she assumed that calm, sweet expression he had begun to call her *m'lady* face.

"The MacQueen laird has sent an answer," Gavin said.

Seeing no missive in his hand, Annys asked, "Did ye put it in the ledger room ere ye came to find me?"

"Nay, he didnae write anything. He told me to tell you he needed to ponder his answer a wee bit and would send it on soon."

"Ponder his answer?" Annys shook her head. "Thank ye, Gavin." The moment the youth walked away, she looked at Harcourt. "What is there for the mon to ponder? I asked him to do something about the trouble his son was causing me. A simple aye or nay, or e'en a *my son can do no wrong* reply was all that was needed."

Harcourt stood up, reached out to her in the hope of easing her agitation, and then tried not to wince

when she smoothly moved out of the way. "He but
delays, makes ye wait."

"Wait for what?"

He shrugged. "For him to see for himself if what
ye told him was true? To keep ye waiting and thinking he might help so that his son has more time to
ready his next attack? All I am certain of is that the
mon plays some game. I am just nay exactly sure
which one."

"Which do ye think is the most probable?"

"That he tries to make ye think ye could find help
there and so will wait and do nothing else."

"Thus, as you said, giving Sir Adam that time he
needs to ready himself for his next strike." She closed
her eyes and took a deep breath to try to tamp down
a rising anger, then looked at him again. "Weel, he
will soon see that I am nay such a weak fool. We shall
continue to do whate'er is needed to protect ourselves. And I *hate* this," she added softly.

When he moved to take her into his arms, thinking only to comfort her, she evaded him again.
"What is wrong? I but meant to try to ease the pain I
heard in your voice when ye spoke."

Annys studied his face, seeing no lie there. She
doubted the embrace would have remained one of
only comfort, however. She was not being vain in be-
lieving that he wanted her, was just not sure it was a
want as whole-hearted as the one she had for him. As
with too many men, Harcourt's wanting probably
sprang from just one part of him while hers was
rooted so deep inside it was as much a part of her as
breathing.

"Then I thank ye for that thought," she said. "And,
aye, this is a matter which causes me great pain. I

simply cannae understand how anyone could wish harm upon a child or a place as fine as this just for their own gain. And that is all Adam sees when he looks at Glencullaich. Gain. *His* gain. He would bleed this place dry if he got his hands on it. I willnae allow that. I willnae play his father's sly games, either."

"Good, although I wasnae verra worried that ye would cry a halt to all we are doing just to wait on that mon's word." He held out his hand. "Sit with me for a wee while and we can discuss it all."

Harcourt inwardly cursed when he saw wariness creep into her expression. He was not surprised, however. It had been an awkward ploy. For reasons he could not fathom, he lost all his reputed wooing skills when dealing with Annys.

"I begin to think ye play a wee sly game as weel, Sir Harcourt Murray."

"Me? What game would I play with you, sweet Annys?"

"Seduction. Weel, ye can cease playing for I am wise to you now."

Harcourt watched her walk away and slowly smiled. It was freeing, in a way, that she now understood he was trying to seduce her. He had discovered that his well-practiced seduction ploys did not work well on a woman who had never played the game. Such ploys were for the more worldly wise ladies, not one like Annys. The fact that he wanted to win this prize with a desperation that surprised him made him clumsy at the game anyway. Now he could openly hunt her down and he found he was heartily looking forward to that.

He walked toward the bailey to rejoin the others in training the men. Annys was still giving him a free

# Chapter Seven

It was not easy to ignore the four big men flanking her as she walked to the butcher's, but Annys did her best to do so. Annoying though it was to be smothered with protection there was one advantage to it all. There were a lot of eyes on Benet, keeping her son in sight at all times. The boy was skipping along next to Sir Callum and as safe as he could ever be.

Benet was also chattering away so much that Annys was surprised he found the time to breathe properly. What truly astonished her, however, was how pleasantly Sir Callum dealt with the child's unceasing talk. The man even took the time to discuss the goats Benet pointed out as if it was some new, fascinating subject to him, one worthy of all his attention. Her son, who was so often shy with men he did not know well, had taken to Sir Callum from the very beginning. So had most of the other children at Glencullaich. The man had a true gift with the young although she had to wonder if he thought it more of a curse at times.

"Callum loves the bairns," said Harcourt, seeing where she was looking and burying a twinge of jealousy over how well Benet got along with Callum. "He made a vow when nay more than a child himself. He said he would always keep children safe, that he intended to become the one to defend them. Lad had a hard beginning himself."

"Mayhap that is what draws the children to him," Annys said. "The children ken it in that way they have." She met Harcourt's gaze, ignoring the way her pulse increased when she looked into his golden eyes. "And mayhap 'tis for the best if Benet doesnae spend too much time with you," she added quietly and tried to ignore what looked like hurt darkening his eyes.

Harcourt pushed aside the pain her words caused him. He had just begun to believe that he had accepted the fact that he could not come to know his son as he wanted to, and then something would be said to make him regret the loss all over again. She was right. The less he and Benet were together, the smaller the chance that anyone would grow suspicious. Too much could be lost if anyone outside of Glencullaich guessed David was not the boy's true sire. It would give weight to Sir Adam's claim that he was the true heir. The people of Glencullaich deserved far better than Sir Adam as their laird.

Benet was alive, much loved by his mother and the people of Glencullaich, and he was both healthy and bright. He also was the laird and had a future ahead of him as a powerful and wealthy noble, something Harcourt could never give him. Harcourt found that he needed to remind himself of that far too often the longer he stayed at Glencullaich. Openly claiming

Benet as his might make him feel better but it would take from Benet far more than he could ever hope to replace.

There were times he cursed the customs and teachings of his family. Many men were all too ready to walk away from a child they bred despite how often they condemned that child to a hard life. Harcourt could never do that. Leaving a woman carrying his child had proven hard enough but he had known that child would be loved and cared for, and would prosper. Now that he had seen his son, come to know the child, that was no longer enough but his vow to David held him silent. Murrays did not break a vow.

When Annys entered the butcher's small shop with Benet, Harcourt took a careful look around before leaving her to do her business with the man. He rejoined his companions and surveyed the village that hugged the hillside. It was a good place. Harcourt made careful note of a few things he would like to do at Gormfeurach.

"'Tis a fine place for a lad to grow into a man," said Callum.

Harcourt winced. "I ken it. Kenned it all those years ago when David asked me to do that one thing for him. After all, I owed him my life. Doesnae make it any easier."

"Nay, I suspicion it doesnae."

"And now? Weel, now I ken more fully why he asked such a thing of me. The kinsmon who wants to take his place as laird cannae be allowed to hold Glencullaich. This land, these people, deserve better than that."

"Aye, they do. That doesnae mean ye couldnae still be a part of the lad's life."

Harcourt smiled faintly. "That could cause as many problems as it might solve."

"Because others might soon suspect what the lad is to you?" asked Callum. "Or because it would be difficult to leave the lass alone?"

"I have been told that most of the people here have kenned that the lad was ne'er David's get."

"And they dinnae care?"

"Nay. They loved David and David claimed the boy, took him straight into his heart. Now that I have seen what awaited them if there was no heir, I can understand such acceptance. As for the lass? Nay, I wouldnae be able to leave her alone. I find it most difficult to do that even now."

"And, of course, if ye stayed here it wouldnae take long for your kin to discover the lad, aye?"

Harcourt grimaced. "They would and that would be a complication I should verra much like to avoid."

Callum nodded. "They wouldnae be able to act as if he was just some other woman's child, a woman ye ken weel and whose husband was a good friend to you. They would treat Benet as what he is—blood kin. But then, they are weel kenned to readily accept stray bairns into their family."

Recalling how Callum came to be so much a part of their family, Harcourt frowned. His clan was indeed well known to take into their homes the children that others cast aside so callously. It was that reputation that had landed Callum in his brother Payton's home so many years ago. The woman Payton now called wife had hunted him down to aid her in the rescuing of Callum and his friends. Payton and Kirstie still rescued children, a crusade Callum had taken up as well. It could mean that he could tell his kin about Benet yet not risk the boy's place as David's heir. His kin were also very skilled at keeping secrets.

"I need to decide what I do and dinnae wish to do about Annys ere I decide on how to deal with my kin," he said.

"What is there to decide? Ye want her. That isnae much of a secret. Ye wanted her five years ago and ye still do. A wanting that lasts that long is much more than a simple lusting."

"I ken it. Just dinnae ken if it is enough. And, she isnae rushing into my arms now, is she. My vanity has taken a mighty beating as she remains unmoved by all my seduction skills."

Callum laughed softly but quickly grew serious again. "I can see the want in her eyes when she looks at you. But, do ye ken what else I see? Guilt."

"She has naught to feel guilty about."

"Nay, but that doesnae means she believes that. The rules are written clearly, old friend. The Church preaches them to one and all from the time we are all too young to e'en ken what they are actually saying or what they mean. She broke a verra big rule and it doesnae matter much if her own husband told her to do it. Big sin. Big guilt."

Harcourt cursed. "I wondered on that. Cannae say I dinnae feel the bite of it myself from time to time. Ne'er mind what the Church preaches. Adultery is darkly frowned upon by my kin. I didnae break a vow to a wife but that wouldnae completely save me from their censure." He frowned as he caught the glint of sun on metal on the side of one of the many hills surrounding the village.

"What is it?" asked Callum as he looked in the same direction Harcourt was intensely staring in.

"Someone is up there."

"One of the herdsmen or shepherds?"

"Would they start a fire on such a fine day?" Seeing how Callum squinted, Harcourt pointed to where he had seen a thin curl of smoke rising above a cluster of big stones. "There. Just behind that wee cairn." He soon saw two more signs of smoke.

"Ye have eyes like a falcon. Ah, aye, now I see it or something akin to what ye say ye are looking at. What are they doing? And, aye, now I see the other two."

"I dinnae ken. Spying on us. They are close enough to see a lot if they have good eyes. But why the fire? 'Tis a warm day." He mulled over that very question for a moment and then cursed.

"What?"

"How close do ye need to be to hit one of these roofs with an arrow?"

Callum cursed. "Since he but has to put one onto a roof, that is close enough. I now see the problem with having the village nestled in these hills."

"Two choices. Warn the village or try to get to them before they shoot any arrows."

"We can do both. Only need to bellow out an alarm and make sure they dinnae get so afraid they hurt each other in fleeing." Callum whistled, bringing Tamhas and Gybbon to his side.

Both men cursed freely when they saw the problem and raced for their horses, held by Joan's boys at the edge of the village. Harcourt was just trying to think of a way to quietly spread the word that people needed to move when the first arrow came toward the town in a pretty if deadly arc of flame. He slapped Callum on the shoulder and the man began running to warn people as he turned and raced into the butcher's to get Annys and Benet out of the shop.

Annys turned quickly to see who had just slammed into Master Kenneth's shop. The look on Harcourt's face had her reaching for Benet who was patting a lamb, blissfully unaware that it was soon for the block. Something had gone terribly wrong, she thought, and a heartbeat later she heard the sounds of alarm outside the door.

"Out of the building," Harcourt ordered. "Someone is trying to set the roofs alight."

Master Kenneth grabbed what he cherished most and headed straight for the door, snatching up the lamb as he walked past it. Annys clung to Benet as Harcourt pulled them out onto the street. For a moment it looked like complete chaos but she quickly began to see that Callum was working to get everyone out and to begin work to save as much as they could.

"Get to the edge of the village but stay in sight so I ken ye are safe. By Old Tom's rowan tree."

"I should help."

"Ye will. I mean to send the women and children to gather there with ye."

A cry and several people pointing caused her to look up. Even though she knew that what was headed their way was viciously dangerous, Annys was fascinated as it sailed over her head and landed on the roof of Old Meg's little home. That woman was already hurrying out of the house dragging two sacks of her meager goods. Annys hurried to her side, grabbed one of the sacks, and then led the woman to where Harcourt had told her to wait.

"My bonnie wee home will be gone," cried Old Meg, tears streaking the dirt on her wrinkled face. "What will I do?"

"If they cannae save it, Meg, then ye shall have a new one," Annys promised.

She soon saw that she had been given an important job, alleviating the last of her unease about not being right there in the midst of it all alongside Harcourt and the men of the village. The women who had the strength and agility to help, stayed with the men to try to save what could be saved but they readily sent their children over to Annys and the older women. Annys soothed whom she was able to but her anger over the destruction was a hard knot in her belly. Keeping children and old women calm and corralled at the tree took all of her energy and she was grateful for that. Something inside of her was demanding she have a screaming, fists-and-heels-pounding-on-the-ground fit, the kind that had been quickly beaten out of her as a child. Giving in to that would be too humiliating.

Men from the keep raced into the village and swiftly moved to help. Annys tried to see where the fire had come from and saw Callum send a few men toward the hills. She then recalled seeing Tamhas and Gybbon ride that way as she had hurried to get Old Meg to the tree. It frightened her to think that men that far away could wreak such damage but she could not move the village or flatten the hills. She was worrying about that danger when she was distracted by a wrinkled, dirty hand patting her on the arm. She realized she must have let her alarm show for Old Meg was trying to comfort her.

"Everyone got out, m'lady, and that be what matters." The old woman squinted toward the hills. "I suspicion those fine knights ye fetched for us will think of something to fix that weakness now that it has been seen clear and all."

"I suspicion they will indeed," replied Annys as she finally set Benet down. "Stay right here with all of us."

"I will, *Maman*," he said, his bottom lip trembling. "I dinnae like the burning. Why would someone want to burn our village?"

"A mon who wants us to leave so he can have this land for his own," she replied. "All the people got out of the houses, love. We will be fine."

"The animals are running about all scared. They could get hurt."

Annys had noticed that. Needing to flee quickly meant not being able to gather up one's pets or livestock and it appeared the solution had been to just open wide the doors, gates, and hutches. The bigger animals had swiftly moved to the edge of the village away from the smoke, milling around nervously as each kept a close watch on the fire. The smaller animals scurried around squawking, quacking, barking, and just making a general, dangerous nuisance of themselves.

"I dinnae think there is much we can do about that, Benet. We cannae get in the way of the ones fighting the fire."

She yelped and leapt out of the way when a large cat raced between her legs followed by a barking dog. Spinning around she watched the cat leap into the tree while one of the boys grabbed the dog by the ruff and pulled it away. Several people laughed and Annys's concern for everyone eased a little more.

"We can go down and gather up some of them, m'lady," said a young girl with a face splattered with freckles. "We willnae get in the men's way. We ken how to get most of them to come to us." She pointed at the two girls with her.

"Be verra certain ye stay away from the burning areas and the men, Annie. Ye as weel, Una and Beth. None of those poor animals are worth any of you getting hurt."

"We will be careful, m'lady."

With so many women watching the children, Annys felt safe keeping her attention on the girls slipping around the edges of the area that was on fire. They had collected two boys to help them. Soon the small livestock along with dogs and cats, most of which made a quick retreat up a tree as soon as they reached one, joined the women and children by the rowan tree. She made certain to congratulate the girls and boys on a job well done and meant every word of it. Without all of the smaller animals cluttering up the road in their mindless panic the men working to put out the fires moved a little faster.

Soon no flames could be seen although a few things still smoked. The ones who could see that their homes remained untouched began to cautiously return to them and the crowd gathered by the rowan tree began to thin out. Holding firmly to Benet's hand, Annys carefully made her way to where she could see Harcourt and his men studying the damage, occasionally ordering a few men to throw some more water on something that appeared to be still smoldering. She had just reached his side when

Gybbon and Tamhas returned with three men from the keep who had raced to help them hunt the ones who had committed this crime. Annys needed only one look at their faces to know those men had gotten away from them.

"They were already mounted as they shot their last arrows and rode off the moment we started up the hills," said Gybbon. "I think those three men were hired because they were so skilled. It was only a wee lead they had on us but it was enough."

Tamhas nodded his agreement. "And they rode off leaving their fires still burning which meant someone would have to stop to put them out. Aye, these men were far better than any of the others we have faced."

"No trail?"

"A wee one. We decided to nay go too far ere we discussed it with you."

"I think we should make some attempt to hunt them down," said Harcourt, his anger evident on his face as he looked around at the damage done to the village. "Aye, we cannae go far from here but we might get lucky and catch one, or gain some useful information just by seeing which way they were going."

"Then we must try," Annys said. "We can keep working here. Ye go hunting." She, too, looked around, counting six destroyed structures and nearly that many needing extensive repairs. "There is certainly more than enough to keep us busy. Between the ones who still have a home and the keep, we also need to make certain everyone has some shelter."

"Oh, look, *Maman!*" cried out Benet. "Master Kenneth saved *my* lamb."

Annys sighed as she watched the butcher stop, his

broad shoulders tensing. The little lamb tucked under his arm looked round at Benet and bleated, its legs moving as if it wanted to get down and run to the boy. Benet pulled free of her grip and ran over to pat the lamb. Whatever the child was telling the butcher, it made the man look even more morose.

"I best go and fetch Benet so that Master Kenneth can put his belongings back," she said and started to walk toward the sad-faced butcher.

"Ye do that," said Harcourt. "I will go fetch a horse to join in the hunt and tell Dunnie to expect a lamb soon."

Ignoring the snickering of the men, Annys kept walking, reaching the butcher's side just as he set the lamb down on its feet. It ran straight to Benet who laughed with delight. Benet began to talk to the lamb, testing out names, and Annys softly cursed.

"I ken it, m'lady. Could see the threat of it when ye were in my shop," the butcher said.

"Is it a boy or a girl, Master Kenneth?" asked Benet.

"'Tis a ewe, laddie."

"Nay, we cannae do that; we cannae take a sheep in. Ye were prepared to butcher it," she added, lowering her voice so that Benet could not overhear her words.

"Truth is, I wasnae looking forward to that. My own fault. It was cast aside by its dam and none of the others wanted it so I got it for a pittance. Fattened it up a bit but the cursed thing is too friendly. Kept telling it it was for the pot but kept telling myself it needed just a wee bit more fattening up before I killed it."

"Roberta! *Maman!* I am going to call her Roberta." She silently echoed the butcher's mild curse.

"How much is it worth?" she asked the man and he named a price so low, she frowned suspiciously at him. "I mean to pay ye the fair value."

"I ken it, m'lady, but I am nay sure that ewe will be a good breeder for ye as the one it came from wasnae, but it will eat a lot and will need care, aye? Unless ye have a starving time at the keep, that ewe will be with ye until she dies of old age and I dinnae ken exactly how long that will be."

Annys did not even want to think about that. She promised to send him the coin. Then she told him that he should make a list of his losses and damages and send her that information. While the butcher tied a rope around the lamb's neck so that Benet could lead the animal back to the keep, Annys took one last look at the village. Due to the efforts of Harcourt and his men, no one had died or been seriously injured and the damage was far less than it could have been had they not been there to warn everyone and lend them aid. There was still a lot of work to be done now to get the village looking better and return homes to the ones waiting to get inside them again.

Harcourt slowly rode by as she and Benet walked back to the keep. Annys looked up at him, idly considering how handsome he looked astride his mount, and caught him grinning at her. He looked at Benet and then the lamb, then looked back at her and cocked one dark eyebrow. She thought wistfully on shaving it off his face while he slept.

"Look, Sir Harcourt," Benet said, dragging his lamb forward so Harcourt could see it better. "The butcher gave me this lamb. 'Tis a girl lamb, ye ken. I am calling her Roberta."

"A good name for a ewe. Dinnae ye think so, Lady MacQueen?"

"Dinnae ye have some hunting to do?"

He laughed, nodded, and rode away to join his men. Annys glared at his broad back and saw his shoulders shaking with laughter. She ached to throw something hard at that back but a quick glance to the side showed her that Benet was watching her. Sighing at the lost chance, she started walking again and had to smile at the way he walked and talked with his lamb.

Once in the bailey, Annys turned coward. She did not want to face Dunnie so she sent Benet and his lamb off to the man without her. A quick look around revealed there were plenty of men within the walls of the keep and they all took a moment to notice where the child was going.

By the time Annys got to her room, she had lost the humor of Benet's wanting the lamb and the annoyance caused by Harcourt's amusement over that. She shed her gown and washed away the stink of burning buildings. All the while her spirits sank lower and lower until she knew she was very close to sitting on the bed and wailing like a bairn.

Tugging on a clean gown, she poured herself a tankard of cider and went to sit on the bench in front of the window. It overlooked her gardens and could often lift her spirits. Annys was not sure they would this time as gardens were pretty to look at but they offered one no advice on how to save people or land. Seeing the destruction in the village, knowing how easily there could have been many people killed or scared by burns, she felt helpless.

She had to wonder if it was all worth it. It was just

land, just a building, yet she was fighting for it as if she had no choice. There was a choice. She could hand it all over to Sir Adam, pack up her things, and find another place to live, something small but comfortable, something that would never draw the greedy eye of a man.

"Nay, Mary Two, ye must nay touch the flowers. They are Lady Annys's and they are to look at and smell, nay to pick or play with."

"They are verra bonnie. And they do smell verra nice. Like ye do, Mother."

"Thank ye, love. Come let us sit here for a moment."

Annys struggled to hear the words and leaned closer to the window. Below in her garden a young, large with-child woman walked with a little girl. The child looked to be about Benet's age. She thought a moment and then realized she knew who these people were. Mary Two was what Dougal the weaver called his little girl because his wife was also named Mary. They had all come to the keep because their home had been badly damaged.

"Do ye think we can have a bonnie wee garden at our house?"

"That would be lovely, dear heart, but we really dinnae have the room." Mary idly picked the dead blossoms off the roses. "I do love this, however. Mayhap your da can think of a way for me to have a wee corner for a few flowers." She sat down on the bench and Annys could almost hear the sigh of relief the woman gave as she got off her feet.

"Did ye have a garden when ye lived with your family?"

"Nay, but there was a lady near to us who did and she would allow me to help her tend the flowers. My

da thought it a waste of time and good earth that
could have grown some food."

"Nay, I like it. Do ye think we can come visit this
every day?"

"We will go home soon, dear heart. It willnae take
your da that long to fix what needs to be fixed. But,
mayhap, someday, if we ask verra nicely, Lady Annys
will let us come back for a visit."

Annys watched as the woman suddenly looked in
the direction of the gates. She whispered something
to her child who smiled widely and they hurried off.
The men had returned and Annys suspected Dougal
the weaver was amongst them.

Her sense of hopelessness had eased and her bat-
tered spirit had strengthened. Mary and Mary Two
were the best reasons of all to keep fighting for Glencullaich. They would find no welcome in any garden
Sir Adam might have. It was such a small thing but
she knew it was almost a sign, something showing her
what she had to do and why.

For the sake of the two Marys, mother and daughter, for Master Kenneth who raised a lamb and was
doubting he could now kill it although he made his
living as a butcher, and even for Old Meg who wept
at the loss of her tiny cottage, she made her choice.
They were but a few of the many reasons she had to
hold fast and fight. A man like Sir Adam would crush
such people beneath his boot. Annys was determined
not to give the man the chance to do so.

# Chapter Eight

Sweat dripped down from his forehead and stung his eyes. Harcourt wiped it away with the sleeve of his shirt. He was ready to ride back to the keep. He, Callum, Tamhas, and Gybbon had been riding around the boundaries of Glencullaich since dawn, trying to find any sign of Sir Adam and discovering nothing. It appeared that Sir Adam had directed his attention elsewhere although Harcourt knew that could not be true.

It was not easy but Harcourt beat down a creeping concern for Nathan and Ned. They had been gone for three days and there had been no word. It was not an unusual length of time to spend trying to gather information on an enemy. Harcourt knew that. His concern was born of the fact that spying was dangerous work and he had been the one who had asked the MacFingals to do it.

"They will be fine," said Gybbon as he rode up beside Harcourt. "MacFingals are hard to kill."

Harcourt looked at his cousin and frowned. The

younger man was neither sweating nor dusty despite the long hours they had all spent in the saddle. His hair was still neatly tied back with a leather thong. That was grossly unfair in Harcourt's opinion.

"Did ye stop for a bath in the burn and change your clothes?" he asked, not even trying to hide his suspicions.

Gybbon laughed. "Nay. I simply dinnae ride about in a frenzy when I am looking for something. Or someone."

"I wasnae riding about in a frenzy. Dinnae see the sense in ambling along like an old mon, either. And how did ye ken that I was thinking of the MacFingals? Or can say that they are fine with such confidence?"

"I just ken it. Decided ye were looking for signs of them as hard as ye are looking for signs of Sir Adam."

"Weel, I sent them out on the hunt, didnae I. It has proven to be a heavier weight than I had kenned it would be."

"They are MacFingals, Harcourt," said Gybbon, smiling. "What ye asked of them is what they do with a skill unmatched by any other. They were born kenning how to slip about, hearing secrets, finding lost things, or people, and, of course, stealing."

"Thought they stopped stealing."

"Hard to break such a habit. 'Tis nay a way of living for them anymore, though. As Nathan likes to say, at times ye come across someone who simply doesnae deserve to have all he has so ye feel compelled to relieve him of some of it. But, as to them being hale, I just ken it." He shrugged.

"Ah, ye have a wee gift then. I just ne'er had cause

to notice it before now. Runs rampant in the clan, doesnae it. Missed me."

"Nay, it didnae. Ye just have one that doesnae raise any questions."

"Gybbon, I dinnae have one."

"Ye do. Ye can see the patterns of things, look at something and see it as if 'tis drawn up by the finest mapmaker in the land. The defense of Glencullaich looked fine to all of us yet ye could look about and see the smallest of weaknesses."

Harcourt shook his head. "'Tis just a good eye."

"Then ye have the best eye I have e'er seen. Wheesht, ye could fill a purse or two just offering your skill to those who wish to be certain their defenses are as strong as they think they are. Ye cannae see it because ye just do it, but 'tis a gift. By my oath, I think ye could look out on a cleared field and find that one tiny hollow or dip and rise that could be used by an enemy. 'Tis as if ye can see it all played out from the field itself to how the enemy could use every blade of grass. That is indeed a gift. Trust me to ken it. I have seen enough to ken how different what ye can do is to what any other soldier can do, even the most skilled and experienced one."

"Weel, I am nay sure I agree, but I am pleased that, if I do have a gift, 'tis nay one that causes the trouble some of our kin have to deal with."

Harcourt tensed. Something was wrong. A moment later Gybbon tensed as well. Before he could ask Gybbon if he had any idea what had them both on alert a sound reached his ears and he cursed. A quick glance at Callum and Tamhas told him that they had also heard the sound. Some herd of animals was headed their way at a gallop.

"I would guess cattle," said Gybbon.

"Aye." After looking all around, Harcourt pointed toward a small hill, the faintest hint of a dust cloud rising above it. "O'er there and headed straight for us." When the other two men joined them, Harcourt advised, "As soon as they are in sight we will ken which way we need to go to get out of their way. Dinnae hesitate, either. Just move. They are nay interested in harming us, only in getting away from whate'er is driving them."

"Ye think they are being driven?" asked Callum.

Harcourt nodded. "'Tis a panicked run. Ah, there they are."

The cattle poured over the hill, thundering toward them at a reckless pace. Following them were four men on horses driving the beasts onward with whips and even swords. As he rode to the side of the stampede he had to wonder how many cattle would be lost to this new attempt to get at him and his men.

The waste infuriated him. That anyone would think he and his men too stupid to evade such an attack deeply insulted him as well. As soon as the cattle had passed, Harcourt drew his sword and went after the men driving them on, his men quickly following him.

It was a quick battle much to Harcourt's disappointment. One man escaped, turning his horse quickly and fleeing over the hill. Tamhas pursued him for a while but turned back before getting too far away from Harcourt and the others. Harcourt killed one and Callum killed another. Gybbon wounded then captured the man he had fought with. Dismounting, Harcourt walked over to where Gybbon held his captive at sword point and looked down at the man who was clutching his bleeding arm and wailing like a bairn.

"Cease that noise," he ordered and lightly kicked the man in the hip.

"I am bleeding to death!"

"Then ye will miss your hanging." Harcourt folded his arms over his chest and nodded in approval when the man paled and grew quiet. "One of Sir Adam's men, are ye?" The man nodded. "Where is the bastard?"

"I dinnae ken. He sent us to stop ye looking about."

"And ye thought sending noisy, scared cattle at us would do that?"

"Nay, I thought it a witless plan but Jaikie"—he glanced at one of the dead men—"he thought it was brilliant. Boasted how we would be trampling ye into the mud and finally be rid of ye all. Told him ye were on horses and could just ride out of the way but he cuffed me offside the head and did it anyway."

"Where is Sir Adam?"

"I dinnae ken. Done told ye that."

Harcourt placed his sword point at the man's throat. "He gave ye the orders. Ye saw him."

"Nay, I didnae and ye will get nay more answers from a dead mon than ye get from a live one. The mon sent another mon to tell us what to do. We are nay more than his hirelings. Mon wouldnae spit on one like me if I was on fire. I saw him but the once when we were hired. He came to look us o'er like cattle he meant to buy and slaughter. Nay more than that. When he wants us to do something he has Clyde come and tell us. Clyde be his second, ye ken."

"Aye, we have learned that much. Now we take this fool back to Glencullaich."

"Och, mon, I told ye all I ken," the man said, his voice a pain-filled whine as Gybbon none too gently yanked him to his feet. "Why dinnae ye just let me go?"

"So ye can go back to Sir Adam? Mayhap tell him all ye ken?"

"I dinnae ken a thing, do I?"

"Nay, ye will come with us. We may yet have need of what little ye do ken."

Annys gaped at Harcourt and Gybbon when they strode into the hall. It was not that they appeared as if they had been in a battle that shocked her for a quick look at them revealed no wounds. It was the body Gybbon had flung over his shoulder. A body that was filthy, bloody, and very still.

"Where do ye keep your prisoners?" Harcourt asked.

"Ah, so he isnae dead then," she said as she stood up and started to walk out of the great hall, waving at the two of them to follow her. "I wasnae sure."

"Nay, he is nay dead," said Gybbon. "Does have a wee wound that he should probably have tended to though."

"That might be best," she said as she led them into the ledger room. "E'en if he is one of Sir Adam's hired swords, I am nay too fond of letting anyone rot down there."

She unlocked a door at the far end of the room, one that blended perfectly with the heavy wood panels covering the walls quietly telling the men that it was also the door that led to the bolt-hole. She shivered a little as she lit a torch with Harcourt's help. The air drifting up from below was cool and a little damp. Annys knew that small shiver was also born of a deep dislike of going down into the bowels of the keep. As she led them down the narrow steps, she repeatedly reminded herself that her fear was no more than a childhood scar on her heart and had no place here. This was not her parents' holding nor was it as cramped, dirty, or smelly as those few cells her father had kept for the occasional prisoner awaiting the sheriff.

As her right foot touched the floor of the cellar, something ran by and she had to clap a hand over her mouth to hold back a scream. Harcourt reached around and took the torch out of her trembling hand. He lit the torch stuck in a sconce on the wall at the base of the steps and she breathed a sigh of relief. Out of the corner of her eye, between her and the cells, was a mouse.

"Oh, that is nay a rat, thank the Lord," she muttered only to tense when it started to run again.

A heartbeat later something much larger raced out of the shadows only to disappear into them once more as it ran after the mouse. Annys heard a strangled high-pitched sound escape her and she leapt up on Harcourt. He caught her to him with one strong arm, still holding the torch in his other hand. It took a moment for Annys to calm down enough to begin to feel embarrassed by her fear.

"What was that?" she asked, trying to look around without losing her grip on Harcourt. "A rat?"

"Ah, poor Roban to be so cruelly insulted. Nay, t'was no rat. I cannae see that far down into the shadows but I suspicion there is no mouse now, either."

Attempting to pretend she had not just climbed the man like a tree in her blind panic, Annys eased her stranglehold on him and put her feet back on the ground. "That was Roban?"

"Aye, it was chasing the mouse."

"But, how did he get down here?"

"How does the cursed beast keep getting into the keep, into your bedchamber, and solar?"

"Mon's getting heavy," said Gybbon. "Can we discuss the cat's skills later?"

"Oh, Gybbon, I am so sorry." Annys took one cautious step toward the cell, looking everywhere for any sign of a rat.

"Give me the keys, sweetling," Harcourt said, and gently pried them from her clenched hand. "Ye can walk behind me. I will protect ye from the wee mousie if that cat hasnae killed it yet."

Annoyance at his teasing did a lot to banish her fear, as did walking with him between her and anything lurking in the shadows. "The wee mousie doesnae bother me. 'Tis rats I cannae abide. They bite and they gather in the dark like some army so that they can hunt their prey with nay fear."

"So, 'tis rat armies ye fear. Weel, that does sound frightening. Just where did ye come by the knowledge that rats wander in the dark gathered up in little rat armies?"

Annys softly cursed as they stopped before one of the three cells and she pointed to the key he needed to use to unlock the door. Harcourt stuck the torch he held into another sconce set in the wall next to the door, unlocked it, and helped Gybbon get their unconscious prisoner settled on the narrow bed. They were quick and efficient but, in the short time that the men left her side, her panic began to rise again. Having avoided coming down into the bowels of the keep for any reason, she had forgotten how deep and strong her fear of rats was.

Harcourt handed her back the keys and wrapped his arm around her shoulders as they walked back to the stairs. "Now, tell me why ye fear rats so much ye tried to sit on my shoulder just to get away from one."

It was a humiliating story but Annys decided he deserved some explanation for how she had just behaved. "I got locked into a wee, dirty cell in the cellars at my parents' holding when I was but a child. My father had a prisoner brought up from them and he was so filthy, a bit bloody, and shaking. He answered all my father's questions and begged the mon to please nay put him back down there. He was babbling and crying and I couldnae hear what troubled him about the cellars. I was hiding in the room, having tucked myself behind a chest in the corner. I wasnae supposed to be in that room and I was verra afraid of being caught there. My father assured the mon that he wouldnae have to go back into the cell. The mon thanked him but then my father informed him that he wasnae going back there because he was being taken out to be hanged. I thought that was rather cruel."

Gybbon grunted. "Aye. Cold. What had the mon

done?" he asked as they paused at the bottom of the stairs leading up out of the cellars.

"He had stolen a bag of food scraps meant for my father's pigs," she answered quietly, shamed by her father's harsh treatment of a man who had just wanted to feed his family.

A low whistle of shock escaped Gybbon but Harcourt asked, "So ye decided to go see why that mon had hated that cell so verra much."

"Aye." She shook her head at the memory of her foolishness. "Foolish but I *had* to see what would frighten a grown mon so verra badly. I think, too, I was ready to do anything to avoid watching that hanging."

"Your father would make ye watch a hanging?"

She shrugged. "He said we should see what happens to those who break the law. But, I didnae want to see it so I went exploring in the cellars. The door to the cell the mon had been locked up in was open and the cell already mucked out. I think I must have bumped whate'er was holding the door open because it shut behind me when I stepped inside. I couldnae get it open again, screamed myself voiceless, and then had to wait for someone to come looking for me. Thought I would be searched for when Father saw that I wasnae at the hanging."

"How long did ye have to sit there?"

"Three days," she whispered.

Both Harcourt and Gybbon stared at her in shock but it was Harcourt who finally growled out the question, "They left ye in there for three days? Didnae they look for ye at all?" He winced, realizing that was not a kind or well-thought-out question.

"After no one had seen me for two days, aye, they started a search for me. My brothers just wouldnae stop asking where I had gone. They were nay the most loving of brothers and we are nay truly close, but for that alone I will ne'er turn my back on them. They pestered and pestered until my parents finally decided it was a little odd that no one had seen me for so long."

"And it was there that ye found the rats."

She shuddered. "There were so many of them and I think they didnae get much to eat. I had to sit on the cot with the slops bucket and a stick broken off the bed to fend them off whene'er they came round. I still came out of there covered in bites. So, aye, it appears I ne'er have gotten over a verra big fear of rats. And they do have little armies."

"I have no words. Weel, aye, I do," Harcourt said as he took her by the arm and escorted her up the stairs, "but they are a lot of foul ones I would like to spit at your parents."

Annys smiled at him as they emerged back in the ledger room. "I suspect I have already used most of them." She shrugged. "They are what they are, what they have always been."

Seeing that Gybbon had left the room, Harcourt took her into his arms and kissed her. He had begun the kiss with sympathy in his heart but it soon fled beneath the onslaught of an aching need. Harcourt slowly turned and pressed her against the wall as the kiss deepened. He trembled when she stroked her hands up and down his back and desperately wanted to feel them against his skin.

Fighting to keep some control over himself, he eased his hand up from her waist and over her breast.

The weight of it in his hand, the press of her nipple against his palm, made his mouth water with a need to taste her flesh. For a moment she pressed eagerly into his caress, but then that tension he dreaded began to return to her body. Knowing it was the last thing he wanted to do but that it was the wisest thing to do, he ended the kiss, put his hand back at her waist, and stepped back a little.

There was still a dazed look in her pretty eyes and the flush of desire still on her cheeks, when he looked into her face. Harcourt could not completely resist the urge to kiss one of those lightly colored cheeks. He was pleased when she did not flinch away from that kiss. Her resistance to the passion between them was slowly easing. He just wished he could find out what caused it.

"I will send a maid down to tend to his wounds," she said as she started toward the door only to turn back to take the keys from him, lock the door that led to the cellars, and reattach the keys to her belt. "There should be a guard with the maid, aye?"

"Aye. I dinnae think the mon would hurt anyone but he is verra frightened and could do some harm if he tried to escape."

"I will see to it." At the door she again halted and looked back to the door to the cellars. "Did ye see where Roban went?"

"After the mouse."

"How *is* that cat wandering about the place with such freedom?" Annys shook her head and left.

Harcourt stared at the door she had just locked and frowned. That was a very good question she had tossed out before leaving, although he doubted she fully understood the import of it at the moment. Cats were agile and could get in and out of places one would never have expected them to fit through. Yet that cat appeared in places where there really was no way to explain its presence.

There had to be some secrets David had never shared with Annys. Another bolt-hole or some passages in the walls. It was the only explanation. Cats might be clever and agile but they could not climb up stone walls to squeeze through a narrow window or walk through those same walls. As far as he knew, animals did not know how to open doors or turn into spirits that could slip past you as you opened doors. The door to the bolt-hole she had mentioned needed the keys she carried but he would get her to show him where it was. But, in this keep there had to be ways to sneak in and out that Annys did not know about. He grew more certain of that by the minute. He just had to figure out a way to search for them without letting any of those secrets become too well known.

Inspired and fleetingly praying he did not end up looking like an idiot, he went to find Callum. That man had been forced to learn how to hide and how to find the ways in and out of a place at a very young age. Over the years, even as his life had greatly improved, he had honed the skill. If there were ways in and out of the keep that David had neglected to tell Annys about, Callum would sniff them out.

"Weel," Callum drawled as he gave a futile attempt to brush the dirt off his clothes, "it would be a trial but someone could get in and out of there. A wee bit of work and it could be made a more comfortable little bolt-hole. I just dinnae understand what use it is. It goes under the wall and little else."

Harcourt nodded slowly. "But it gets ye outside the walls without having to walk across the bailey where there are so many eyes to watch you."

"Why dinnae they just use the bolt-hole ye said David had made for everyone to use?"

"Because the door to it is locked and Annys keeps the keys with her all the time."

"Another set of keys?"

"That is a possibility but how would one get the key one wanted without her kenning it and it takes time to make a new one. The other keys, if there are any, would be given to someone she and David trusted completely. It is also accessible only from the ledger room and she is in there a lot. Nay, I think we need to look for things like this, although more accommodating. This would work for that cursed cat though. Any sign it has been used lately?"

"'Tis packed tight. I wouldnae have gotten so filthy if I had been a wee bit smaller."

"Back to it being a woman again, aye?"

"Aye. I will keep looking though. Ye may take time to question Annys about any knowledge she might have about such bolt-holes. Just because she doesnae have a key to them, doesnae mean they are not there, or that David had nay done the work himself."

"Weel, I would certainly have believed that ere he was mutilated as the mon did love the lassies but his parents were verra religious, verra pious, and he wouldnae have wanted them to ken he was sneaking out to tumble about with some wench." Harcourt smiled as he recalled some of the tales David had told him while he had been so long abed while healing. "From the time he had his first taste of a woman until he was gelded by that jealous oaf, he was a randy beast."

Callum nodded. "So, to go off rutting without having to endure the pious lectures of his parents, he would indeed want some secret way out of the keep. And it would nay be one he would have told Annys about, if only because he wouldnae have wanted to explain the reason he had it. I will keep looking."

"Good. We need to find out how the traitor is slipping in and out of here nay matter what is going on or how many we have watching. That is a weakness that could end up costing us dearly."

# Chapter Nine

"Where is the wretched child?"

Annys bit back a smile as she heard the annoyance in Joan's voice. Her son had a true skill for arousing that emotion in Joan. Joan's children were quiet, well-behaved little boys, unless they played with Benet. She looked up from her sewing to smile at Joan.

"Has my son led your lads astray again?" she asked.

"Nay yet. He was meeting with them to play ball but they have been waiting for near to an hour they said and he hadnae come."

A closer look at Joan revealed that worry was behind her annoyance and Annys felt an icy chill flow down her back. "Mayhap Benet got distracted doing something with whichever mon was charged with watching him today."

"Nay. That was Sir Gybbon. He thought the boy was with mine. Said the lad needed to go to the garderobe first and then said he was meeting my lads right here in the bailey. Weel, my lads finally came to get me because they couldnae find him."

Annys tossed her sewing aside, leapt to her feet, and started out of the solar. "Then we must find Sir Gybbon now."

"He waits in the bailey with my lads," said Joan as she hurried after Annys. "Ye cannae think something has happened to the wee lad. Everyone was watching o'er him. He hasnae gone a step in any direction for a sennight without someone kenning exactly where he is."

"It appears that this time he may have eluded that constant watch."

Annys told herself to control the fear welling up inside of her. A clear head was needed now. One could not plan if one's head and heart were both lost in the fog of fear. But terror was gnawing at her and it was difficult to fight.

She saw Sir Gybbon pacing in front of Joan's sons. The young man looked both upset and angry. A part of her wanted to yell at him but she silenced it. He had done as he had been told. This was not his fault. She was certain of it. He had simply allowed Benet to go to the garderobe. Somehow the boy had been snatched or led away from there.

"M'lady, I dinnae ken . . ." Sir Gybbon began, his blue eyes dark with guilt.

"Nay, dinnae apologize," she said and patted his arm. "There is no need. No one said ye should follow the lad right into the garderobe. He was also inside the crowded keep. Nay a place we thought extra eyes needed to be." She turned to Joan. "What we need now is for everyone to search the keep," she told her, and Joan quickly began to order people inside to hunt for Benet.

"Do ye think he is hiding in there?" asked Sir Gybbon.

"I *hope* he is. I hope he is just being a naughty boy and thinking he is doing something funny by hiding on us." She lowered her voice so that no one else could hear her but Gybbon. "My fear is that the one who poisoned my husband has betrayed us again."

"Och, nay." He dragged his hands through his thick black hair. "Mayhaps watched closely for those few times when the lad was alone." He grimaced. "Such as when he had to visit the garderobe. But, how would he get the lad away from here with none of us seeing anything?"

"Every keep has a bolt-hole, Sir Gybbon. Recall I mentioned one when we took your prisoner to his cell. 'Tis nay a secret for all it can be locked from inside the ledger room. David felt it unfair for only a few chosen ones to ken how to escape an attack so most all here ken where it is. Joan and Dunnie both ken where the extra keys are hidden. I suspect David told Nicolas as weel, giving him one to hide. There is another bolt-hole just for the laird and his closest kin or guards, but, if someone took Benet, it wouldnae be so verra hard to get him outside the walls through that bolt-hole if they uncovered it as it is nay locked. I can only pray that didnae happen for it would mean that they could have already gotten him far away from us."

Sir Gybbon gave her shoulder a gentle squeeze. Annys knew it was intended to reassure her. It did not, but it did stop her from racing into the keep yelling Benet's name. Someone needed to stay in one place so the searchers could quickly report to her whatever they might find. She soothed her need to join the search by reminding herself that Joan, and several of the younger girls, knew every one of Benet's hiding places. There was no need for her to direct the search.

One by one her people came out to say that they had found no sign of her son. Each report was a blow to the heart. Annys forced herself to thank the person reporting, say something comforting, and then calmly wait for the next person to report. Joan was the last one to walk up to her and it took every scrap of strength Annys possessed not to fall to the ground and weep at the look upon the woman's face. Joan had not found her child either.

"He isnae in there, Annys," Joan said, her voice thick with tears.

When Joan moved to embrace her, Annys held out her hand to stop her advance. "Nay, I will break. I will fall to the ground and be of no use to anyone." She looked at Sir Gybbon. "Where are Sir Harcourt and the others?"

"They went to ride the boundaries, to talk to people, see what may or may nay be happening," he answered. "Been some reports of cattle and sheep being stolen. At least one place found where some-one was certain one of the stolen animals had been butchered."

Annys clenched her hands in her hair, barely stop-ping herself from tearing at it like some madwoman. "The bastard has ceased playing with us."

"Thought that myself when the village was fired," said Sir Gybbon. "That was so quickly stopped, the damage so slight and quickly mended that I decided I must be wrong. I now wonder if what drew the others away was naught but part of a plan to grab the wee lad. Fewer people watching the lad today."

"Of course. I would ne'er have thought Sir Adam capable of devising such a clever plan, an almost intricate one, but he may have one or two men with him who are more sharp-witted."

"True." Sir Gybbon signaled to Gavin, drawing the tall, thin youth to his side. "Ye need to hie yourself to Sir Harcourt and tell him someone has taken the boy. Fast as ye can, lad. Go now." He looked at Annys. "Where does that bolt-hole come out?"

Silently thanking the man for giving her something to do, Annys took him to where the tunnel beneath the walls of Glencullaich came out. He carefully studied the ground and Annys found herself doing the same. It looked very much as if someone had dragged something, or someone, along until he reached a place just beyond the tree line where two horses had waited. Footprints clearly marked that person's return to the bolt-hole. Someone she did not ken about had a key. Someone had handed her child over to the enemy, someone from within the keep itself.

Annys felt a stinging in her palms. She slowly opened her clenched hands and winced at the marks her nails had left in her palms. Several of them seeped blood. She needed to rein in her fear and anger. Neither would help her find Benet.

"I would like to go into the bolt-hole from the other end now, m'lady," said Sir Gybbon.

"Do ye think ye will find anything to help us?" she asked as she led him back to the keep.

"Cannae tell until I have a look."

"Then look, please. We need to find the traitor within these walls."

Although she could only hear the tone of his words as he answered since he was already dropping down into the tunnel, she knew it was an agreement. It had just been a particularly profane one. Annys wished he had not hidden his words. She would like to use a few curses, she decided as she followed him into the tunnel. Soon she held the torch so that he could better study the ground as they walked along.

Sir Gybbon retrieved the torch when they reached the end and Annys climbed out first. He was just climbing out of the bolt-hole when the sound of swift horses reached her ears. Annys spun around and saw Harcourt and his men returning with a gratifying speed.

She knew exactly when Harcourt saw her and Gybbon for he and his men turned their mounts to ride toward them. Her heart pounded with hope and she realized she was expecting him to fix this. Annys cursed that weakness, sternly reminding herself that he would not be staying with her and she could not start to depend on him so much. This time, however, she would take whatever help he could give, do whatever he asked of her, if he just brought their child back home safely.

"What has happened?" Harcourt asked as he reined in, swiftly dismounted, and went to Annys.

"I begin to think we need that question engraved on the coat of arms," she said in a shaking voice. "Benet is missing," she replied and felt every word as a stab straight to the heart.

He pulled her into his arms and Annys did not resist. She wrapped her arms around his waist and held on tight, trying to draw some of his strength into her own body. There was no doubt in her mind that Sir Adam had taken her child. She could only pray that he did not actually have his hands on Benet yet. There was just one reason Sir Adam would want her baby. Benet gained the man nothing unless he was removed as the laird of Glencullaich. Annys prayed her baby was not being led to the slaughter.

"I willnae waste time asking if ye have searched for him," Harcourt said, knowing full well that Annys and her people knew every single place the boy would hide and would have turned over every stone in the place looking for the boy. "Why are ye here?"

"Someone took the boy out this bolt-hole," said Gybbon.

"Are ye certain?" Annys said, pulling away from Harcourt enough to look at Gybbon. "I saw what ye did but, although I cannae think of anything else that could have caused such marks, I am nay skilled at reading such signs. And I am nay sure I am thinking too clearly, either."

"Verra sure. Someone dragged the lad over there"—Gybbon pointed to the small cluster of trees where they had seen the signs of horses having waited in place—"where two riders waited. Then only one person returned here. By the depth of the prints, I believe that person wasnae carrying the boy back. He had to have been given over to the riders."

Harcourt studied the ground and then signaled to Callum. "Go see if there is a trail for us to follow." As Callum and Tamhas hurried off to have a look, Harcourt held Annys close again. "We will find the boy."

"He must be so afraid," she whispered, fighting the urge to weep and rant.

"He is a sturdy lad." He glanced down at the drag marks. "He fought hard."

"Why didnae we hear him calling out then?"

"Tied and gagged." He tightened his hold when she shuddered. "We *will* find him, Annys, and if anyone has given the lad e'en a bruise, he is a dead man." He looked down at her. "Ye must find out who the traitor is. That will be your task. Ours is to find Benet and make certain the ones who took him pay dearly for it."

"Harcourt," Callum called as he ran back to them. "Look there." He pointed back in the direction he had come from. "As far back as ye can look but be quick or ye will miss it."

A small white shape caught Harcourt's eye. "Is that Roberta? A sheep cannae track anyone."

Callum shrugged. "Try to look closer to the ground."

Harcourt did and cursed in surprise. "'Tis that cat."

"Roban?" Annys pulled out of his arms and stared hard in the direction all the men were looking. "My cat is following them? Can ye nay use that?"

"Aye, we can, although I willnae swear it will be all that reliable, 'tis worth a try. Be at ease, love." He gave her a quick kiss. "We will bring Benet home."

A moment later she was alone. She watched the men until they disappeared from view but could not tear her gaze from where they had last been. A hand touching her arm startled her out of the stupor of blind fear she had fallen into. Annys abruptly turned and nearly knocked Joan to the ground.

"Oh, I am so verra sorry, Joan," she said, catching the woman by the arms to steady her.

Joan hugged her. "I startled you. Ye have naught

to apologize for." She looked in the direction the men had gone. "Do they have a trail to follow?"

"Aye." Annys took Joan by the hand and showed her everything she and Gybbon had found. "One of our own took my child and gave him to someone who wants him dead." She was torn between the aching need to rage and to weep.

"And when we find the one, she will pay dearly," Joan vowed.

"Ye think it is a woman, too, dinnae ye."

"Aye." Joan pointed at the drag marks in the dirt. "No mon would have dragged the lad along like that. A mon would have just picked him up. Aye, might e'en have just knocked the lad senseless. A woman will oftimes just keep pulling a recalcitrant child along, using her greater strength that way." Joan looked closer at the footprints. "Smaller feet than a mon would have, too."

Annys stared at Joan in surprise. "How do ye ken such things?"

Joan shrugged. "I just notice things more than some do. And with all the footprints I have had to help mop up, I just ken some of the differences."

"I truly need to pay more attention to the world around me. There is one odd thing that has happened that might actually prove helpful. That lamb and my cat were going in the same direction as the ones who took Benet rode in, as if they were tracking him like some pack of dogs."

"Both can follow a scent verra weel."

"A sheep can?"

"Aye, a dam can find her lamb e'en in a packed flock. Ye want to find water then put a thirsty sheep in the field and follow it. I suspicion that lamb kens just what our lad smells like. Come back to the keep. We shouldnae be out here unguarded and ye need to eat something."

"Someone has a key to the bolt-hole. Someone other than me, ye, and Dunnie."

"And Nicolas," Joan whispered, stunned by that news. "We need to find out whose key is missing." She looked down at the keys hanging from Annys's belt. "Nay yours then. Food and then we hunt down all the keys."

With a last look in the direction the men had gone, Annys allowed Joan to take her back to the keep.

Harcourt held up his hand and everyone stopped, dismounting when he did. At times he had felt foolish following a lamb and a cat but what signs he had seen along the way had revealed that the men who had taken Benet were indeed riding in this direction. Crouching low, he and his men crept forward until they found the campsite of the men they had been following. The cat was up in a tree close by, lying on a branch overlooking the boy, and the lamb stood at the base of the tree, staring in the direction of Benet.

Rage seized Harcourt when he saw the boy tied up and sitting on the ground. He had to fiercely battle the urge to race into the camp and begin killing every man there. The risk to his son was all that held him back. There were eight men in the camp and only five in Harcourt's group. Planning was needed. He signaled the others to move back so that they could talk without risk of being overheard only to have the chance to plan anything taken away. Roberta trotted into the camp, bleating, and heading straight for Benet.

All eight men stared at the lamb and then the tallest one grinned. "Seems we will be feasting on lamb tonight, lads."

"Nay!" screamed Benet, struggling to stand up. "Run, Bertie! Run away!"

Chaos erupted as the men tried to grab the lamb, Benet screaming all the while and trying to wriggle free of his bonds. Harcourt shook his head. He looked at his companions and they just grinned and shrugged. Harcourt thought it over for a moment. The only real cost to waiting for things to settle down and make an attack easier would be the life of the lamb. One look at a frantic, crying Benet told him he could not do it.

"Kill or hobble, but get as many of the fools down as ye can." He sighed and shook his head. "Dinnae risk yourselves but try to keep that witless animal from being killed."

They all stood up, drew their swords, and charged. Three men fell quickly due to the shock of the attack. Out of the corner of his eye, as he faced off with the tall man who had wanted Roberta for his meal, Harcourt saw Benet still huddled on the ground but much closer to the trunk of the tree and with the lamb pressed hard up against his chest. He was safe, the fighting going on away from where he was, so Harcourt turned all his attention to the man he was facing.

The man turned out to be skilled with his sword. Harcourt found himself in a true battle for his life. He took a wound to his leg but kept standing as he repaid that with a slash to the man's sword arm. The man staggered and Harcourt took quick advantage, driving his sword deep into the man's chest. He fell but, to Harcourt's surprise, still had enough breath to bellow out an order to the survivors still fighting for their lives.

"Kill that brat!"

Harcourt ignored the pain in his thigh and the feel of the hot blood running down his leg, and raced to reach his son. As he drew near, one of the kidnappers eluded Nicolas, knocked him down, and turned toward Benet, raising his sword to strike at the boy. Harcourt did not think he could make it in time and Nicolas was struggling to his feet, dazed from a hard blow to the head. Just as he bellowed out in pain, fearing he was about to see his child murdered, Harcourt saw a golden ball of fur drop from the tree limb and wrap itself around the attacker's head, a whirlwind of claws and teeth.

Stumbling to get by Benet's side, Harcourt watched in amazement as the man screamed and tried to grab hold of the cat that was tearing his face apart. Nicolas rose to his feet, steady again, and called the cat by name, telling it to get down. It did and Nicolas killed the man, not even waiting to see if he was still able to use a sword.

Benet looked at Harcourt. "They were going to eat Roberta." He burst into tears.

Making certain it was safe to do so, Harcourt untied the boy and tugged him into his arms. The lamb moved to be by him and rest its head on his unwounded thigh. Harcourt watched Roban sit down and begin to delicately clean its claws and he shook his head. It was going to be impossible to complain about the beast now.

"All dead," said Callum as he came to crouch by Harcourt and started to bandage his leg wound. "This will take a while to heal." He glanced at Benet who was watching him. "Are ye hurt, lad?"

"Nay," Benet said, stroking the lamb's head. "They were going to kill Roberta." He glanced at Roban. "I think that made *Maman's* cat angry and he tried to rip out that mon's eyeballs."

"He certainly put up a good fight but I really think he was saving you."

"Aye, that too, but I could hear him growling when the men were chasing Roberta around." He frowned. "Why did ye bring them with you?"

Harcourt laughed even though it hurt. "Och, lad, we didnae bring them. They brought us. They were following you so we followed them." It was weak but the smile that curved the boy's mouth eased his concern for Benet.

"Now, we need to get ye back to Glencullaich so that the women can tend that wound with more care than I can," said Callum. "Can ye ride?"

Gently setting Benet aside, Harcourt rose to stand on his own two feet. The pain was bad but he believed he could get back to the keep without causing too much damage so he nodded. He felt a little pang of regret when Callum took Benet up with him and someone settled the cat in his saddle pack. With a sigh he patted the cat's head and decided it was better than having to carry the lamb. Nicolas had taken that animal up with him.

By the time they reached the keep, Harcourt was not sure he would remain conscious when he dismounted. Pain and blood loss had made him grow increasingly light-headed. They were swarmed by people when they rode in. Harcourt's last clear vision was Dunnie walking up, taking one look at the lamb and the cat, and laughing so hard he was clutching his sides. Then Harcourt heard someone yell out in alarm as he slid out of the saddle.

"*Maman,* is he going to die?"

"Nay, Benet. He just had a lot of pain and lost a lot of blood. He needed to sleep."

"Why didnae he get off his horse first?"

"Sometimes sleep just reaches out and takes you. Ye have done it a few times."

"Oh, aye. I have. I wanted to tell him I am sorry."

Harcourt wanted to tell Benet he had nothing to be sorry for, that it was not his fault. He found it difficult to form the words, however.

"Ye have nothing to feel sorry for, love. Ye did naught wrong. Those men who took ye away from us were the ones who did wrong."

"But Sir Harcourt got hurt fighting the bad men and he wouldnae have had to do that if I wasnae with them."

"Ye didnae ask to be with them, love, and that is the important thing. Now, have ye fed Roberta yet?"

"Och, nay. I best go do that now. They wanted to eat her," he added in an unsteady voice.

"Weel, they didnae understand that she is precious to ye, love. We all do so ye dinnae need to fear that while she is living here."

Harcourt heard the boy sigh with relief and then run out of the room. "He ne'er walks anywhere."

Annys was so startled by hearing Harcourt talk she nearly dropped the basin of water she was using to bathe him. The man had lain there like the dead for two days. His friends and family had assured her that he would wake when he was done recovering from the blood loss, that a good long sleep after a wounding was not uncommon amongst the Murrays. She could feel tears stinging her eyes and fought against the urge to weep.

"So, ye have decided to rejoin the world," she said and watched his eyes slowly open.

"Aye, although my leg is protesting it."

"It has actually been healing verra nicely while ye snored away the days."

"How many days?"

"If we dinnae count the part of day that was left after ye fell off your horse, then two days. 'Tis the night of the second. I was told again and again that this was a normal way of healing for a Murray and must say, it did seem to work verra weel."

He allowed his mind to mull over every ache and pain and said, "I dinnae feel like I hit the ground."

"Nay, Nicolas moved verra fast and caught ye ere ye finished falling."

"How is Benet doing? I could hear him saying he thought it was all his fault and ye seem to get him realizing it wasnae. But, he saw a lot of things that could badly trouble a wee lad."

"What he appears to have latched on to is that those men wanted to kill and eat Roberta and that no one should get Roban angry."

Harcourt laughed and winced. "The cat was a fury of claws and teeth. Ne'er seen anything like it. One could almost think the fool beastie placed himself in the tree where it did intending to do just what it did if anyone got too close to the boy."

He took a deep breath and let it out slowly when she bathed the area around the wound on his thigh. It was not pain that caused his sudden tension either, but the fact that she was touching his leg. Even the damp cloth she held between her skin and his did not dim the pleasure of that touch.

"How did someone get the lad out of the bolt-hole?" he asked in an attempt to get his mind off the way her bathing of him made his passion rise.

"Whoever did it stole a key. We are still trying to find out whose key was taken but the search for that got set aside when Benet was returned and ye were brought to bed with a serious wound. Now that ye are awake, we shall deal with that. The bolt-hole is being watched. Callum has found that odd one ye discovered filled in and he looks for more."

"We will get the traitor now."

"I hope ye are right. I was so hoping that Benet could tell us who took him but he said they covered his mouth and eyes until he was in the camp. Put a sack o'er his head. He is too young to have noticed anything such as scent or sound, and too scared. So we still dinnae ken exactly who is doing this. It is verra difficult to fight an enemy who lives within your home and kens all your secrets."

"But ye now ken a few of hers. Ye ken how she is slipping in and out and ye ken that she has stolen a key. Small steps toward discovery but more than we had."

"And then we can put an end to Sir Adam's source of information. Next we have the final battle with the fool. And then ye can return to your life at Gormfeurach. So, best ye heal fast and weel as I dinnae want to have to explain a lingering injury to your family. I hear it is verra large."

He reached out and took her hand in his. "It would be nice if the business with Sir Adam is finished so precisely, but, Annys, mayhap the ending ye speak of doesnae need to happen."

Annys abruptly stood up. "Nay. Dinnae ye make me any promises. I couldnae bear it to hear them and then watch ye ride away. I watched ye do that once and I ne'er want to do it again. Ye didnae e'en find me to say good-bye." She cursed at her loss of control and ran out of the room, praying every step of the way that he would forget that short emotional outburst.

Harcourt stared at the door. He wished his head were clearer, not so foggy with the remnants of a long sleep and pain. There was something in that little rant that was important. He was certain of it. Closing his eyes as the need for sleep returned, he struggled to make his mind store those words so that he could examine them later.

# Chapter Ten

Annys paused at the door to Harcourt's bedchamber and carefully looked over what was on the tray she carried. She wondered if it was too much for a man who was still recovering from what had been a serious wound. Then she recalled that it was Joan who had laid out the meal and the woman had enough experience in healing to know what she was doing.

The moment she entered the bedchamber, Annys decided Harcourt was healed enough to eat the hearty meal she had brought him. He was sitting up in bed, idly scratching his broad chest, and playing chess with Callum. She returned his smile as she set the tray down on the table next to the bed. It eased her fear for him as well as the guilt she had suffered. He had been injured while helping her to retrieve her son. It was her enemy he had been fighting. It was her call for help that had plunged him into the middle of her mess.

The fact that he made no mention of her little emotional rant on the night he had finally woken up from what he liked to call his healing sleep had made it easy to return to caring for him. She would have hidden away for longer than the day she had if Benet had not demanded she take him in to see the man. Harcourt had given no sign that he even recalled talking to her the first time he had woken up after falling off his horse. That could simply be because he was too polite to do so, but she did not much care about his reasons, only that she was not going to have to be reminded of that loss of control.

"Ah, sustenance," said Callum. "By the look of what is set out for you, the ladies have deemed ye weel on your way to being healed. No more gruel." Callum carefully moved the chess set to the table in front of the fireplace. "Am I right to assume the meal has been set out in the great hall?"

"Aye, the platters were being set upon the table as I left the kitchens," Annys replied.

"Then I shall leave ye for now, Harcourt. M'lady."

He bowed slightly to Annys before leaving. She could not fully still her curiosity about the man. Sir Callum was so handsome the maids sighed whenever they saw him. Children adored him. He was also faultless in his courtesy and yet he bristled with weapons. The fact that, despite how finely he dressed, the many knives he carried were not much better than what one of the villagers would have puzzled her. It was just another one of those things that kept her curiosity about him sharp.

A soft hiss of pain drew her attention. She turned to catch Harcourt wincing as he pushed himself into a more upright position. Shaking aside the last of her thoughts concerning Sir Callum she moved to assist Harcourt.

The moment she put her hands on his warm, smooth skin, Annys knew she had made a mistake. Memories of their lovemaking all those years ago crowded into her mind as they too often did since his return, heating her blood. She gritted her teeth as she fought the urge to release her firm hold on him and stroke his strong arms until he wrapped them around her. Harcourt settled himself firmly against the pillows and she immediately released him. Annys clasped her hands together behind her back to hide how they trembled.

Harcourt wasted no time in helping himself to the rich stew she had brought him. It was not the hearty piece of roasted meat he craved, but it was not a tasteless broth either. It also distracted him from the need to yank her into his arms, to pull her body beneath his and repeatedly feed the hunger she stirred within him.

"Has Benet come to see you since the first time when I brought him in?" she asked.

"Aye, many times," Harcourt replied. "I think he finally believes I havenae been killed."

Annys smiled. "He was verra fearful. It took me quite a while to convince him that it wasnae his fault. He was so certain he should have fought harder. I fear he doesnae like to be reminded that he is just a wee lad."

"Of course not. No lad does. From the day they understand they are to become men like those they see walking about with swords, fighting, and drinking ale, they take on that pride."

"Hmmm. So they try to become men with all that swagger and arrogance."

"Aye." He grinned at the look of annoyance on her face.

"Weel, he is calmer now. Ye will be pleased to ken that Joan believes ye can get out of bed for a wee while. It has been a sennight and ye are healing weel."

"We Murrays do heal weel, and oftimes fast."

"A fine gift. But, ye are to be careful to nay do too much or stand on that leg too much."

Harcourt nodded, frustrated but not foolish enough to ignore good advice. "The healers in my clan would say the same. Aye, and be verra annoyed if I didnae heed their warnings."

"Glad to hear it."

"And I suspicion if I was fool enough to ignore Mistress Joan's advice, she would show me that she could lecture me with all the power of my mother."

"Aye, she would. Joan has always been an expert at a good, ear-reddening scold."

Annys reached to take away his now empty dishes and squeaked in surprise when he put an arm around her waist, pulling her close. She put her hands on his broad shoulders to keep some space between them but decided that was a mistake. The warmth of his skin beneath her hands had her pulse leaping. When he moved, the shift of his strong muscles under her hands made her flush as her blood heated.

"Ye ken, 'tis custom to kiss a wound to help it heal," he murmured as he kissed her blush-tinged cheek.

"That is only for bairns," she said, fighting the urge to look at his strong thigh, the one now bearing stitches and snugly bandaged.

"A poor wounded mon is much akin to a bairn."

"Ye willnae hear me argue that."

He was still smiling when he kissed her. Annys knew she ought to pull away, to admonish him for his attempt to seduce her, but she failed to gather the willpower to do so. He tasted too good. Despite the slight awkwardness of the position she was in, it also felt far too good to be held in his arms again. She wanted to push all the dishes aside and climb into the bed with him.

A hard rap at the door jerked Annys to her senses. She scrambled free of Harcourt's grasp so quickly she barely stopped herself from falling on the floor and rattled the dishes. Only his quick action saved him from a lap full of dirty dishes. Fussily patting her hair to fix any dishevelment and plucking at her skirts to be certain they were in place, Annys ignored Harcourt's grumbled objections to being disturbed and moved toward the door. It surprised her to find Callum there, his expression far more serious than she was used to seeing.

"Is something wrong?" she asked, her fear still running strong after what had happened to Benet.

"Nay, but I need to talk to Harcourt for a moment," he said.

"Just give me a moment to collect the dishes," she said and hurriedly did so.

It was not until she found herself out in the hall, the door shut securely behind her, that Annys began to be a little annoyed. If they were about to discuss Sir Adam or some trouble at Glencullaich she should be involved in the discussion. Then she shook aside that moment of pique. She had handed the problem of Glencullaich over to Harcourt and his men. It was unfair for her to now complain about how they went about it. If there was anything she truly needed to know or do as the lady of Glencullaich, Harcourt would tell her.

Although, she mused as she made her way back to the kitchens, it might not be a good idea to be alone with Harcourt for too long. Annys knew he had been working hard to seduce her into his bed. She also knew she was weakening fast. It was past time for her to come to a decision about Harcourt. Her heart and body yearned for him but she had to try to silence them and think clearly. If nothing else, if she bed down with him she wanted it to be her choice, a clear-headed, well-thought-out decision.

"The traitor is in the kitchen," said Callum as he sat on the edge of Harcourt's bed.

"Ye discovered which one is betraying us?" Harcourt wanted to leap from the bed to go confront the one who had given his son into the hands of his enemy, probably with sword in hand, and he was not sure the fact that it was a woman he was hunting would stop him from killing her.

"Nay yet, but 'tis one of the lassies who work in the kitchens. Three of them have some secret. The lass I play with is certain that two of them have a lover they meet with, one they dinnae want anyone to ken about. She isnae sure what young Minna is doing but doubts 'tis anything bad."

"Annys's kitchens are a true pit of sin from what ye say. Can ye trust your lass?"

"Aye," Callum said without hesitation. "I havenae told her why I ask so much, but she isnae a fool and I think she has guessed my game. She quickly began to tell me anything and everything about each one who works there. Peg grew even more of a fount of information after Benet was taken. The shades of outrage within the kitchens was another way I have fixed my interests and suspicions on but three of them, although I do believe Minna is innocent of betrayal. 'Tis only her closely held secret that makes me wonder."

"Ye didnae discover this all between here and the great hall. Why come to tell me right now? Did ye e'en get a bite to eat?"

"Peg was waiting for me just inside the door of the great hall to quietly say that she had thought long and hard on what I was trying to discover and it suddenly occurred to her that 'tis nay just the problems with Sir Adam that have me asking questions. She said she thinks I have decided the laird was killed and am looking for the killer. Seems someone might have overheard our talk of poison. She told me that only three women dealt with the laird's food."

"The three ye already watch?"

"Aye. Biddy, Minna, and Adie."

"Do ye ken why it is the maids in the kitchens who are the only ones amongst who a traitor has emerged?"

"Aside from the fact that the easiest way to poison someone ye badly want dead is to get to him through his food?"

"Aye, aside from that."

"Weel, they are nay watched verra closely, are they. They go where they want as long as the meal is done weel and on time." Callum smiled faintly. "No one wishes to cause trouble for the ones who feed them. 'Tis also verra easy for one of them to slip in and out of the keep. There are always errands to run and supplies needed. No one questions what they are doing. The entrance to the bolt-hole is verra close at hand so it is easy to sneak into. Those two things alone were why I set after one of those lassies."

"Have ye found who nay longer has the key to the bolt-hole?"

"Dunnie found his. Nicolas found his yet seems to think something isnae right about it. It works so it is the key. Or *a* key. Joan found hers. So, Nicolas and I are thinking it may have been his key, stolen, and used to have another made. I have also made certain that the place where the tunnel comes out is weel guarded, but not too obviously."

"We need to find which one of them is the guilty one as quickly as we can. Sir Adam is preparing for something, I am certain of it, and we cannae have anyone here who is willing to help him," said Harcourt.

Callum nodded and stood up. "I mean to follow each one of them. May e'en get Nicolas to help. First will be Minnie. I need to ken what her secret is before I can dismiss her as the traitor."

Harcourt settled back against his pillows after Callum left. They were close, he could feel it. Ending Sir Adam's ability to get information about them would be the first true victory they had gained. Most everything else they had done had been little more than successful acts of defense. More was needed.

He greeted Nicolas with relief when the man arrived. Although he would do his best not to do too much that might risk aggravating the healing wound in his leg, he had to get out of the bed he had been trapped in for a sennight. Laughing at Harcourt's eagerness, Nicolas helped him dress. When the man handed him a walking stick, Harcourt swore but took it.

It did not take many steps for Harcourt to realize a week in bed sapped a man's strength. He should have remembered that, he thought as he almost collapsed in the seat at the table in the great hall. A few drinks of ale, set before him by a freckle-faced maid, were enough to revive him and he was pleased when the others joined him. They needed to make plans because he could not shake free of the certainty that Sir Adam would soon attack Glencullaich in force.

Annys scowled at what remained in the spice cupboard. Either Maura, the cook, had been too caught up with the troubles they were suffering from to notice how low their supply was getting or was just old enough now to become forgetful. There had also been a lot of the villagers staying at the keep who had needed to be fed, although most of those had been able to return home by now. If their spices were not replenished soon they would all be eating some very bland food.

Realizing she had nothing to make a list of their needs with, Annys decided to go get some writing materials from the ledger room. If they were running out of something as important as spices they undoubtedly needed other things. She started out of the storeroom only to pause just inside the door to study the women there.

When she saw Biddy, a plump, fair-haired young woman who was one of the cook's assistants, slyly tuck some bread into her apron, Annys stepped back a little into the shadows and kept her gaze fixed on the woman. Since Biddy had no desperate need for food, she had to wonder why the woman would steal some bread. It could be something as innocent as wanting to share some food with a lover, but Annys was still wary. The moment she had learned there was a traitor within the walls of Glencullaich, the number of people she trusted without question had dropped alarmingly. Annys wanted the traitor gone so that she could feel safe again within her own home.

Biddy told Maura she needed to get out of the hot kitchen for a while. Maura did not even look up from the work she was doing, just grunted in reply. The moment Biddy walked out, Maura began to mutter to herself, a long list of complaints about how often Biddy walked away from the work she was supposed to do. The fact that Biddy did not go out the door leading to the kitchen gardens was suspicious. Annys decided that was more than enough reason to follow the woman.

Biddy slunk her way to the door leading into the ledger room and Annys felt her suspicions grow stronger. One thing she did know about the woman was that Biddy could neither read nor do her numbers. There was nothing in the ledger room that could possibly be of interest to her except the door to the bolt-hole.

Annys waited outside the door, keeping close to the wall and using the shadows there to hide in. A moment later Biddy slipped out of the room, something the shape of a small book weighing down one of the pockets in her apron. Torn between rushing into the ledger room to see just what the woman had taken and following her to see if she went to meet with anyone, Annys finally picked the latter course of action.

When Biddy slipped into the small room meant for the lady of the keep to entertain her female friends, Annys's heart sank into her boots. That was where the special, very secret bolt-hole was. She doubted David had confided that information to the cook's assistant so Annys had to think that she had been spied on by the maid. Every so often she would check that bolt-hole to see if it needed any repair. It was just another part of her duties in the keep and it would probably have been easy enough for Biddy to see her do it or even overhear the occasional remark made to Joan after she had done the chore.

She waited outside the door a few moments and then slipped inside, working furiously on a reasonable excuse for being there if Biddy was still in there. No one was in the room and she sighed. There was only one way out of this small solar if one did not choose to use the door, and that was the bolt-hole David had made for a select few. It really did not matter how Biddy found out about it, only that she had. If the woman was just using it to meet a lover, it could be a forgivable crime, but Annys's instinct told her it was far more than that.

Sliding aside the wood panel that hid the opening to the bolt-hole, Annys slipped inside. She could see the light from Biddy's torch just up ahead. Trying to be as quiet as possible, she followed the woman just far enough to remain unseen or duck into the shadows, but near enough to take full advantage of the torchlight. Her heart was pounding and she knew it was not all with the anticipation of solving an important puzzle. The fear she had for such tight, dark places was stirring to life inside her.

When Biddy reached the end and opened the hatch that led outside, Annys pressed herself hard against the wall and inched back a few steps, deep into the dark she so hated. Then all the light was gone as Biddy silently put the hatch back down and the full dark of the tunnel pressed in on her. Annys realized she was panting, her nails digging into the stone she leaned against. It took a long time for her to calm down enough to run over to the hatch and test it to be certain it would open easily.

She reached up and cracked the hatch open just enough to let some light inside. Annys stood there for a little while, savoring the light and breathing deeply of pine and grass, before cautiously peeking outside, her eyes just above the thick grasses covering the hillside. She could see Biddy running toward some trees. It was not until the woman was just inside the wooded area that the men arrived.

Thinking she was about to completely ruin a very good dress, Annys pulled herself out of the hole and sprawled in the grasses. It was not easy but she squirmed around until she could reach the hatch and quickly closed it again, letting the small bushes crowded around the hatch fall back into place to hide it. A quick look told her that the people meeting in the wood had all their attention on each other so she scurried closer until she was crouched behind a clump of saplings.

"I fetched that ledger ye asked for, Clyde," said Biddy, barely releasing her grip on him to pull the book from her pocket and hand it over.

Annys had to clamp her hand over her mouth to smother a gasp of shock. That was the book in which David had kept his accounting of all he had given to Sir Adam's family over the years. He had told her that he had also begun to keep a record of all that he knew or did not know about Nigel's death. She had to wonder which matter Adam was most interested in.

Clyde hugged Biddy and gave her a kiss. Annys listened as he told the foolish woman what a beauty and a joy she was. That soon they would live well because he was Sir Adam's second and she would be his woman. She would be but one step down from whatever lady Sir Adam chose as a wife once he was laird of Glencullaich.

"I dinnae ken if I can do that again, Clyde," she said when he started to speak of trying again to get Benet. "They are watching the lad verra closely now. Someone e'en follows him to the garderobe now. And a knight sleeps in his bedchamber. And I think someone is closing up all the ways I use to slip out to you."

"Do the best ye can, my love. Our path to the laird's chair will clear quickly if the brat isnae standing in the way."

Annys clenched her hands into tight fists, wishing she was a sword-wielding knight. She would cut them all down where they stood and smile as she did so. Benet was but a child and they spoke as if he meant no more to them than some pebble they needed to shake from their shoes.

"How fares the knight? The one wounded when they took the boy back."

"Sir Harcourt is out of his bed, healing weel. He walks with a stick though."

Even from where she crouched, Annys could see that that news displeased Clyde.

"I tried what ye asked but only Joan tends to his meals."

"Keep trying, love. The woman cannae keep that up for long since she must answer the demands of her ladyship."

The way Biddy nodded told Annys the woman thought that the truth. She began to wonder if Biddy had ever really seen what it was like where she lived. If she had, she would never believe what this man was saying.

There was more kissing and Annys decided it was a good time for her to make her escape. She started to wriggle her way back, never taking her eyes off Biddy, her lover, and the men with him. The lack-witted Biddy was completely enraptured by the man. Annys prayed she did not look at Harcourt with that slack-jawed adoration.

"How I wish we had more time to spend together, my love, but I need to get away from here before I am seen. Our time is coming soon. I will send word when it is time for ye to do that last favor for us."

"It willnae be easy for me to slip away to make certain all the ways inside the keep are open to you, Clyde. I may nay be able to get to them all."

"Do your best. It could be what saves my life in the coming battle." He gave her a pat on the backside and pulled up the dark hood Biddy had worn to hide herself from any possibly prying eyes.

"Oh, Clyde, I wish we could be together now. Tonight."

"Soon, my love. Soon. Just a little more patience is

all I ask. Now, back ye go." He gave Biddy a little nudge in the direction of the bolt-hole she had used.

Annys realized she was now between Biddy and her way back into the keep. It was tempting to just get up and run but she hoped to get away unseen, small though her chances were. She scrambled back to the bolt-hole but even as she reached out to open it, Clyde looked her way.

# Chapter Eleven

Fear cut through Annys like shards of ice. The man who had seen her was drawing his sword and three others were stepping out of the shadows, also arming themselves. Biddy squealed in fright and ran toward the keep. It was a long run back to Glencullaich, she thought even as she hiked up her skirts and began to run, heartily cursing Biddy and the men now chasing her for robbing her of the chance to take the shorter path back home.

"Dinnae kill her," yelled out one of the men. "Sir Adam will be wanting to get his hands on her."

Sir Adam could just keep on wanting, Annys thought. She had no intention of falling into that man's hands. Her heart pounded as she ran, fighting to keep herself moving fast enough not to lose the small lead she had on Adam's men. They might not be planning to kill her but Sir Adam wanted her dead. She had no doubt about that.

If she had breath to spare, Annys knew she would have cheered when the walls of Glencullaich came into view. She could see the men upon the walls. The outcry from them was sweet music to her ears. Thinking herself safe, she allowed her fears to ease a little.

A small divot in the ground took her down a heartbeat later. Annys cried out as pain shot up her leg when it was twisted badly as her foot sank into the small hollow in the ground. That ground proved to be very hard when she hit it. The speed she had been moving at when she tripped caused her to slide and roll over the ground for several feet, adding even more aches and pains. Hearing the men chasing her drawing close, she tried to get to her feet, ignoring the ominous dampness at her waist, but unable to ignore the pain in her leg when she tried to stand on it.

Men raced out of Glencullaich, stopping the terror rapidly rising within her. She looked behind her when she heard a guttural curse and her fear receded even more. Sir Adam's men had turned and were running away. Annys sighed and slowly sat down. When Nicolas halted by her side while the other men continued after her pursuers, she forced a smile for him to try to ease the concern she could see on his face.

"If that look is meant to fool me into thinking ye are fine, it failed." He crouched down next to her. "Did they hurt ye at all or is this just from the fall?"

"Just the fall," she replied. "I suspicion I am covered in bruises, have at least one cut, and I have hurt my leg."

"Broken?"

"Nay, I think not. There wasnae that horrible crack such as I heard once when I broke my arm as a child.

Didnae feel the same, either. I am fair sure I just twisted it in a direction it was ne'er meant to go."

"Ah, I ken what ye mean." He carefully lifted her up into his arms. "Hurting?" he asked when she winced.

"Everything hurts right now," she replied, curling her arm around his neck to steady herself. "It has naught to do with ye carrying me. And, I suspicion 'tis far, far less painful to be carried than to try to walk back myself just now."

"Why were ye outside the walls?"

"Ah, weel, I was following Biddy, the cook's assistant. She was meeting with one of those men."

Nicolas muttered a curse. "Weel, she is long gone now. Most like fled with the men."

"That would have been the clever, sensible thing to do, aye. I believe our Biddy isnae verra clever or sensible. She ran back to the keep the moment she saw me." Annys almost smiled when there was the slightest falter to his step, revealing his surprise.

"Mayhap she believed ye wouldnae be returning to the keep."

"That may be so, but I believe there was no true thought behind her actions. She just ran. Mayhap she thought that cowl she wore was enough to hide who she was so that e'en if I did return, I wouldnae ken it had been her I saw. 'Tis clear she forgot I saw her earlier and kenned what she was wearing today."

"Ye are right. Nay verra clever our Biddy. As soon as we get ye settled with Joan to tend to your wounds, I will have a wee word with her."

Annys sighed. "Aye, ye must. I ken it. Just . . ." She frowned, uncertain of what she wanted to say.

"Just what? Dinnae hurt her? Dinnae put her in a cell? She killed David."

She could hear the anger in his voice and shared it. Biddy had lived well at Glencullaich. She could claim no mistreatment. Although there was no proof or confession, Annys also believed that Biddy was the one who had doled out the poison that killed David. There could be no mercy for that. Yet she had seen how Biddy had fawned over Adam's man, how he had flattered her and touched her. His attentions had undoubtedly been false but Biddy had believed in them, Annys was sure of it. As a woman who was fighting to have her head rule over her heart, she could not completely suppress a twinge of understanding.

Then she thought on all Biddy had cost her. David had done nothing to deserve the miserable, painful death he had suffered at the woman's hands. Benet had certainly not deserved being kidnapped and nearly killed. Harcourt had done nothing to deserve his wounds. She had not done anything to deserve two attempts to kidnap her. The village could have been destroyed and was still doing some repairs. They had lost sheep, cattle, and crops. Sir Adam wanted her and Benet dead. Biddy had not given any thought to those crimes and for that she certainly did deserve her punishment.

"Aye, she deserves whate'er punishment is due her," she said finally as they entered the keep.

Annys found herself hurried off to her bedchamber, Joan barking out orders for all that was needed to tend to her injuries. Nicolas set her down on the bed and left. In the brief moment the door was open before it shut behind him she could hear Harcourt bellowing. A little smile curved her mouth as Joan and two maids arrived to help her. Harcourt had sounded both furious and afraid. It raised her hope that it was more than the way the passion flared between them that stirred his interest in her.

"What happened?" Harcourt demanded the moment Nicolas entered the room. "And what took ye so long to get here?"

"I had to put Biddy in a cell," replied Nicolas, watching as Harcourt carefully sat up and swung his legs over the edge of the bed. "Lady Annys is naught but a bit bruised so ye dinnae need to leap up and rip out your stitches in some mad rush to get to her side."

"The stitching is to be taken out tomorrow anyway."

"Taken out, nay ripped out."

"Verra weel then. Help me get my clothes back on. This is what happens when a mon lets a woman fuss o'er him. Come up here like a weel-behaved child to have my stitching peered and poked at and the moment I do, that fool lass goes wandering about outside the safety of these walls." He ignored the way Nicolas just grinned as he helped him get dressed. "What happened to Annys then? All I could hear in here is that she was hurt and almost grabbed by Sir Adam's men."

"Annys was watching Biddy, saw the maid steal some bread, and followed her as she slipped out of the kitchens. Kept following her and saw her meet with Sir Adam's men. Then she was seen by the ones she was watching and they gave chase. That could have ended verra badly as she had gone beyond the sight of the men on the walls. She proved to be a verra fast runner though, and would have made it back to the keep unharmed save that she tripped on some uneven ground."

"She didnae break anything, did she?"

"Nay. Twisted her leg, got a wee bit bruised in the tumble she took, but by then the men on the walls had seen her and were calling out the alarm. Sir Adam's men ran off. Think one of them was Clyde. A shame we didnae get our hands on him."

"How did ye catch Biddy? Alive, I pray."

"Ah, aye, she is alive. It appears Benet's Roberta probably has more wit than Biddy. She ran back to the kitchens but, as Lady Annys said, the hooded cloak the woman wore wasnae enough to hide who she was. Also m'lady had seen the woman earlier so kenned just what she was wearing."

"*Jesu*, are ye telling me that all this trouble was caused by some lack-witted cook's assistant?" Dressed now, Harcourt stood up and grabbed the walking stick he had reluctantly agreed to use.

Nicolas laughed. "Weel, ye could choose to look at it that way. Nay, she was but the tool and 'tis the one who wields the tool that has the skill."

"True enough. 'Tis good news to have that weakness ended." He paused at the door. "It will be hard on the people here when she is judged and punished for the murder of their laird."

Opening the door for him, Nicolas said, "For her close kin, aye, it will be verra hard indeed. For the rest? I dinnae think so. I was lucky to get her out of that kitchen alive once the women kenned why I was taking her."

"Poor Nicolas stuck in a kitchen with angry women and a lot of knives. Aye, ye are lucky."

Harcourt moved as fast as he dared and reached the door to Annys's bedchamber just as it opened and Joan stepped out. Two young maids slipped around the woman, gave him a brief curtsey, and hurried away. He almost stepped back a little when he saw the anger on the woman's face.

"Nicolas should have let the women in the kitchens have Biddy," Joan said before striding off down the hall.

Shaking his head, Harcourt decided Nicolas was right. There would be few tears shed for Biddy when she met her fate. He stepped into the room and closed the door behind him. Annys lay on her bed in her linen night dress, salve smeared on several scrapes and bruises on her arms and legs, and a tightly bandaged ankle and foot resting on top of several cushions.

Relief swept over him. He had been told she was not badly hurt, but now knew he had had to see that for himself before his concern eased. It all looked a bit painful but he knew her injuries were all small ones that would heal quickly. Soon only the bruises would linger as they would take a longer time to fade. He gently lowered himself to sit down on the side of her bed, smiling when she looked at him.

"We are a fine pair," he said.

"At least I didnae have to be sewn back together."

Harcourt laughed. "True." He glanced at her ankle. "I think your bandage is bigger than mine was though."

Annys looked down at her ankle, her toes the only part of her ankle and foot that were still showing. "I havenae any idea why Joan did all that. Her husband fell a lot, ye ken. It was all part of the illness that finally killed him, and he was always twisting his ankles when he went down. Joan kept trying new ways to help the wrench heal and swears this way is the one that worked the best. She near to froze my foot off with cold water right from the burn, smeared handfuls of salve on it, wrapped it up so tight I cannae e'en wiggle my toes and it throbs, and stuck it up on these cushions." She shrugged and then said, "It had best work or I shall ne'er let her hear the end of it."

"I think I would trust her to ken best in this matter." He frowned when her expression abruptly changed until she looked as if she was about to cry. "What is wrong, sweet?" he asked, taking her hand in his.

"I am certain Nicolas told ye all about Biddy."

"Ah, aye, he did."

"I just cannae understand why she would do such horrible things."

"Mayhap she loved the mon she was trysting with."

"She was trysting with Clyde." She nodded when his eyes widened in surprise.

"He has been coming that close to us all this time?"

"It would seem so. But, I thought on how she did it all out of love, e'en though I couldnae see how she could love such a mon. E'en if she did, that still doesnae excuse her. Something inside of her should have been appalled by the things he was asking her to do. Mayhap nay when her victim was an adult, though poisoning your laird, a mon who ne'er mistreated you, was vile. But then she helped them steal a child. They even talked about her trying again."

"What did she say?"

"There was no refusal to hurt a bairn, but a lot of

talk about how she wasnae sure she could get to him again. No more than that. And she did it all for greedy reasons. She believed Clyde would wed her, they would set Sir Adam in the laird's chair, and, since he was Sir Adam's second, Biddy would then be second only to the lady of the keep once Sir Adam married. Greed. Nay more than that."

"Some people are incapable of seeing that what they have is good and always seek to get more."

"Weel, all she will get is a hanging. At first I didnae think I could stomach doing it to one of our own, but then realized she has ne'er been one of us. Nay if she could do what she has done. Her next gift to her lover was to be the opening of any bolt-hole in the keep, any way he and some of his men could slip in and attack us from behind."

"We could have been slaughtered."

"I ken it and she ne'er e'en gave that a thought. I am sad only because I now ken that e'en in the best of places, e'en if ye treat a person kindly and fairly, they can still betray you."

By the time she was finished speaking her eyes were closing and Harcourt knew she needed to rest. He kissed her gently and left her. It was time to talk to Biddy. It might be a good thing to leave her sitting in a cell for a while so that her fear of what was going to happen to her built. Then he shook his head. That could still be done, but he would ask at least a few questions now. He went to find Nicolas.

"Ye have made a terrible mistake," cried Biddy.

"Nay, I think not," said Harcourt, nodding his thanks to Nicolas who brought him a stool to sit down on. "Ye didnae have a verra good disguise, Biddy. Lady Annys had already seen ye once and kenned the gown ye were wearing. Ye also bared your head and face when ye met your lover."

"Is she going to be in here for verra long?" asked their other prisoner.

Harcourt looked over at Geordie. They had gotten that name out of him after he had woken up and Joan had seen to his injury. The man still refused to give them a clan name and he was beginning to think it was because Geordie was banished from his clan, a broken man. They were still not quite sure what to do with him.

"Nay, Geordie, as I believe she will be hanged before ye are." He ignored Biddy's wailing protest.

"What did she do?"

"Poisoned the laird."

"Nay, nay, nay! It was only supposed to make him sick and too weak to fight."

Harcourt looked at Biddy who looked as startled by her words as he felt. That was a confession. He glanced at Geordie who was looking disgusted and shaking his head. There might be hope for Geordie. He was now witness to the woman's confession. Harcourt suspected that Geordie would point the finger of guilt at anyone just to save his own neck, but at least this time it would be the truth.

"So ye are the bitch that killed him," Geordie said. "I told Jaikie it was a lass but he wouldn't hear it. He didnae listen much and look where that got him. Shame he isnae here any longer to find out I was right."

"Hush, Geordie," Harcourt commanded in his coldest voice.

"Hushing," he mumbled and sat in the far corner of his bed.

"So, Biddy, ye would have us believe ye kept feeding your laird a poison but just thought he would get ill, nay die," Harcourt said.

"That was it. That was all. 'Tis nay my fault he was a weakling."

It made him furious to hear her call David weak and Harcourt made no secret of his anger, allowing it to coat his words. "Ye put the poison in his food. It doesnae matter whether ye were mistaken about what would happen. Ye gave it to him. He died. So, ye are the murderer."

"I was just doing as I was told."

"Certainly nay by your laird." He noticed that Geordie was listening closely. "Ah, then it was your lover."

"Nay, he was just doing what he was told as a loyal second should."

"So ye were both obeying Sir Adam MacQueen then."

"I didnae say that!"

"Your lover used you, made ye the knife he was too cowardly to use himself."

"Clyde is no coward," Biddy snapped.

"Clyde?" Geordie said. "Ye were Clyde's wee whore? Wheesht, ye are a witless lass, arenae ye?"

"He was going to marry me!"

"Och, aye? Ye believed that?"

Even Harcourt felt like wincing at the sharp scorn in Geordie's voice. "Ye ken Clyde weel, do ye?" he asked the man.

"Nay, just another of his hirelings. Although I suspicion he didnae pay ye much," Geordie said to

Biddy. "He ne'er pays the lassies he uses. Weel, nay in coin. 'Tis rumored he has paid a few with cold steel though when they thought he had made promises he wasnae keeping and made too much noise about it." He looked around the cells. "Ye best be careful. He might consider this making too much noise."

"Clyde is going to marry me and when Sir Adam gains this place, Clyde will be his second. Then I will be a lady."

Geordie hooted with laughter and Harcourt watched Biddy blush. Not from shame or embarrassment, however, but with a growing fury. Geordie was, in his strange way, doing better at getting information out of Biddy than he had been. He had also stopped her crying, replacing fear with anger.

"I shall tell Clyde about you," she hissed.

"Oh, I be so scared. What is he going to do? Toss me in a cell? Hang me? Missed his chance there."

Biddy looked at Harcourt and he realized Geordie had become the new target for her anger. Anger was good. Anger made people say things they would not under other circumstances. It made them lose their guard over their tongue. It was almost as good as pouring ale down a prisoner's throat until he was too sotted to care what he told the one asking questions.

"What is there for me here? Cooking for people who dinnae e'en notice me. Clyde was going to get me out of the kitchen."

"And right into a grave," muttered Geordie.

"Shut up!"

Biddy glared at the man but Harcourt could see the glint of fear in her eyes. He could not be certain if it was because she knew she had lost what she sought or if she feared Geordie was right. Her confidence in

Clyde's promises might not be as strong as she wanted them to believe. Shaking his head, he decided he actually had enough information to hang her but he wanted something else. He wanted information on Sir Adam.

"How did ye come and go to your trysts with no one kenning when and where ye went?" Harcourt asked.

"The bolt-hole."

"That is locked."

"The one they made for us peasants, aye. But I got a lock maker to make me a new key. I also looked about for other places where I could come and go but ye have already found most of those."

"It will make it easier if ye tell me where they all are."

"And why should I do that?"

"Did your lover promise to nay hurt your sisters when he and his men sneak in here to slaughter us?" Her look of unease gave him his answer. "Where are the bolt-holes ye used, the ones aside from the two your laird made?"

Biddy hesitated and then reluctantly told him. As Harcourt left, he had the feeling she may have kept one secret. Since she would have done that for her own purposes, he would have to consider what the best approach would be for getting that piece of information from her.

He hunted down Gybbon and told him where Biddy said her other bolt-holes were, not all of them tunnels. It annoyed him that he had missed those places in his work to strengthen Glencullaich's defenses. Gybbon promised he and the others would leave no stone unturned. The fact that Biddy would try to keep one hidden despite how it could be used against Glencullaich angered him. The woman was far more selfish than anyone had guessed. She might be a bit witless, but she was also cunning and cold. Even the concern for her sisters had not fully deterred Biddy from what was her most important concern—herself.

Deciding he needed to have his questions well planned out when he next visited Biddy, Harcourt chose to exercise his leg a little with a careful stroll around the inside of the wall. He also intended to keep a close eye out for any sign of that bolt-hole Biddy was keeping secret. Every instinct he had told him that it was important to get Glencullaich as tightly sealed and secured as he could, as soon as he could.

War was marching their way. Sir Adam MacQueen had tried to take Annys, tried to get hold of Benet, tried to destroy the village, and had played a long game of trying to make life so miserable many of the people fled. None of those things had gained him the prize he thought he was owed. There really were only two choices left to him—fight to take it or give up. Harcourt did not believe they would be so fortunate as to have the man walk away and leave them alone. That left them with a battle to take Glencullaich. Harcourt just hoped the man would wait until his leg healed completely.

# Chapter Twelve

Harcourt wondered what the punishment was for beating a sheriff. The man seated at the table eating and drinking too much from Glencullaich's larder was not going to be any help. It had been a waste of time to even send for the man. Sir Thomas Mac-Queen was not actually interested in doing his job. That he was kin to Sir Adam should have warned him that the man would do nothing, but other sheriffs dealt justice out to their kinsmen all the time and without hesitation when it was deserved. It was possible, he thought, that Sir Adam had bribed the oaf in some way.

"The mon kidnapped the laird of Glencullaich and twice tried to take Lady Annys as weel," said Harcourt. "Ye cannae just ignore that."

"I am nay ignoring it but ye have no proof any of that was done by Sir Adam."

"They were his men. Ye spoke to the mon we hold, the one who stampeded the cattle. He told ye he was hired by Sir Adam MacQueen."

"Aye"—the sheriff sat back and rubbed his rounded

belly—"but Sir Adam wasnae the one who told him to do that, was he. And that lass? Weel, she wasnae talking to Sir Adam, either, was she. Best ye have is the right to accuse Sir Adam's man Clyde and t'will still be that mon's word against some witless kitchen maid."

"Get out," Harcourt said, wanting the man out of his sight as quickly as possible.

"What?" The sheriff lumbered to his feet looking a strange mixture of shocked and afraid.

"Ye heard me. Get out."

"Why so harsh? Because I willnae let ye falsely accuse a mon who has been cheated of what is rightfully his by some wee bastard?"

Harcourt was not surprised when the sheriff paled for he suspected the glare he sent the man revealed just how murderous he was feeling. "Nay, because ye have no respect for the law. I suspicion Sir Adam has bought ye, although I hope he didnae pay verra much. Sir Adam has no claim here, nay by any law, for Sir David MacQueen, the laird, clearly declared Benet his son, born within the bounds of marriage to Lady Annys. And, Sir Adam will lose this game. Ye will have disgraced your office and your name for naught. Now, leave."

After the man hurried away, Harcourt poured himself a tankard of ale. He had almost finished it all before his fury receded. He sighed when Nicolas and Callum arrived and joined him at the table.

"No help at all, was he," said Callum as he helped himself to some cider.

"Nay. He sits firmly in Sir Adam's pocket," replied Harcourt.

"Then we will deal out justice on our own."

"I was trying to avoid that tangle."

"I ken it, but that fool has tossed it all right into our laps. He will regret that."

"Oh, aye, he will." Harcourt heard the force of a vow behind his words and could see that the other two men did as well. "I cannae understand how the mon e'er became a knight, let alone a sheriff. His corruption runs bone deep."

"Happens more often than ye may think," said Nicolas.

"Any more from that idiot of a maid?" he asked.

"Nay. She still does naught but cry and she continues to claim she didnae ken what she was doing. Geordie demanded he be moved to someplace quieter or just to get his hanging over and done so he can get some peace." Nicolas grinned when the others laughed.

"Ye dinnae believe her."

"Nay, dinnae believe a word she says. If it had been a quick poison she gave David, I might, but it was a slow one. She may be dull of wit but no one is so much so that they wouldnae see what they were doing was causing a terrible sickness in the mon."

Callum nodded. "I think she kens verra weel what she did, e'en what she was helping Sir Adam to do. When I spoke to her about an hour past, she said something to make me think she believed she was about to better herself, that she would come out of all this placed far above a mere kitchen maid."

Harcourt shook his head. "Witless lass. Annys said she heard something similar when she listened to what Clyde and Biddy said to each other. It appalled her. Biddy is an utter fool to have ever thought she would get what was being promised. Within minutes after Sir Adam set his arse in the laird's chair all she would have been is dead."

"Weel, what she is now is gone," said Gybbon as he entered the hall. "Someone set her free."

"How?" asked Harcourt.

"Nay certain but do suspect it was one of her sisters who did it. They must have given Geordie something because he is surrounded by tankards and snoring loud enough to shake the mortar out of the walls. The lass was facing a hanging and mayhap they couldnae bear the thought."

Rubbing his head to ease a growing ache there, Harcourt said, "Pick some men and try and find her."

"She will try to reach her lover," said Callum.

"And if she reaches him before we find her, she will die."

"Aye, probably ere she e'en finishes asking for help."

Harcourt sighed and rubbed his leg. His stitches were out now and the wound fully closed, but it still ached from time to time. It had been exactly a fortnight since he had been wounded and he knew he had healed well, even quickly, considering the severity of the wound, but that reminder did not always still his irritation over a lingering weakness.

"Any word from those two idiots?"

"Just that they are still alive. Hard to kill Mac-Fingals. Sometimes 'tis hard to realize ye probably should kill them."

Harcourt smiled briefly. "Still alive is enough although I hope they can give us some useful news soon. I best go and report all of this to Annys," he said, reluctant to give her what could only be called bad news.

"I think a part of her will be a bit relieved that Biddy has fled," said Callum. "She wasnae looking forward to having to mete out the justice needed."

Standing up, Harcourt nodded. "I ken it. 'Tis a hard thing for anyone with heart to see done nay matter how certain they are of the person's guilt. But, I also think she was hoping for some answers, some reason for why Biddy did what she did."

"She heard the reasons. She just doesnae want to believe that could be all."

"It will be hard for her to accept that sometimes greed is all there is that makes some people do the evil they do."

No one argued that and Harcourt left to go talk to Annys. She, too, was healed now, although the signs of all the bruises she had suffered still lingered as did a faint limp. He smiled as he rapped on her bed-chamber door. They now had matching gaits.

Annys called out an invitation to enter and he let himself in, quietly shutting the door behind him. He stood and savored the sight of her for a moment. She still wore her hair unbound though he knew the ache in her head caused by her fall had faded. A simple green gown flattered both the blood-red color of her hair and her green eyes. When she smiled a greeting at him, his heart skipped and he had to smile back at her, a little amused by how besotted he was.

"I saw the sheriff ride away," she said.

"Aye, that proved to be a great waste of my time,"

he said as he moved to sit beside her on the bench by the window. "Ye have these benches everywhere."

"I like the natural light to do my sewing and needlework. Joan likes to say that she just looks to see where the sun is in the sky if she needs to find me."

"Something to remember." He ignored the wary look she gave him "The sheriff isnae only a kinsman of Sir Adam's. I strongly suspect he is bought and paid for by the mon. He had no interest in what I was telling him, the accusations and proof I offered, and is obviously a believer in Sir Adam's claim that Glencullaich is his by right."

"So yet another MacQueen does his duty by Adam whilst giving no blood or coin to the fight." Annys shook her head as she put her needlework aside. "They are all in league with him if nay actually armed and standing by his side. They are like carrion crows, sitting about in the trees waiting for the winner of the fight to emerge so that they may get a few scraps to feed on. I cannae believe David or Nigel shared blood with those people."

"Aye, their relationship is hard to see." He took a deep breath and said, "Biddy has escaped."

"Och, nay." Annys shook her head, her pleasure in the day quickly dimming. "We should have banished her sisters from the keep, but I dinnae have the heart to do it since I kenned Biddy would hang. She will be running to her lover, aye?"

"That is what I think."

"Then she will soon pay for David's death, just nay at our hands."

Harcourt put his arm around her and held her close. "Unless we find her first. We will search for her. Callum told me they will begin the search for her.

We may find her before she foolishly seeks out her lover." He kissed her temple, savoring the light brush of her against his face.

"And then we will be forced to hang her. There is no victory to be found here."

"She chose her path, Annys. And she is no innocent, for all she claims she didnae ken the laird would die. Her reasons for what she did are nay innocent ones, either. Nay honorable at all. She was doing all of it for her lover because he told her she would find herself in a position far above the one a mere kitchen maid holds."

"She would be but one step below a laird's wife," Annys murmured. "Clyde spoke of how he was going to raise her that high. I wanted there to be more reason, e'en if that more made no sense to me. I wanted David's death to have been for a reason, nay just greed. 'Tis so hard to believe he was murdered because a cousin wants more coin and a foolish kitchen maid wants finer gowns and someone to cook for her as she has always cooked for others. Murdering a good mon for such petty reasons makes it all seem far more evil."

"Aye, it does. But, Annys, greed and envy kill many a good mon. Always has. Always will."

Annys leaned against him and wrapped her arms around his waist. The steady beat of his heart, the warm strength of his body, soothed her even as it stirred her body's interest. David was gone. There was no bringing him back or changing the sickening reasons he was murdered for. All she could do was hold fast to the land he loved, keeping it out of the hands of ones who would destroy it in their greed, and make his murderers pay for all their crimes.

She hummed her pleasure as he stroked her hair. Annys decided she was weary of her own lingering indecision. The man could still stir her blood like no one else ever had. She was no virgin lass, no innocent maid. Their trysts by the burn years ago had taught her a great deal. Sadly he had also shown her what she was missing in her marriage to David. There was something missing in her life now as well. It was past time she reached out and took what she wanted even though she knew it could never last.

"This is dangerous, lass," Harcourt murmured, his whole body tightening with want as she pressed her body against his and idly caressed his back and arms.

"Mmmmm. So is life, I have discovered." She lifted her head from his chest and smiled at him. "Mayhap I have just decided that I like poking at the fire."

"Ye dinnae have to poke too hard, loving. 'Tis burning hot already. It has been for five verra long years. I could find naught to fully douse it."

He saw the brief flare of hurt in her eyes but refused to lie to her. She had been married and out of his reach. He had had every right to seek comfort, maybe even more. He knew she was not so naïve, or even witless, that she would believe he had spent the years since they had parted celibate and pining for her. The urge to soothe pain, no matter how brief and prompted partly by the knowledge that she had been alone, could not be completely smothered, however.

"Of course, I havenae e'en bothered to try for a verra long time so 'tis somewhat quick to flare up now."

"Is it now." She kissed the hollow at the base of

his throat and heard him inhale sharply. "I ne'er even tried."

"Weel, ye were married."

"More or less."

Harcourt could not wait any longer. He slid his hand under her chin, tilted her face up to his, and kissed her. She slid her arms around his neck and began to return his kiss with all the heat any man could ask for. Still uncertain if he was really seeing the willingness he thought he was, the willingness he ached to see, Harcourt struggled to keep his need for her from overwhelming him and making him push her too hard, too fast.

Annys could sense his caution but was not sure how to break the control he was exerting on his lust. She had done all she could to let him know she was willing to be his lover again. Even when they were lovers, Harcourt had always been the one to start the dance. Annys thought back to those days, fighting to recall something that she could do to end his caution with her.

Harcourt's control was hanging by a thread, a very thin, frayed thread. He was considering just bluntly asking her if this time she wanted to go beyond kisses, when she slid her small hand over his thigh and lightly brushed her fingers against his groin, as if testing his interest. He groaned softly and began to undo her gown.

Ending the kiss, Harcourt said, "Annys, if ye are going to say nay, say it fast so that I may crawl out of here without having offended or frightened ye in some way."

Annys just smiled and began to unlace his shirt. He decided to take that as an *aye*. It amazed him that

he got her gown off without tearing it. One she wore
nothing under but her shift. He decided she was
being too slow in removing his shirt so he quickly finished the job himself. He pulled her back into his
arms and felt a small tremor go through her. That
sign that her need might match his own only increased his desperation to be skin to skin with her.

And in a bed, he thought, and suddenly grew still.
Annys was a small woman and lifting her into his
arms would be no trouble at all. But, walking her to
the bed when he still limped might not be as easy. In
fact, it could prove humiliating.

Beneath her hands Annys could feel the tension
in Harcourt's body. It was not due to passion, she was
certain of that. She chanced a peek at his face, afraid
she would see something there that would cause her
pain. It puzzled her to see that he was staring at the
bed with a look of consternation. That was not an expression one expected to see on the face of one's
lover.

A heartbeat later she understood. He still had a
limp and an occasional weakness in his leg. They
were going to have to either make love on the floor
or get to that bed in the least awkward way possible.
Annys smiled, stood up, and grasped him by the
hand.

"Ye can be all romantic some other time," she said
as she tugged him to his feet and started to lead him
to the bed.

"Ye would find me carrying ye to the bed romantic?"

"Weel, since we have ne'er made love anywhere
but on a plaid or the grass, I believe I find the verra

idea of making love in an actual bed romantic right now."

He laughed, picked her up, and gently tossed her onto the bed. Harcourt then shed the rest of his clothes, his desire renewed when he saw how she looked at him as he did so. Climbing into the bed beside her, he kissed her even as he began to remove her thin shift.

His breath actually caught when he finally bared her to his gaze. Her breasts were fuller and her hips a little rounder, but she was still as beautiful as he remembered. His gaze fell to the faint scars bracketing her womb and his heart clenched with the meaning of such marks; they were the marks of her work to give his son life.

When she suddenly covered the marks with her hands, he gently removed them. Harcourt bent his head and kissed each one before turning to face her. She was blushing just as she used to and he still found it endearing.

"I may nay be able to openly claim the boy, may nay e'en have the right to think like that since I held to the plan to breed him and hand him to David, but I still thank ye." He traced each scar with his fingers. "With so many healers in my clan, I am nay as ignorant of the risk a woman takes to bear a child, as weel as the pain she endures and the strength she needs to bring life into the world. So thank ye."

Annys reached up and stroked his cheek. "I am the one who has had the blessing of Benet so I think I should thank ye."

He grinned as he leaned over her. "Then what do

ye say to us heartily thanking each other for a wee while?"

She lifted her hand and gave a *come here* wave with her fingers. When he growled softly, she laughed and he smothered the sound with his kiss. Annys had the thought that it was pure heaven to at last be skin to skin with him before passion's fire cleared her mind of everything but the taste and feel of him.

Harcourt kissed her until his head swam from the heady taste of her. Then he began to kiss his way down to her breasts. The way she gasped and squirmed beneath his caresses strained his control over his own passion. He needed to be buried deep in her heat but he was determined that she share in his pleasure, that she get the full measure of her own. He slid his hand down over her belly and between her legs. The fact she was already wet nearly snapped those last threads of control he clung to.

Annys thought she ought to be feeling pain as the fire inside her grew and grew. She caressed every part of his strong body she could reach, loving the feel of his skin beneath her hands. His every caress and kiss only made her hungrier for him. She realized she needed him joined with her soon, if not sooner. The tightness in her belly was growing so fast she knew she risked being done before he had even entered her.

She slid her hand down his body until she reached the erection she could feel pressing against her leg. He certainly felt ready to her, she thought as she stroked him and lightly rubbed the dampness from the tip with her thumb. The groan he gave sounded as if it welled up from some place deep inside of him. Then he grabbed her hand and pulled it away. A flicker of panic went through her as she feared she had overstepped.

"Och, lass, that broke me," he said, his voice little more than a low growl. "I apologize now if it is too soon for you."

Before she could tell him that it was not too soon, he was thrusting inside her. Annys gasped and shook with the pleasure of him inside her. She had the odd thought that it was where he belonged and then he began to thrust in and out of her, the tightness in her belly growing almost painful. She clung to him and was returning his kiss when that tightness suddenly broke apart. He growled when her cries of release fell into his mouth.

Annys was still shaking from the force of her pleasure when he found his. The warmth of his seed as it spilled inside of her made her shiver with another small wave of pleasure. She wrapped her arms around him when he slumped over her, careful to fall a little to the side so as not to put his full weight on her. It was just as wonderful as she had remembered, she mused, as she held him close while she fought to catch her breath.

This was what had haunted her dreams for five long years. At the time the memories had caused her to sink into a sadness it was difficult to shake free of. Benet had helped. She would look at him and tell herself whatever heart pain she suffered over Harcourt was worth it for the blessing of her son.

It was several moments before she became aware of the less beautiful parts of lovemaking. A little longer before the stickiness between her legs and sweat drying on her skin became a bit irritating. Just as she was about to try to get out of bed with some semblance of dignity to wash off, Harcourt rose and went to get the bowl of washing water and a couple of rags. She had to smile as they both hurriedly cleaned themselves off, both of them clearly eager to be done with the chore so they could be skin to skin again.

Harcourt put away the bowl and washrag and quickly slipped back into bed. He sprawled on his back and tugged Annys into his arms. A sigh of pure contentment escaped him as her soft skin pressed against his. He took her hand from where it rested on his chest and kissed her palm.

"I was a wee bit worried there that I was going to be as quick as an untried lad and leave ye wanting," he said.

"Nay, ye werenae. Truth tell, I was beginning to think ye were moving too slowly."

He laughed. "Then, as always, we were matched in our pace."

"I often thought of those times we spent together," she said quietly. "I confess, at times I could almost hate ye for showing me how much was missing from my marriage but then I would remember that I wouldnae have Benet if nay for all that."

"I often thought of them, too," he confessed in an equally soft voice. "As I became less of a reckless lad in heart and mind and became the mon I should have been even back then, I was always torn about it."

"I dinnae think ye were so verra reckless and ken weel how skilled David was at getting people to do what he wanted them to."

"He did convince me when everything I had e'er been taught by my family should have held firmly against him. But"—he kissed the top of her head— "I was lusting after ye and I think that pushed me to agree when I might have stood on my principles otherwise."

"I am sorry that David made ye agree to all that but I will ne'er be sorry that ye did."

"Because there is Benet."

"Aye, there is Benet. And whate'er else was wrong or hurtful and may still be, without it all happening as it did, there would be no Benet."

"And that is a gift I wouldnae wish to see lost."

He stared up at the ceiling and thought on all that stood between them for a moment. Then he decided he was wasting a moment that should be peaceful and quiet, and, just maybe, would work to soothe any of those hurts she spoke of. He idly stroked her arm and wondered when he could make love to her again.

# Chapter Thirteen

The pounding on the door made Harcourt curse.
He was enjoying the warmth and peace of lying
naked with Annys. His body was pleasantly sated and
he could savor the feel of her soft curves without the
press of a frantic need. He had even been ready to
enjoy that pleasure for a second time.

Just as he opened his mouth to order the one
banging on the door to leave, a small, soft hand
covered his mouth. He looked at Annys and she
shook her head. He muttered another curse when
she slipped out of bed and began to dress. Knowing
there would be no returning to their lovemaking, he
got up and started to dress as well. He comforted
himself with the knowledge that, now that her resistance had ended, there would be other times they
could enjoy.

"M'lady?" Joan called from the other side of the
door.

"Just a moment, Joan," Annys called back.

Annys struggled to bury all sense of embarrassment as she hurried to dress. Not only had Joan

made it very clear that she thought Annys should take Harcourt as a lover, she was a widow, a mother, and five and twenty. She had earned the right to do as she pleased. Glancing back at a now-dressed Harcourt who was tidying the rumpled covers on the bed, she nearly blushed. There was no question that she had been pleased, she thought, and then went to let Joan in.

"What is it, Joan?" she asked as the woman stood before her, wringing her hands.

"Biddy has been found," Joan said.

"Alive?"

Joan shook her head. "Nay, they found her hanging from a tree a few miles from here."

"I was afraid that was what she would find when she ran. I ken who let her out but I still cannae understand how she found a way out of here. She must have gone to a great deal of trouble to get out without being seen and all she found was death." Annys shook her head. "Is she being brought in now?"

"Nay, they want Sir Harcourt to come meet with them where she is. Said they want to be certain there is naught there to lead them to that bastard causing all this trouble." Joan glanced at Harcourt. "If ye move fast there may still be enough light to find something."

Using every drop of willpower she had, Annys stopped herself from blushing. She had not realized how late in the day, or night, it was. She narrowed her eyes when she saw the hint of a smile curve Joan's mouth. Joan clearly could not wait to start her crowing.

"Ye are verra certain that no one saw her leaving

here or e'en running away from here?" Annys asked, attempting to distract Joan from what she was seeing.

"I think the men on the walls are looking for someone trying to get in. Might nay be looking for someone using the shadows and all to get away from Glencullaich. And when ye think of how often she slipped in and out of the keep with none kenning what she was doing, weel, she obviously had one skill."

"We shall have to make a verra thorough search for the place she used to slip out of the keep this time when the light allows for it."

"Ye ken she willingly ran to her death, dinnae ye?" Harcourt asked the two women in a quiet voice.

Annys lowered her head and sighed, but Joan nodded and said, "I ken it. She courted it the first time she fed our David that poison. S'truth, I heard ye warned her about exactly that. Aye, e'en that other prisoner warned her. She was facing a hanging and none of us wanted a part in it e'en though we kenned it was weel deserved."

"So ye came to tell Sir Harcourt that he must go to his men?" asked Annys.

"Aye, and that the evening meal is being served. Didnae think ye wanted to miss that." Joan nudged Harcourt toward the door. "Go on with ye. I need to tidy m'lady's hair so she doesnae look like she just crawled out of bed."

Harcourt heard Annys's outraged protest as Joan closed the door behind him.


"Joan, ye presume too much," said Annys, trying to sound as haughty as possible even as she allowed the woman to push her into a seat and begin to fix her hair.

"Are ye going to try to tell me that I am wrong?" When Annys said nothing, Joan nodded. "Didnae think so. Ye ne'er did like to lie."

"It wasnae right," Annys mumbled, guilt sneaking back into her heart to replace the lingering warmth of passion. It was clear that her moment of making a firm decision had not been the epiphany she had thought it to be, but merely a momentary change of mind.

"Huh. I would have thought that one weel skilled in the loving of a lass."

Annys laughed but the burst of good humor faded quickly. "Och, nay doubt. I suspicion he didnae spend many nights alone whilst we were apart. Truth tell, he said as much."

"Weel, ye were still another mon's wife."

"I ken it. I leap from pleased to guilty, from wishing he would stay to wanting him to leave, and from thinking of how he spent those years we were apart and hating every woman he has e'er bedded. 'Tis a madness. I dinnae like it."

Finishing with her hair, Joan moved to stand in front of Annys. "Ye are just a lass in love. 'Tis a madness of a kind. Always has been. Always will be. I suffered the like for my mon, Nial, whilst I had him, God rest his sweet soul. It eases."

"Mayhap, but what happens if that love isnae returned?"

"Ye think he doesnae care for you?"

"He cares, but does he love? And if he loves, does he plan to stay? The mon has his own keep to run, the people there depending upon him. I have to stay here to care for Benet's inheritance. 'Tis nay a simple matter of sharing a love. It ne'er was."

"Ah, nay." Joan frowned for a moment and then shrugged. "Then take what ye can, savor it, and revel in what ye can have now. Ye have certainly earned it."

"'Tis what I told myself. But, the people . . ."

"Willnae care. I have told ye that but 'tis clear ye didnae heed me. Wisdom wasted. Ye are a widow, lass, and ye ken weel that foolish men believe we cannae abide being without one of them sharing our bed. 'Tis a witless belief we widows have long used to our advantage. All the world expects is for one to be discreet. Dinnae flaunt it and no one will care."

Annys was not sure she believed that, but would consider it. She doubted she could step away from Harcourt now anyway. Not only would he not allow it, she had now had a memory replaced by fact and her body already craved more. She also knew enough widows to know that Joan spoke the truth. There was the hint of freedom in widowhood as long as a woman was discreet. The fact that everyone knew who fathered Benet actually aided her. Harcourt was an experienced lover, one she had known before through her own husband's prodding. And she would not be surprised to discover that, since David had approved of the man, they did, too.

"I had thought I had decided but then I began to be not so decisive again but, I promise, I will try to clear away all this confusion in my head," she told Joan.

"Fair enough," Joan said as she joined Annys in walking down to the hall.

* * *

The evening meal was almost finished when Harcourt and the others came in. She could tell by the looks on their faces that it had been a gruesome task. A shiver went through her when she all too clearly recalled the hangings her father had made her attend.

When Harcourt sat down next to her, she briefly tensed, afraid of what people in the hall might think. A quick look around showed her that they were barely paying any attention to the fact that their lady was sitting with the man who looked so much like her son. Something inside of her breathed a huge sigh of relief. Joan was right. They did not care. It would be a long, long time before she ever admitted that to Joan though.

"It was bad?" she asked quietly.

"Aye." Harcourt took a long drink of ale as a young boy put some platters of food near him. "Probably nay a thing to speak of during a meal."

"Nay, although I do have a verra strong stomach. Recall what I told ye about my father and his rules."

He frowned, angered yet again by what her father had made her do as a child. "There is one thing I wanted to ask about all that," he said as he began to eat. "What happened to the family of the mon ye saw that day."

"They survived," she muttered, and turned her attention to the stewed apples she had put on her plate.

Harcourt studied her face and began to grin. "Nay with pig scraps though, aye?"

"Nay, no more pig scraps." Then she saw by his grin that he knew exactly why that poor man's family had survived and she sighed. "I stole the food. May have been silly but I was almost certain that my father wouldnae hang me if I was caught."

"And are they in the village here?"

She rolled her eyes, not very pleased that he could guess what she would have done so easily. "Aye. She and all six of her children. She is Master Kenneth's wife."

"How did ye manage that?"

"I took a chance and sent Nigel, my newly betrothed husband, a letter. I told him about the family and why I was helping them and asked if I could bring them. E'en asked if he had any good ideas about how I could explain why they were coming with me. He wrote a letter to my father and informed him that I should come with my own maid and that he would prefer it to be a grown woman, preferably a widow. Weel, my father had no idea who was in the village unless they did something he felt he needed to hang them for so I kindly offered a suggestion, got Ilsa all cleaned up and dressed well but nay too well, and presented her to my father. He grunted and waved us out of his way so we took that as an aye and off we went. Master Kenneth took one look at Ilsa when she went to the village to see the cottage Nigel had readied for her and that was that."

"E'en with six bairns at her skirts?"

"Ye would have to see the way Master Kenneth looks at her. He would have taken her if she had had ten bairns at her skirts."

"And probably if she also had one in her belly," said Joan from the other side of Annys. "I recall thinking there would be some jealousy for Master Kenneth was a fine catch as a husband but Ella, who had fancied him, told me she took one look at the way the mon looked at Ilsa and gave it all up. Said the fool would ne'er see anyone else anyway."

"And so Ilsa and her bairns live weel in the village now. A fine ending."

"Aye," agreed Callum who sat across the table from Harcourt. "A verra fine ending."

"Got better when she brought Ilsa the fruit to grow."

"Joan," Annys hissed but her maid ignored her.

"Annys is gifted with plants and Ilsa had skill enough to learn to tend them. She also makes some verra fine things with the fruits, too. But it helped make her enough coin that she could stay in her cottage and for Annys to cease taking the risk of stealing food." She saw Annys scowling at her. "Ilsa told me that years ago. I was wondering why she brought those plants all the way here when she was supposed to be watching you."

"I didnae plan that far."

"I think ye did a lot of planning for a child," said Harcourt. "And I thank ye ladies for the tale. It was nice to hear the good of life after seeing what we did." He looked around and saw that most of the others were gone now.

"It was verra bad, wasnae it," Annys said and could not stop herself from touching his hand in a soft stroke of comfort.

"She fought until the end." He decided not to tell them that it was not only the hanging Biddy had had to fight and prayed the skilled Joan would not say anything if she happened to look at the body and see how it had been cleaned up. "'Tis always worse when ye can see that. I think the bastard must have hoisted her up there himself and just held on until it was over."

"And a mon like that is Sir Adam's second?" she asked, horrified.

"So says everyone we talk to who kens the mon. My first thought upon seeing it was that she must have truly irritated him all the time he was playing her devoted lover. There was that kind of cold cruelty to it."

"Poor Biddy. I wish we had kenned what she was about. We might have stopped her before it went too far."

"He would have hunted up another one. And Biddy may nay have been saved for she had that want in her, that greed for more than she had, and a willingness to do anything to get it. I could hear it when I talked to her."

"Aye," agreed Callum. "She had that greed inside her. She felt she had been wronged by nay being a lady proper, just a kitchen maid. And as we have all said, she had a good life here and a good mon for a laird. There was naught here to breed those feelings that ate at her. I often wonder if they are in there when one is born, just waiting for a chance or a nudge to awake. Her sisters dinnae have that same belief that they are so deserving of things they dinnae have that it excuses anything they do to get those things."

"But they freed her."

"Family. Just because ye dinnae like one of your siblings all that much doesnae mean ye will turn your back on them when they are in trouble."

"Then what should be done about her sisters? I have been thinking on it and just cannae decide.

Some punishment should be dealt out but that is hard to do when ye ken so weel why they did it."

Harcourt nodded. "Ye need to think of something that looks like punishment to all the others yet isnae too harsh."

"Garderobes. Slop buckets. For at least a fort-night."

"Och, ye have a cruel side, Joan," said Nicolas and he laughed.

"It serves me weel from time to time." Joan looked at Annys. "Shall I tell the girls that?"

"Aye, but mayhap nay until they have buried their sister," said Annys.

"Agreed. I will give them a wee bit of time to grieve and pick a day for them to come to me to hear what their punishment will be. Let them ken one is coming. 'Tis best."

Annys nodded and then looked at Harcourt. "Ye found nothing to help ye hunt down Clyde or Sir Adam?"

"Nay. We followed the mon's trail for a wee while but it grew too dark to read a trail weel. We will return there in the light of day and see what we find." He glanced toward the door. "And I think ye will be sorting out Biddy's sisters earlier than ye had planned."

Annys looked to the door and watched two young women walk toward her. Their faces were blotched with the marks of a long time of heavy crying and they held hands as they moved toward her. She immediately felt sympathy for them but was determined to be firm. They had done something that was seriously wrong and needed to be punished for it.

The two girls curtsied and the taller one said, "We

have come to beg your forgiveness, m'lady. I am
Florence and this is Davida. We did wrong, m'lady.
We ken it. 'Tis just that Biddy was so scared and
crying and . . ." She fell silent when Davida nudged
her in the ribs.

"Biddy was the eldest and we have long done what
she told us to. This time we should have found the
backbone to say nay. She had done a terrible thing.
Nay, a lot of terrible things and would have done
more with no care to who might suffer. I am shamed
by what she did. I helped let her go simply because I
couldnae bear to watch her die e'en though she deserved such punishment."

Annys was a little stunned by the blunt honesty of
Davida, the girl's gaze never faltering as she had
spoken. This girl was the strong one in the family, she
suspected, with none of Biddy's weaknesses. It was
tempting to say they were forgiven and send them on
their way but she could not, as the lady of the keep,
be that lenient over what was a very serious crime.

"'Tis good that ye ken how wrong ye were and
there will be a punishment handed down. Howbeit,
your sister is dead and it can wait until ye bury her.
Good or bad, she was your kin. When that is done, ye
go to Joan and she will tell ye what ye must do to pay
for this."

Annys reached out and took each girl by the hand.
"I understand and I forgive ye. But, it was a grave
wrong ye did, so I will also see that ye serve your punishment. Aye?"

"Aye," said both girls and they turned to leave
but halted after a few steps and Davida looked back
at her.

"It was a grave wrong but, do ye ken, it was also

foolish. One of the saddest things is that we risked ourselves to try and save her from hanging, but she kenned full weel her plans and her betrayals would bring an army to these gates, mayhap right inside when we were nay looking so that we could be slaughtered more easily. She didnae e'en consider that that could mean we die, too, and all so she could sit higher at the table.

"So I bless ye for being kind enough to forgive us but, weel, I am nay sure I have that kind a heart. Help her though I did, it will be a verra long time before I e'en consider forgiving Biddy."

Annys sighed as she watched the two girls leave. Having a sister who had blackened their names as deeply as Biddy had meant the girls were already being punished. She would not relent though for the people of Glencullaich had to see that she could be firm, forgiving but also ready to give punishment when it was deserved.

"That Davida bears watching," said Joan. "She has a good sharp wit and backbone."

"Aye, she does. And isnae easily fooled."

"Nay. Florence has a tender heart and I suspect Biddy kenned how to use that to her advantage. Davida did what she felt a sister must but wasnae fooled for a moment." Joan stood and brushed down her skirts. "I will go see if they need or want any help preparing the body after I make sure Benet is abed as he should be."

"I could check on Benet if ye wish, Joan, so that ye can go to the girls," said Harcourt.

Joan just cocked one brow at him and nodded. "Ye do that. And if he has that cursed lamb in the room be sure to take it back to the barn. Lad has been trying to keep it close because he fears someone might try to kill and eat it again."

Seeing the look of motherly concern on Annys's face, Harcourt placed a hand on her shoulder and held her in her seat. "I will, Joan."

Joan looked at Annys. "Let him deal with it. Benet might still be little more than a bairn, but he is a boy, and maybe hearing a mon talk some sense into him will sink into his head and ease his fear for the beastie."

Annys frowned as Joan walked out of the hall in search of Biddy's sisters. What Joan said about letting a man talk to Benet made sense but she felt a little annoyed that she couldn't fix everything for him. She looked up at Harcourt and inwardly sighed. She would let him go to Benet. At some point in his life Benet would have to learn about Harcourt. It would not hurt if he had a few good childhood memories of the man when that time came.

"Shall I go?" he asked, praying she would not say no.

"Aye, go on. I had not realized he was still doing that. And, after all, ye were right there when it happened and helped rescue him as weel. Might add some weight to what ye say. I think at times he just thinks I am being a mother and saying things to calm him down just as mothers should do."

Harcourt laughed and kissed her on the forehead. She fought not to reveal her excitement tinged with a hint of embarrassment when he whispered the word *later* in her ear. A moment later he was gone, eager to do something to help the boy he could not claim.

"So," said Gybbon as he looked at her after watching Harcourt leave, "I must assume that there will ne'er be a nice roasted lamb served at a Glencullaich table then."

Annys gaped at him then clamped a hand over her mouth when Callum slapped him on the back of his head. She started to laugh and soon they were all laughing. It felt good and she welcomed it.

Harcourt walked into the room after greeting the guard outside Benet's door and looked at the boy as he shut the door behind him. He could see no lamb in the room, just the cat sprawled rather obscenely on its back at the end of the bed. It opened one eye to look him over and closed it again. When he looked at Benet again, however, he noticed that the boy was sitting up in his bed, his small hands clasped and resting on his lap and an angelic look on his face.

"Benet," he said, "ye ken ye are nay supposed to bring the lamb to your bedroom, dinnae ye?" He sat on the edge of the bed and pretended he did not hear the soft bleat coming from beneath it.

"Do ye see a lamb here?" the boy asked.

"Nay but it is here, isnae it?"

Benet sagged, his thin shoulders slumping, and he nodded. He reached over and banged twice on the bed frame. There was a brief scramble and the lamb appeared from beneath the bed. The fact that he had actually trained the lamb was astonishing, but Harcourt was not going to praise his skill this time.

"Why cannae it stay?"

"It is cute and small now, Benet, but it will grow. Ye have seen a grown ewe, havenae ye?" The child nodded. "Ye cannae have that expecting to join ye in your bedchamber every night, now can ye?" Benet shook his head. "Roberta needs to sleep in the stable." He sighed when he saw the child's lower lip wobble and his eyes turn shiny with tears.

"I dinnae want anyone to kill her and eat her."

Harcourt moved to lie beside him on the bed and put his arm around his thin shoulders. "Benet, people do eat lambs, but there are a lot of them at Glencullaich. No one needs your lamb to survive. They also all ken that Roberta is your special lamb and not one person here would e'er think of hurting it. Those men were bad men, mean men. They didnae care whose lamb it was or that it was making ye unhappy to see them trying to kill it. We dinnae have those kind of men here."

"Nay, we dinnae. I just get afraid for her. What if someone thinks my lamb is one of the ones they can eat? She looks like some of the others."

"That is easy enough to fix."

"It is?"

"Aye, we shall put a collar on it. I suspicion your mother can think of something. Mayhap e'en something with Roberta written on it so no one can mistake it for just any lamb." When Benet started to scramble out of the bed, obviously intending to have it done immediately, Harcourt caught him up in his arms and put him back in place beside him. "Ye can talk to your mother in the morning and ask her if she can make something for Roberta."

"Oh. Aye. Dunnie will keep a watch on Roberta, aye?"

"Aye. Now, go to sleep and I will take the wee beastie to the stable."

He kissed the top of the boy's head and then got up. Even as he picked up the lamb Benet leapt out of bed and stood in front of them. "Benet?" Harcourt asked, hoping he was not going to get a fight about the lamb now.

"I need to give her a kiss good night. She expects it."

Harcourt looked at the animal he held who was trying very hard to dip her head down to Benet and sighed. He crouched down and waited as Benet kissed the lamb on the head and gave it a little pat.

Then Benet climbed back into bed but kept staring at the animal.

"Benet, I give ye my word as a knight, the lamb is safe in Glencullaich."

"I just worry, ye ken."

"Do ye trust Dunnie?"

"I trust ye, too. But, aye, I do trust Dunnie. He has been teaching me how to care for Roberta."

"Weel, that is where your lamb will be. With a mon ye trust in a stable ye go to all the time in a keep that doesnae have men as bad as the ones who scared you." He was relieved to see Benet smile and lie down. "Now, sleep and ye can see the wee beastie in the morning."

He took the lamb to the stable and shook his head when Dunnie just laughed. Yet he found himself watching how the man treated the lamb for a moment to reassure himself. Harcourt shook his head again and headed back into the keep. Discovering that Annys had gone to see a new baby born to the weaver's wife, he sat with his men and talked over what they should do on the morrow to continue readying themselves for the war they were certain was headed their way. When he heard Annys return, he waited what he considered a reasonable amount of time and then, ignoring the teasing of the others, went up to her bedchamber.

Annys opened the door at his knock and smiled at him. Harcourt smiled back, stepped inside even as he picked her up in his arms, and kicked the door shut behind him. Carefully he walked her to the bed, tossed her down, and started to take off his clothes as she laughed. It was, he decided, a perfect end to the day.

# Chapter Fourteen

Muttering a curse, Harcourt made his way up onto the walls to take a turn at the watch. On the one hand he was more content than he had been in a very long time. He had a willing Annys warming his bed. On the other hand, there was still a lot that stood between them that could turn what they shared from a blessing into a curse.

She had to stay at Glencullaich. His son had to remain David's heir. There was Gormfeurach and its people waiting for him to return. His brother had entrusted the care of his son's lands to him. Back at Gormfeurach there was also the chance of gaining some land of his own. If he turned his back on that then he became no more than a landless knight, not a man worthy of the lady of Glencullaich. And that was the one thing that bothered him the most, he decided. He loathed the idea of coming to her empty-handed. She deserved better than that.

"I would have thought ye would be in a much lighter mood," said Gybbon as he joined Harcourt at the wall. "Ye have certainly been smiling a lot this past sennight."

Harcourt laughed but the moment of good humor passed quickly. "Aye, and most times I still am despite nay having solved this trouble with Sir Adam. Yet, although I am nay sure if I or she looks for this to last, every so often I find myself thinking of all the reasons it cannae. She must stay here and I must go back to Gormfeurach."

"Ah, aye, that is a trouble. Especially since ye could gain yourself some land for the care ye are taking of Gormfeurach."

"'Tis already chosen." He nodded at Gybbon's look of surprise. "'Tis but a matter of drawing the boundaries. Many things to consider when doing so. Then I hand o'er a token payment for the deeds to it and 'tis all mine. If I stay here, I really have no right to it."

"And Annys cannae take the laird of this land away from it, especially with such greedy kinsmen eyeing it. They may have sat back as Sir Adam tries to take it but they all want it."

"Nay, she cannae."

"'Tis a shame the elder brother died."

"Aye, but, if he hadnae, David wouldnae have wed Annys, and, in the end, there wouldnae have been a Benet. That would be a loss. As she said once, for all that is wrong in this tangle we put ourselves in, there is one bright blessing and that is Benet. Change one little thing and he wouldnae be here."

"How did the elder brother die?"

Harcourt shrugged. "In some battle in France. David always bemoaned the fact that he didnae ken the how or even the where of Nigel's death. Nay e'en the when. The letters, though ne'er plentiful, just stopped coming about seven years ago. Every inquiry David sent out brought back naught."

Gybbon looked out on the land beyond the wall. "Ye could always set Nicolas here to watch o'er the land just as Brett set ye in Gormfeurach."

"Nicolas has no kinship to me or to Annys. It wouldnae hold long."

"Nay, mayhap not." Gybbon clapped Harcourt on the back. "Ye will think of something if ye find ye have the need to do so."

The need to do so was growing stronger every day, Harcourt thought. Each time he had to hold back because her people were around watching them, or he had to slip out of the bedchamber with a care to get away unseen, his resentment of such secrecy grew. He wanted to openly claim Annys as his. The thought of riding away from her once Sir Adam was defeated stung more sharply with each passing hour. It would be as if he had left behind a piece of himself.

He began to think he had done just that when he had left her years ago.

It was far past time that he took a good deep look into his own heart, Harcourt decided. Far past time to make a few hard choices as well. Not only was his indecision embarrassingly clear to his men who knew him so well, but he was finding it irritating himself.

"Who is that?"

Gybbon's question pulled Harcourt from his thoughts. He followed the direction of Gybbon's pointing finger and looked out at two distant figures riding toward them. A moment later he breathed a sigh of relief, one heavy weight lifting off his shoulders.

"'Tis those cursed MacFingals returning," he replied.

"Ye can see that from this far away with naught to aid ye but a weak setting sun mostly covered by clouds?"

"I can see the shape of them, how they sit a horse, and e'en a wee bit of the horses. Enough to recognize the beasts as the ones the MacFingals took when they left. Those vain fools near always wear their hair loose as weel, just as those two riders do."

"So, ye didnae send them to their deaths as ye had begun to fear."

Harcourt scowled at Gybbon as he turned to begin his way down off the walls. "I didnae think that. They sent word now and then. I kenned they would be back when they found something we needed to know." He ignored Gybbon's mocking snort of laughter.

The MacFingals were riding into the bailey by the time Harcourt got there to greet them. He noticed that both men had returned with more than they had left with. Extra very full packs were secured on each horse.

"Did ye go to a market on your way back here?" Harcourt asked even as he prayed the thievery they had so clearly indulged in was not something he would have to strenuously object to.

"Aye, in a way," replied Nathan, grinning widely. "We decided Sir Adam's men didnae need to be carrying so much about on Lady Annys's land so we kindly lightened their burden a wee bit."

Harcourt shook his head. "And they are nay hunting ye down?"

"May be but nay this way. They think we came from the far north."

"Come inside then. We can talk while ye have some food and drink."

It did not trouble Harcourt when he caught no sight of Annys as he and the others entered the hall. All that had occurred in the last few days, from discovering Biddy's betrayal to her own close escape, had exhausted her. It would not surprise him if she had slipped away for a brief nap before the evening meal was all set out. He knew he should feel guilty over the fact that his greed for her lush body had undoubtedly added to that weariness he had seen in her of late, but he found that he did not.

"So, what have ye discovered?" he asked the Mac-Fingals after they all sat at the table and the two men began to fill their plates with food. "Ye were gone a long while, long enough that I was thinking on which of my kin I would be willing to sacrifice by sending them to Scarglas with the news that I had lost you."

Ned laughed and shook his head. "Those fool men of Sir Adam's ne'er suspected us. Thought we were naught but two more men who thought to earn a few coins for swinging a sword around. Only one I was worried about was Sir Adam himself for I wasnae certain if he had remembered us here with ye that time he came or e'en when someone was watching Glencullaich."

"But he hadnae."

"He may have," said Nathan as he refilled his tankard with ale, having downed the first drink with unhesitant greed, "but he is one of those men who doesnae notice the soldiers or servants, only those of a higher birth. He didnae e'en like coming round to speak with us, always using that fellow Clyde to do his talking for him."

"Clyde is a verra busy mon."

"Ah, aye, we heard about that poor lass," Ned said. "She had to pay for all she had done and planned to do but it was a verra hard death. I suspicion ye didnae tell the women everything, aye?"

After a quick glance to make sure they were alone, Harcourt shook his head. "'Tis why the body wasnae brought home for a while. Cleaned her up a bit although ye cannae hide everything, can ye. Callum sent word that I needed to come and help find a trail for the ones who hanged her. So I am hoping all that will nay be known. For the sake of her sisters if naught else. Joan has made no mention of it and she helped them prepare the lass for burial so that may be the end of it."

"It will be hard for those lassies for a while but I think the people here are nay the sort to hold the sins of one kinsmon against a whole family."

"Nay," agreed Nathan. "Good, kind folk here."

"The lassies are still working out their punishment for setting their sister free," said Harcourt. "Couldnae just let that go e'en though they didnae hide their crime. Oh, and now that ye are back, ye will probably start wooing the lassies again." He ignored their grins. "Word of warning. Biddy's sister Davida is young and verra bonnie and no fool. She e'en saw the wrong in her sister and there isnae any mercy in her heart for the woman."

"Yet she set her free."

"Family." Harcourt was not surprised when both MacFingals nodded.

"Weel, the most important thing we discovered is that Sir Adam is verra busy gathering an army and 'tis a sizeable one."

Harcourt cursed. "I suspected that. He has failed to kill either Annys or Benet, failed to drive her away with everything from stealing stock to setting the village on fire. Only thing left is to just take the place. He wasnae e'en planning to do that fair. He was using Biddy to find him all the secret ways in so he could send men inside and slaughter as many as possible that way."

"And Biddy failing in that, getting herself caught and questioned, enraged Clyde," said Ned. "When the word first came that the fool lass had actually run back to the keep, and then that ye had kenned about her meeting with Clyde, he killed two fools before he grew cold again. And, nay, I am nay sure how he kenned it. Thinking he has one or two lads just sitting round in ale houses gathering news. Only thing I am sure of is that no one here, aside from Biddy, has e'er helped him. The lack of another spy was what so enraged Clyde and he was verra clear about that when he was ranting."

"It is the kind of news that would travel far and fast. But, she was nay clever enough to have kept it all to herself when she went to him anyway. So, do ye think this army a worthy one?"

"Some of it. He has a small number of men sent from half a dozen kin and money to hire more swordsmen. The quest to take Glencullaich from a four-year-old boy has stirred up a lot of MacQueens. I suspicion they are hoping for a wee piece."

"It sounds as if Sir Adam will have to fight hard for a long time to get his arse in that laird's chair. And, if he works some miracle and wins the battle, that knowledge will give me some comfort."

"Och, we willnae lose," said Ned. "Got more skills, more wits, and more strength. And big, thick walls. Dinnae forget the big thick, walls."

Harcourt laughed. "Nay, let us ne'er forget those walls. Especially since we are mostly confident we have sealed all the bolt-holes. The two we might have to use have been heavily secured but are still able to be used. I am nay one to think it noble to die to the last mon, woman, and bairn. Ye can see when that time comes that a loss is racing toward ye. That is when ye start to get the women and bairns out, while ye can still have men ye can set on the walls to protect their retreat."

"Agreed," said Nathan. "A large number of Sir Adam's forces are just hired swords, and the number of those whom I would call skilled is but a small part of it all. There is only one group he hired that ye need to be verra wary of."

"His archers," Harcourt said. "We saw a showing of their skills when they fired the village. Are they still with him?"

"Aye and there are about twenty of them." Nathan nodded when the others cursed. "They will be busy replacing their arrow, however, and it appears there is a scarcity of fletchers in the area."

"Had a great need to be south of here for a wee while," added Ned.

"We dinnae need an army," said Callum with a laugh. "Just a few MacFingals. Let us hope Sir Adam demands to begin his fight ere his archers can replace those lost fletchers. Now, I have a confession to make." He grinned when everyone looked at him. "'Tis nay that exciting.

"I am still looking for ways to go in and out of Glencullaich unseen. I was doing it all by myself, inspecting every inch of the wall, every space between buildings, and walls, every floor, wall, and roof. But then I was telling Peg about how Roban keeps appearing in places where we cannae see how it could get in and the lovely Peg said, when she could stop laughing, 'Why dinnae ye just follow the cat for a while?'" He looked at the stunned expressions on his friends' faces and nodded. "So, ere I bared my moment of humiliation to the world, I tried it. Yesterday. And I found three places."

"Three? When did this place become riddled with holes?" demanded Harcourt and he dragged his fingers through his hair. "I looked this place over from top to bottom when we first arrived and do so regularly now."

"Only one of the three is big enough to have been used for a person to crawl through and might be able to be quickly widened to let in some men. My guess? The dogs and cats roaming around here dig the holes, especially the dogs as 'tis what they do, and Biddy occasionally widened and lengthened one for her own use or because it was one of the things Clyde was telling her to do. Then the other two lassies creeping in and out as they please started to do the same. So what ye get is a mess and one that doesnae go away because the ones doing it keep making new ones."

"Wheesht, what are ye lads doing round here that is making those lassies dig their way out?" said Ned, laughing heartily as he put his arms over his head to protect himself from the empty tankards hurled at his head.

"Am I interrupting something?" asked Annys as she stepped into the great hall, fighting against the urge to laugh along with the men so thoroughly enjoying themselves.

"Nay, 'tis just Ned being a lackwit," said Harcourt as he held out his hand in a silent invitation for her to join them.

"Actually, I found it quite witty," said Nathan and he grinned.

"Did ye want something?" asked Harcourt when she sat down next to him.

"Sir Adam's father has finally sent a letter with his long pondering decision in it," she replied and placed the letter on the table in front of her.

"What has he said?"

"That I am a liar and a whore, my son is a bastard and no true get of David's, and that Glencullaich belongs in MacQueen hands."

Annys could feel the heat of their collective anger despite how some of them had actually gone into what many would call a cold rage. Harcourt was most certainly in the grip of one. She could see it in his eyes. The other was Callum, which surprised her a little. He was usually the most pleasant and calm of the men.

"He is a dead mon," Harcourt said.

"Weel, that would be a verra nice gift to give me,

but I fear I must refuse," Annys said. "Ye cannae go about killing a laird simply because he is an uncouth, foul-mouthed piece of midden heap slime."

Those odd words slipped through Harcourt's mind and reined in his temper enough for him to think more clearly and he looked at Annys. "Midden heap slime?" She shrugged while the others chuckled. "This goes far beyond insult, Annys. Half of what he wrote are words no weel-bred mon would e'er say before a lady. Ye cannae say this didnae upset you."

"I can but t'would be a lie. T'was like a knife to the heart. Then I got angry. And because I was so verra angry, I started stomping about and threatening to go to his keep and drop Roban on his head." She nodded when the men winced. "I should probably nay send him this reply." She removed a rolled up letter from where she had tucked it into her sleeve. "One should ne'er write letters while angry."

Harcourt snatched the letter from her hand, unrolled it, and read, "*Sir William MacQueen, self-proclaimed laird of Duncraoch: I thank ye for your prompt response to your promise to respond in your first response to my grave concerns about your son. Ye may have considered waiting until your attack of bile had receded, however. I am a very truthful widow, which ye would have discovered had ye ever visited us here at Glencullaich and ever actually spoken to me since David died. My son, David's son, has been accepted by both Crown and Church as his heir. And, nay, ye will not have Glencullaich. Ever. I would also like to remind you that I am not David. My husband was a kind man, always prepared to help when ye arrived with your wagons and your hands out. The laird of Glencullaich filled your larders, your purses, and your stables many times. The laird is now a boy of not yet five years of age and will do as his mother bids him. As said, I am not my husband, sir. Ye and all your kin will no longer feed off the charity of Glencullaich. Your wagons will always be turned away unless your clan's children are close to dying of starvation in the street. If that dire circumstance comes to pass, I will assist them by sending precisely what they need to precisely where they need it as I am most weary of finding goods my husband gave you when ye cried poor being sold for a profit in a market. As for your son, Sir Adam, whom ye refuse to rein in, he now prepares to attack Glencullaich. He will not ever get Glencullaich, even if I must burn it to the ground, salt the fields, and taint the water. There is still time for you to call him back from his folly but, if ye choose to remain ignorant in this matter, then I have but one more thing to say to you. I hope you have more than one son. Cordially yours, the whore, Lady Annys Helen Stuart Chisholm MacQueen, widow of the late Sir David William MacQueen, a victim of Sir Adam MacQueen's greed.*"

The laughter of the men did lift her spirits and she was pleased it had dimmed some of the terrible anger that had gripped them. "See? Something I most certainly shouldnae actually send to him."

"Och, aye, my love, ye most certainly should," said Harcourt and he called for Gavin.

Annys tried to stop him, but he easily held the letter out of her reach. The moment Gavin appeared in the doorway, Harcourt took him the letter. Annys looked across the table and found Callum and Gybbon grinning at her.

"I just needed to spit all that anger out. I ne'er intended to send it to him," she said.

"Oh, but it must be sent," said Callum.

"Aye," agreed Gybbon, the other four men nodding their agreement. "After what he wrote to you, ye deserve to *spit it out,* all over him."

"Perhaps, but when dealing with a mon who could e'en write such a letter, I am nay certain it does much good." She shrugged. "Then, too, what matter if I spit? 'Tis nay as if being polite, mayhap e'en pleading gently for him to come to his senses, will make any difference at all."

"Nay, I am thinking the moment he kenned what his son was about, heard that 'tis naught but a woman and child ruling here, a keep monned by ones who have ne'er fought a battle, and where there are but six or seven men he and his son might consider of any worth, he lost all reason."

"Greed stole his wits and his honor."

Gybbon silently toasted her with a raise of his tankard and then took a drink.

When Harcourt returned and sat down beside her, Annys asked, "Is it safe for Gavin to leave Glen-cullaich now? Ye told me the area round here fair crawled with Sir Adam's spies and that none of us should wander verra far."

"True but Gavin is marked as a messenger," Harcourt said. "I dinnae think e'en Sir Adam would harm the boy. 'Tis a thing that would blacken his name, his clan's name, so deeply he might ne'er wash it away. Messengers are usually left alone. The worst Sir Adam might do is read the message if he stopped Gavin on his way. And, as Sir William's son, could e'en accept it in his stead."

He would not tell her yet about the added message he had sent. Although he did not like to boast, this time he had made a point of naming himself, every well-set, powerful relative he had, and named his companions in arms. It should have the effect of making Gavin as untouchable as a leper. If nothing else the very size of his family, the number of their allies through marriage or treaty, should make Sir William certain that his threat held the sting of truth. When a man with a clan the size of his, one with so many allies, told you that you would be made to regret any and every bruise on a lad, you made certain that boy stayed safe if you had any sense at all.

"Welcome back you two," Annys said as she looked at the MacFingals. "I beg your pardon for being so consumed by my own troubles that I didnae say it the moment I arrived."

"No need to do that," said Nathan. "We ken that ye were a wee bit distracted."

She looked at each man, all of whom had gone very quiet, and asked, "So, ye were successful then."

"Aye. Decided it was time to come back."

Not only was it very strange for Nathan to be so reticent, she also caught the way he sent Harcourt a faintly panicked look. "What have ye discovered then?"

Nathan sighed. "The mon is assembling an army about half a day's ride from here."

"A big army?" she asked, pleased with how calm she sounded when, inside her head was a terrified woman throwing valuables into a sack, grabbing her child, a lamb, and a cat and running for the hills.

"That it is, but 'tis mostly hired swords and I wouldnae consider many of them all that skilled with a sword, either. Ye cannae trust such men to hold fast against a good defense."

"Is he soon to start gathering them all together and begin advancing on Glencullaich?"

"Aye. The mon himself isnae there yet though. Dinnae think they will do anything until he is."

"Well then, it appears we probably have a few days to ready ourselves." She stood up, smiled at them all, and left.

"She took that weel," said Ned. "Ow!" he muttered and rubbed the back of his head where Callum had just slapped him.

"Nay, Ned," said Harcourt. "She didnae take it weel at all, but she will settle to the hard truth of it soon." He finished his ale and stood up. "I believe I will go see if I can help her do that."

Despite his concern about Annys, he had to smile at some of the ribald remarks flung his way. They were all good, brave men. He was glad they were with him even as he felt the pinch of guilt for dragging them into this danger. Harcourt knew, however, that not one of them would have refused to come even if he had been able to tell them exactly what they would face. And, if any one of them had had the smallest doubt, the moment Sir Adam had tried to take Annys and then actually taken Benet, that doubt had vanished and the need to stop Sir Adam had hardened into a steely resolve. They would see the man defeated, as thoroughly as possible.

He entered Annys's bedchamber and hesitated when he found her face down on her bed. Crying women had always troubled him, making him feel a little helpless. A crying Annys tore his heart out. He shut the door and cautiously approached the bed.

"I am nay weeping," she said, her voice muffled by the pillow, "so ye dinnae need to approach as if ye fear I will suddenly become some madwoman, wailing and pulling at my hair."

Harcourt sat down on the edge of the bed and rubbed her back. "Ye have earned a fit."

"Nay, I havenae. We kenned this was coming," she said, turning onto her back to look at him. "It was just a shock to hear that it was truly happening. That he was gathering an army but a half-day's ride from here and that within days that army could be at these gates. I have ne'er been in, been close to, or even seen a battle. I left home when I was still rather young and in the few years I was at home naught much happened. Then I came here, to a place so peaceful I am surprised any mon here e'en kens how to wield a sword. Now we are at war."

"'Tis a sin for that bastard to bring that here, to this place," Harcourt agreed.

"Aye and may he rot in hell for all eternity for it. But, after the shock? After the moment of sinking into the well of it-is-all-my-fault, it passed. Then I just felt so verra, verra sad. I am still sad."

He yanked off his boots and settled himself next to her on the bed. "I might be able to cheer you."

"Do ye think so?" Annys bit back a smile and began to unlace his shirt. "I think I can guess how ye might do that."

Harcourt began to undo her gown, kissing each small patch of skin he uncovered. "I suspicion ye can. Ye are a clever lass." He touched his mouth to hers. "I will make ye smile again. I will make ye shout with joy," he vowed and kissed her.


He did. Twice.

* * *

Later, lying naked, sweaty, and pleasantly languid beneath an equally naked, sweaty, and languid Harcourt, Annys smiled. The knowledge that an army would soon be hurling itself at the walls surrounding her keep and that she had a lot to do to prepare for that was easily pushed aside. For now she wanted to cling to this moment. This time out of time when she was sated and content, holding close a man who could make her shout with joy. The world and all the trouble it held was still out there. It could wait for a little while longer.

# Chapter Fifteen

Annys stared out the window at all the activity in the bailey. She had taken a seat on the cushioned bench to gain the best light for her sewing only to have her attention caught firmly by what was going on outside. The preparations for battle were now obvious, far more so than they had been when Harcourt was just seeing to the strengthening of the defenses already in place. Her heart ached as she watched her people work. This was not what she wanted for them, for herself, or for her child. What had always made Glencullaich such a beautiful place had been its peace. Sir Adam had shattered that with his greed.

The cat she had rescued jumped up on the bench, pushing its head into her hand. Annys smiled and scratched its ears, pleased with the diversion. The animal refused to stay in the stables and she did not have the heart to chase it away every time it sought her out.

"There is a dark cloud o'er Glencullaich, Roban,"

she said, the animal's loud purr comforting her for the moment. "It has a name, too. Sir Adam the Bastard."

"Are ye actually talking to that cat?"

Annys ignored the tingle of a blush on her cheeks and smiled at Harcourt. "Aye, and Roban is a verra good listener."

It was absurd but he had to acknowledge that there was a territorial battle going on between him and the cat. This very morning he had woken up, begun to pull Annys closer so that he could kiss her awake, and found himself staring into the cat's eyes. Shaking off an odd unease over being watched, he had bent his head to place his lips on hers only to have the cat place one surprisingly large paw right over her mouth. He knew people would think he was mad if he said so, but Harcourt knew that was when the battle lines were drawn.

"It was in the bed this morning."

"I ken it but I am certain he is verra clean. I just dinnae ken how he keeps getting inside the room."

And now it was *he*. Harcourt inwardly shook his head. The women in his family always did the same, naming the animal first, and then calling it he or she and treating the animal as if it were a part of the family. Harcourt could see the same path being walked here. Then he told himself that, if his brother Brett could deal with little Ella's cat Clyde, which snarled at him all the time, he could learn to deal with Roban.

"Slips inside when it thinks no one is watching it, just waits for someone to open the door."

She nodded. "I suspicion that is just what he does.

Cats can be verra quick. So, tell me, how does the work progress?"

"It goes weel." He sat down next to her, ignoring the way the cat glared at him from the other side of her. "I wish I could tell ye that this is all but a waste of time, that there will be no battle." He took her hand in his and kissed her palm. "I cannae. It would be a lie and I willnae lie to you, nay e'en to put ye at ease. I believe naught short of that fool's death will stop it. Sadly, we cannae find the lackwit so that we might test the truth of that."

"Ye have been looking for him?"

"Aye, but cautiously. 'Tis nay verra safe for any of us to be far from these walls without a large, weel-armed force at our side. The woods fair crawl with Sir Adam's men." He smiled. "And a few MacFingals. Those lads have lessened Sir Adam's army by a wee bit."

"They go out there e'en though ye believe it isnae safe?"

"MacFingals do what they please. They also do some things with an enviable skill the clan has become renowned for. One of those things is slipping out, creeping up on an enemy unseen, and winnowing away at its strength."

"By killing them." She shivered, the cold, brutal reality of what they were all being forced into hitting her hard.

"There may nay have been any formal declaration, any call to arms, but this *is* war, Annys."

It was easy to see how that cruel truth was upsetting her. Harcourt knew she was too sharp-witted to have not seen exactly where the trouble with

Sir Adam had always been headed. Even those who
had not lived the quiet, peaceful life she had at Glencullaich could grow unsteady when the time came
where no choices were left to pick from, when the
army was actually at the gates and all they had ever
cared about was at risk. Hope for a better outcome
could be a stubborn thing, he thought as he put his
arm around her.

"I ken it," Annys said as she leaned against him. "I
have kenned it from the start, or, mayhap I should
say, have feared it from the start of all the trouble.
After all, I was ne'er going to give Sir Adam what he
wanted, was I? What allies I might turn to are ne'er
going to interfere in what they would see as a famil-
ial argument over an inheritance. E'en Adam's own
kin willnae stop him for, in their hearts, they want
him to succeed. Glencullaich has always been the
jewel of the family's holdings. The greed for what it
has was always there."

She looked at him. "There were times when I
thought David was wrong to give his kin so much, as
if he owed some tithing to them just for sitting in the
laird's chair. I cannae help but think that he was
feeding their addle-brained belief that they deserved
this place, nay him."

"That is verra possible. He was doing what he
needed to do to keep the peace and they saw only
weakness." He kissed her cheek, ignoring the way the
cat moved to sit on her lap. "David did the right
thing. He wasnae a warrior; he was a scholar. He
could fight but he was ne'er one who wanted to."

"Ye *want* to?" she asked, doing nothing to hide her
disbelief.

"Nay, not truly. If Sir Adam came to offer a truce,

I would be willing to hear him out. But, I willnae say I dinnae feel a wee bit of, weel, anticipation. 'Tis the nature of a mon."

"But he willnae come forward with any offer of a truce."

"Nay. He is determined to claim this place, so determined he doesnae care how much blood he needs to spill or how much of it has to be destroyed to get what he wants. Nay, I dinnae *want* to fight, but I do *want* verra badly to make certain Sir Adam Mac-Queen doesnae win."

Harcourt leaned down to kiss her, pulling her closer as he brushed his lips over hers, immediately getting the taste for more. Before he could deepen the kiss, however, something moved between them. He pulled back just enough to look down at the cat now sitting on her lap between them. A quick look at Annys revealed her placing a hand over her mouth, her eyes alight with the laughter she tried to hold back.

"I think he may be jealous," she choked out and started to giggle.

Under better circumstances Harcourt would have shared her amusement. He loved the sound of her laughter, an innocent, musical sound that begged anyone who heard it to share in her joy. Being denied the kiss he was craving made the situation a lot less amusing for him, even though her laughter made him smile. He narrowed his eyes at the cat.

"It should be in the stables," he said and watched the cat's ears flatten.

"Which is where he is constantly put," she said as she gently picked up the cat, scratched its ears, and then set it down on the other side of her. "Yet he always finds me."

"My brother's wife has a wee girl who has a cat named Clyde and he always finds her as weel."

Annys thought Harcourt spoke as if that was the worst fate to ever befall his brother, but decided not to tease him about it. "'Tis verra like a dog, isnae it?"

Harcourt did not think the world needed such an oddity, but said nothing, simply stole a brief kiss from Annys and stood up. "I must get back to work. When I saw ye watching out the window here I but thought to see if ye had anything to say about what ye were seeing, about what we are doing?"

"If ye think I have any advice, I fear I must disappoint you. All I ken about battle is that women best be ready to tend wounds or, if the need demands, grab the bairns and run."

"And from all I have seen ye have prepared admirably for both needs though I will pray that ye dinnae have to meet either of them."

Annys stood to watch him leave and heartily cursed Sir Adam MacQueen. She was weighted down with guilt for having pulled Harcourt and his friends into this. She could claim she had never forseen the risks he would have to take, but that was only partly true. The danger Sir Adam had presented had been clear enough that she had sent for Harcourt. Despite that, she had never truly felt she was placing the man in a dangerous position.

"That was some harsh language," said Joan as she walked into the room carrying a stack of linens in her arms.

"I just realized that I may have been lack-witted enough to think that just having a few seasoned knights here might be enough to discourage Sir Adam." Annys waved her hand toward the solar window she had been looking out of. "That was nay what I had envisioned when I sent for Sir Harcourt."

"Weel, I did a lot of praying for Sir Adam to be struck down by lightning or smashed by a falling drawbridge or trampled by a horse. . . ." She winked at Annys when she laughed. "I decided God would forgive me for such prayers as Sir Adam means us harm and I am nay good with a sword."

"I am nay sure but I think ye may be nudging blasphemy."

Joan laughed as she set the pile of linens on the bench. "Dinnae think I be nudging. Think I be giving it a hearty kick or two." She grew serious as she sat on the bench. "Annys, they couldnae have killed Sir Adam for crimes he committed for they really had no proof, only the word of that fool in the cell and what good is a hired sword accusing a knight? Biddy may have been seen as a good witness if we could have ever made her speak out against her lover, but she was the one who killed David. There would have been only her word that it had been ordered by Sir Adam. That family of his may nay be one ye want to claim as kin but they are nay without their own power."

"Aye, it just wouldnae have worked. But now he will be openly attacking us when we have done naught. He cannae lie his way out of that. Witnesses will abound. If the fool survives this he will be hanged. Our David wasnae without his own powerful friends and they willnae allow Sir Adam to escape justice for an unprovoked attack upon his widow and child."

"I ken it. They have people at court, Sir Adam e'en served in the king's army for a time, they have a kinsmon as a sheriff, and they have wed daughters to some verra powerful men. David has much the same number of powerful people on his side. Yet, ye sound verra certain that Sir Adam will be the one who loses this fight."

"I am. We have Sir Harcourt and his men, and we have Nicolas. Our men have trained until they are nay only far more skilled than they were but have far more pride and surety in themselves as fighting men. We also have something that bastard doesnae have."

"And what is that?"

"A deep, abiding love for Glencullaich. This is our home. This is a blessed place that enjoys more peace than most. Yet Sir Adam brings war to our gates because of nay more than his own greed. We also loved our laird and he didnae want this bastard to have Glencullaich. So we will do all we can with the help of Sir Harcourt and his fine friends to make sure he ne'er claims it."

"Such fire," Annys murmured. "It makes me believe all will be weel."

"Good. Now help me tear these rags."

"Didnae we do enough?"

"Best to have too many than nay enough, aye? And have already had to use some on that young Ned MacFingal. He got poked by an arrow."

Despite wishing they would not tempt her maids as much as they did, Annys liked the MacFingals and felt her heart skip with fear. "Is he weel?"

"Och, aye. The arrowhead only went in a wee bit because he was running away. The lad is fast on his feet. Now, come help me with these and then we shall go see if we have enough salve, herbs, and the like."

Annys sat down and began the tedious work of tearing the cloth into strips for bandaging wounds. It was difficult not to think of what they would be needed for, but she did her best to adopt Joan's more hopeful view of the future. The woman was right about the motives involved. The people of Glencullaich would be fighting for the home they loved. Sir Adam was fighting for the riches of the land he hoped to bleed away. That their motives for fighting were more honorable than his should count for something. Annys just prayed that it would be enough to bring them a victory.

Harcourt winced and shifted his body on the ground until the rock stopped digging into his ribs. He and Nicolas were well hidden in a low-ceilinged cave in the hills. They had had to crawl inside and would not be standing upright again until they crawled back out. Harcourt was discovering that he did not like crowded narrow spaces, especially ones where a man was surrounded by rock. It felt too much like a tomb.

What he could see below them, in a pretty little valley that usually held only cattle, was discomforting. Sir Adam was gathering an army, although he could not see the man himself. The man's force almost matched Glencullaich's now but more men contin- ued to join the group. Seeing all the armed men, the cache of weapons, and the horses, Harcourt was certain that Sir Adam's family was giving him a lot of help despite their denials.

"What of bringing our men to fight this army here, while they still gather?" he asked Nicolas.

"Verra tempting but I hesitate to do it," Nicolas replied. "Only a few of the men we have been training have actually been in or e'en seen a battle. I cannae be certain how they would fare when away from the safety of the walls, and the actual hacking and slashing begins. It wouldnae take many of them losing the stomach for the bloody business, mayhap running away, which could start a rout that would make them all easy prey."

"Yet ye think they will fare weel defending the walls? Blood will be spilt there as weel. No one can fight a bloodless war."

"True, but it willnae be a bloodletting close at hand. The men willnae be sword point to sword point. E'en if the enemy tries to scale the walls it will-nae be as harsh. Bodies would fall ere one of the men actually saw what he had just done to another mon too clearly unless it was particularly gruesome. There isnae the chance of walking o'er a blood-soaked field of body parts, some of which might belong to kin or a friend, and, aye, e'en the stench of battle is less."

"So, what ye are saying is that the men of Glen-cullaich are best at defending and may nay be so verra good at offense."

"Aye. Every mon there will fight to their last breath to protect their homes, e'en the ones nay born there. And, if too many of the men fall, those women will pick up the swords and stand in their place. Glencull-laich is more than their home. 'Tis in their blood, their hearts. They all live weel here and we ken how rare a blessing that is."

"Aye. I can see why though. 'Tis true there are ones who like a wee fight now and then to add something to what they think is a dull life, but most just want peace. They want to tend to their shops or their fields, marry, sire a few bairns, and ken that those bairns willnae be cut down whilst still nursing just because some fool wants something he has no right to."

"There will always be such men."

"And that is our curse, isnae it." He stared into the camp when several men arrived dragging three cows. "And mayhap it would be best if Sir Adam would just get on with it so we can kill him. Much more of this and Glencullaich will have to replace a lot of livestock."

"Mayhaps the drovers and the shepherds can find a safer place," Nicolas murmured and then scowled as, after the cattle were taken off to be slaughtered outside the camp, the men who had brought them handed over several sacks to two surprisingly large women. "Foragers. Appears our neighbors are also suffering because of this."

"And I suspicion Annys will be thinking of how to help them if they need it after all this is cleared away."

"Of a certain." Nicolas shrugged. "'Tis what one must do, isnae it, e'en if it is done with as kind a heart as your lady has. This trouble has come here because of her, because of David's kinsmen. She kens it isnae her fault but also kens that this wouldnae be happening if nay for the greed of David's family."

"Ah, look. That is Clyde, isnae it? The tall mon who is picking what he wants from the things the foragers, and thieves by the look of it since no one can eat candles or candlesticks, have returned with."

"Aye, that would be him. Saw him once when Sir Adam came to rail at David. That mon has a darkness in him that e'en gives me the chills. He is the killer we all fear whether we want to admit it or nay. He kills without a hint of remorse or regret, mon, woman, or child, makes no difference. And if the way Biddy died is any sign, he can enjoy himself in the doing of it if he chooses."

"A mon who badly needs killing."

"Verra badly. If I was a good bowman, I would take him down from here and, I promise ye, nary a mon there would come hunting us."

"Weel, I believe I have seen enough."

Harcourt carefully moved away, staying low and quiet until he could stand out of sight of the camp, Nicolas following and doing the same. Then they kept to the cover of the trees and shadows until they reached the place where they had tethered their horses. Harcourt said nothing as they rode back to Glencullaich, keeping a watch for any of Sir Adam's men, until the keep came into sight.

"A part of one can understand the mon's desire for this place," he said as they slowed their pace and let down their guard a little. "Good land, plenty of water, a fine strong keep. But he doesnae want it for the right reasons, for what makes it such a prize."

"The people and the peace of it all."

"Exactly. He *will* bleed it dry and destroy the lives of all these people. Nay just Annys and Benet but every mon, woman, and child here. There can be no bargaining with him."

Nicolas nodded. "None at all, but ye kenned that."

"I did. 'Tis just me reminding myself for I ken the mon has to die. He will ne'er let it be, nay matter what he may promise if cornered and pressed for a vow."

"Do ye think your lady hopes for some bargain, some pact that will end this?"

"Oh, aye, she hopes but she also kens it will nay happen."

As Harcourt rode through the gates he saw Benet on the steps up to the keep. The child smiled and waved at him, while idly stroking his lamb with his other hand. Seated comfortably on the lamb's back was the cat. Harcourt's heart lightened at the welcome from his son. He decided to ignore the boy's strange companions, as well as Nicolas's laughter. It was not as easy as he thought it should be because too many others in the bailey were grinning or laughing at the sight.

"Harcourt?" Nicolas called softly as they dismounted and the stable boys came to take their horses.

"Dinnae speak on it," Harcourt muttered.

"Just have to say one wee thing. Ye do ken that, if ye find a solution to what must separate ye and Lady Annys, that when ye leave here with the lad and her, ye leave with those two creatures as weel, dinnae ye?"

"Mayhap I can find a solution to them, too."

"Ah, sorry, old friend. Ye take them, too, or ye put a pain in the wee lady's heart that could burn ye as weel."

Harcourt knew that. He simply did not want to think about it until it was absolutely necessary. He walked up to Benet and lightly ruffled the boy's hair. When the lamb stretched its neck up, clearly asking for a pat as well, he sighed and gave it one. The cat just stared at him as if daring him to put his hand close enough to get it properly shredded. Harcourt glared back.

"Dinnae ye like Roban?" asked Benet, scratching the cat's ears and laughing when it loudly purred.

"Roban and I are in the midst of a parlay," he said.

"Dunnie says he is a good cat. Kills lots of mice and e'en takes them outside so the wee bodies dinnae muck up a place. Says he doesnae stink up the place like the other he-cats either, so he may nay need to geld him."

It was difficult but Harcourt smothered the urge to look at the cat who had growled softly when Benet had said that, seeing it as giving in to the nonsense of seeing the animal as more than it was. "He can do that to a cat?"

"And a dog." Benet frowned. "It goes wrong sometimes and can kill them so I dinnae think I want him doing it to Roban but *Maman* says they fixed that and she gives them something to make them sleepy and still and it works so maybe I could let them try but since he doesnae stink things all up I dinnae see why we have to."

It took Harcourt a moment to thread his way through that long, long sentence, but then he nodded. "That decision can wait. Where is your mother?"

"In there." He pointed to the door of the keep.

"Ah, I see, weel, thank ye, laddie."

Harcourt went in search of Annys, finally finding her in the herb garden. She sat back on her heels when he crouched down next to her. The welcome smile she gave him warmed him as much as Benet's had, just in a different way. This was what he wanted, that welcome, that home, and he vowed he would find a way around the things that could separate them.

"Herbs for cooking or medicines?" he asked.

"Most are for medicines. Salves for wounds and burns." She studied his face and sighed. "I am going to need a lot of that salve, aye?"

"Aye, love. I fear ye are. An awful lot indeed. And soon."

# Chapter Sixteen

"Sir Adam has arrived to lead his army."

Harcourt frowned at Nathan who sat down opposite him at the table in the great hall. A maid hurried over with a jug of ale and a tankard for the man. Harcourt waited impatiently as the two flirted but a serious Nathan soon dismissed the woman.

"Ye think he is done gathering his army then?" Harcourt asked Nathan.

"Aye." Nathan took a deep drink of ale and sighed with pleasure. "He has left the gathering of the men to Clyde. And, just a thought, when we talk about this to Brett best we be careful mentioning that mon. Dinnae want wee Ella kenning that her beloved cat shares a name with such a mon. Would break her wee heart."

"Ella who didnae blink an eye when her Clyde trotted into the great hall during the evening meal and set a dead rat at her wee feet? If I recall, she smiled, scratched its ears while telling it what a good lad *he* was and then gave him some cheese. Methinks that wee lass is made of much sterner mettle than ye think. But, aye, we willnae let her learn of it if it can be avoided."

Nathan nodded. "It was Clyde doing all the work. I am nay sure Clyde is verra good at leading so many men or judging their strengths and weaknesses. The men he would set out to watch for anyone attacking or spying on them were near to useless. A lot of the men are naught but swords for hire. Some may be skilled but I dinnae think they are tested in any way to be certain Sir Adam is getting his money's worth."

"I hope this leaves the MacQueens naught but beggars."

"After how hard Sir Adam tried to destroy the prosperity here that would be a fine piece of justice."

"It would indeed. So, so ye think he will attack soon?"

"Aye, I do. If he had nay done more than trot through camp to count heads, I wouldnae see this visit as some signal that he is about to act. But, he has had his tent set up and e'en had Clyde bring him a few lassies."

"Willing?"

"I believe so. They acted as if they kenned him and happily scampered into his tent."

"What exactly do ye mean by a few lassies?"

"Four. Think he means to share with old Clyde. That mon didnae look quite as grim as he usually does."

"Weel, then mayhap the fool will be too exhausted to attack us on the morrow."

Nathan laughed. "Now that is a fine thing to wish for."

"And that is just what I am doing. Wishing for some peace from it all, if just for a wee while."

"Ah, and am I right to think that ye want that peace so that ye might woo a fair maid?"

Harcourt nodded. "I want to romance my woman tonight, to give her some pretty words, feed her some fine foods, drink a toast to her beauty, and give her a few sweet memories to cling to during the coming trouble."

"I didnae hear anything about making a few promises in that listing," said Callum as he joined them at the table.

Irritated that he had not heard the man approach, Harcourt took a moment to think on how to respond. "Ah, weel, I am nay sure I can give her any. Nay sure I should, in truth," he said.

"Because she must abide here and ye must return to Gormfeurach?"

"Aye. I have looked at that problem from every side and see no answers. When this fight is over I must ride away from her and Benet again. At least this time I will pause to say a proper fare-thee-weel," he muttered and took a drink of his ale.

"There is a solution. Ye stay here with her and the boy. Aye, ye willnae be able to openly claim him as your son, but that doesnae mean ye cannae still be a father to him."

Harcourt ached to do just that. He wanted to spend his nights wrapped in Annys's arms, perhaps make another child or two, and his days teaching Benet how to be a good man and laird. The desire to have that was growing so strong he was often trying to think of ways to get the land he craved yet not have to go back to Gormfeurach. He did not think Annys would want a husband who lived by selling his sword, however.

"If I walked away from Gormfeurach and that land that awaits me, I would be coming to her with nothing," he said and held up his hand when Callum started to speak. "What I do ken right now is that I must cease thinking on it all. There will be an army at the gates soon and war requires a man's full attention."

"Verra true."

"And the first thing we need to do now is to start bringing the people in, securing a hiding place for as much of the livestock as is possible, and do a careful tally of what we have for drink and food."

"I will gather up a few men and see to that," Callum said as he stood up.

Nathan also stood up after gulping down the last of his ale. "I will join you. First we best tell Dunnie to send whate'er wagons and carts he can to the village and ready a place to put whate'er stock gets brought inside the walls." He looked at Harcourt. "Mayhap ye can get Annys to bring as many of those benches she has under near every window in the keep down here. More places to sit are always best. Mayhap the young ones could begin filling up buckets or whate'er else will hold water and set them close to anything that can burn. We will be soaking down that sort of thing but it can help to have more close at hand to keep it all wet." Nathan suddenly noticed that Callum and Harcourt were staring at him. "Why are ye looking at me like that? Have I grown a fat, hairy wart on my face?"

Harcourt laughed and shook his head. "Nay. It was the e'er-growing, extremely clever list of preparations ye were giving us. It was a wee bit of a surprise."

"Dinnae forget, my da once had near every clan

for a hundred miles round thirsty for his head on a pike. In the years when it was verra bad, we could find ourselves fighting off attackers near to once a month." He shrugged. "I would see what went wrong and think of ways to mend that weakness, or sort out that confusion that took time and attention away from the fight and staying alive. Ewan once told me I could ready them to live under a siege lasting several years without them suffering any real hardship if I set my mind to it."

"I think he may be right in that."

"Warn your lady that the people will be coming in fast once they get the word. She needs to make it clear where they cannae go while inside the keep," he added as he followed Callum out the door.

Harcourt was still shaking his head as he stood up to go find Annys. If he had had to choose one man to plan out how to survive a siege, it would not have been Nathan, but Ewan was right. Nathan was a planner. Even as he and Callum had walked away, Nathan had been working aloud on that long list of what he felt needed to be done, right down to having everyone in the village clearly mark what belonged to them before bringing it inside the walls as it would save arguments when the battle ended and they could all begin to collect their belongings and go home.

He left the great hall just as Annys stepped inside from the bailey. The dazed look in her eyes told him she had already met Nathan and had probably been given a long list of things to do. Harcourt walked up to her and opened his mouth to speak, but was silenced by her raised hand. He watched her lips move as she repeated something several times, even though he could not discern what. Then, abruptly, her eyes cleared and she smiled.

"Sorry, but I needed to set firmly in my mind all Nathan told me and that required me to repeat it to myself several times. I am certain it is fixed firm in my head now. I believe it is going to be verra, verra busy here for a while."

"Nathan did surprise us. The mon has some verra sound ideas and thinks on things I would ne'er have considered need doing or fixing. He might find himself called on from time to time now that his secret is out. 'Tis a most valuable skill he has there."

"Verra valuable. S'truth, having him give me specific things to do, things I can see will be most helpful, e'en safer for us all, makes me feel safer as weel." The last words emerged in a trembling voice that belied her claim and Annys took a deep, steadying breath. "I am afraid and I am also deeply, blindingly furious."

She sighed with relief when he pulled her into his arms for she needed it. Annys refused to think that need revealed a weakness. She knew that if he was not back in her life, she would have been wanting a comforting embrace from Joan, or David if he was still alive. Whether she believed it or not, she just wanted someone to hold her, pat her back, and tell her everything would be well. When Harcourt did just that, she had to smile.

After staying in his arms long enough for his warmth to chase away the chill of fear, Annys stepped back and gave him a quick kiss. "Now I must see to my assigned duties. I may have to borrow a few men to help me move the benches and turn David's bed-chamber into a nursery."

"A nursery?"

"Aye, and 'tis a wondrous idea. 'Tis the one place we will put all the wee ones with a few women or girls to tend them. Not only will they be safer, and easier to collect if we must flee the keep, but it frees their mothers to help if it is needed." She started up the stairs, stopped, and turned to look back at him. "Oh, and Nathan says ye need to speak to Geordie and decide what to do with him."

"I havenae the time for that."

"I think ye may want to find it. Nathan says he is an archer." She tossed him her keys.

Harcourt gaped, retaining just enough of his wits to catch her keys, and then staring at her as she disappeared up the stairs. Shaking free of his shock, he immediately headed down to the cell holding Geordie. The man leapt to his feet and came to the door of the cell as Harcourt approached.

"Something is happening, aye?" he asked, gripping the thick bars. "What is it? An attack?"

"We got word that Sir Adam has joined his men so we are preparing ourselves for the attack that is certain to follow soon." Harcourt leaned against the bars and studied the man. "I am here to talk to you and decide if I can trust ye enough to let ye join our side."

"And how do ye think ye can make such a decision? And why would ye want to?"

"One can always use another mon in a fight such as we are facing but I think ye may have a skill we have a particular need for. First, I need to ken why ye have no clan name. Ye were outlawed?"

"Nay, just tossed out of the clan. Laird said any of

them could kill me without fear of punishment, though few would even try, but I am nay outlawed."

"What did ye do?"

"Put an arrow through the arm of the laird's son. Bastard was beating on a wee lad and ye could see he wouldnae stop 'til he had killed the boy. He had that look, ye ken."

Harcourt nodded. "So, 'tis true. Ye are an archer."

"Aye, though the lad took my bow and all. Only got a sword and a knife or two from, er, collecting them as I wandered about."

"Did ye kill for them, Geordie?"

"Killed only one mon because he had the urge to kill me."

"What are ye doing with Sir Adam then, for I have heard naught yet to mark ye as one of his ilk."

"Mon has to eat, doesnae he. Only skill I have is fighting. Once my laird made me a broken mon I couldnae just walk o'er and join another clan's fighting men. Jaikie took me along with him when he decided to sell his sword."

"But ye didnae tell them ye were an archer?"

"Didnae have my bow but I had a sword."

"How good an archer are ye?"

"Weel, I havenae seen too many better than me, but a lot who be worse."

For reasons Harcourt suspected he could never adequately explain that not quite humble statement decided him. "Weel, best we get ye cleaned up and give ye a bow then," he said as he unlocked the cell.

"Ye are done deciding then?" Geordie asked, stepping cautiously out of his cell as if he expected a hasty killing rather than freedom.

"They have verra skilled archers. Near twenty of

them. I have about a dozen adequate ones." He watched as Roban unfolded himself from the cot, jumped down, and sauntered over to them, only to walk out of the open cell through the bars.

"He does that to taunt me," grumbled Geordie.

"How does that cursed animal still get into these places?"

"He comes out of there," said Geordie, pointing to the storage room across from his cell.

"It! 'Tis a cat, nay a person," snapped Harcourt as he grabbed the torch from the wall outside Geordie's cell and followed the cat."

"'Tis a he-cat, isnae he? Got balls. Makes it a he."

Harcourt sighed. "Calling an animal a name or he or she makes it more than just something to keep the rats out of the meal or put in a stew and that leads to trouble." He ignored Geordie's chuckle.

The cat slipped around an odd stack of old trunks. Harcourt looked at the torch he held and saw the flame move as if there was a breeze in the cellars. He moved closer to the wall, looked behind the trunks, and then swore. There was a door there and whoever had used it last had not shut it all the way thus giving Roban a way in. Somewhere at the end of the passage would be another opening and Harcourt needed it shut.

"I believe we have just found one of the tunnels David used to leave the keep for a tryst. He was a randy fellow cursed with overly pious parents." He handed Geordie the torch. "Ye go first."

"Ah, and here I thought ye trusted me."

"Nay," he said as he followed Geordie into the passage. "I need an archer. Need doesnae require trust. That takes longer."

At a few places they had to bend a little to clear the ceiling, but it was a sturdy, well-built tunnel in all other ways. It curved upward near the end leading to a set of stone steps. Harcourt got to the top, moved up next to Geordie who had opened a rough slat door, and looked into the stables. One of the slats was broken at the bottom, leaving just enough room for Roban to come and go as it pleased. He stepped farther inside the stable, startling Dunnie so badly the man fell back against one of the stall doors.

"Where did ye come from, sir?" asked Dunnie as he struggled to compose himself.

Harcourt showed the man the door, realizing that it was cleverly situated at the far back of the stables and blocked from sight by worktables and old blankets. "How long have ye worked here, Dunnie?"

"Near all my life, sir. My da was the stable master before me though. He died nay so long after the old laird did."

"Ah, and obviously held fast to this secret, taking it to the grave with him."

"Is it a bolt-hole?"

"In a way. David liked the lassies but his parents were verra strict and pious."

Dunnie nodded. "Ye think he met with the lassies in here?"

"Nay, too great a chance of being caught. There has to be another door."

It took all three of them an hour to find the hidden way out of the stables. Just before they were about to give up, Harcourt carefully walked in a straight line from the door he had come through to the opposite side of the stable. It was not easy due to a vast array of obstacles from buckets to tools but the last and largest obstacle was an ill-tempered gelding in a stall who quickly revealed why he was called Biter.

Dunnie managed to get the animal moved into another stall without injury so the three of them could work to clear away the straw covering the floor. In the far corner was a hatch in the floor. Harcourt had to scrape out years of debris from around the edges before he could open it. Beneath it was a set of worn stone steps, not steep but definitely leading down and toward the wall the stable had been built against.

"This wasnae built by David," he said. "Torch, Geordie." As the man worked to relight the one they had brought with them, Harcourt carefully studied the sloping, narrow steps. "This is verra old."

"Weel, Glencullaich is verra old," said Dunnie. "There has been something on this place e'en before folk began to keep records. But dinnae ken why this is here." He shrugged. "Though stories told let one ken that the lot who lived here back in that time wasnae always made up of good men. Looks to me that, if ye follow that, ye will end up in the burn."

Dunnie proved right. With a grumbling Geordie leading the way with torch in hand, they followed the sloping tunnel all the way down to a small cave on the banks of the burn. Not certain if anyone was watching the keep from this side, Harcourt stood at the back of the cave with the two men. It was big enough to stable a horse, he realized and shook his head. David must have found an ancient bolt-hole and used it to enjoy a few secret trysts. Few of the men on the walls watched this side of the keep for the bank of the burn was high, solid stone, and the tall walls of the keep were built nearly to the edge of the banks. It was going to be difficult to secure but he knew it would be the height of foolishness to destroy it. As they returned to the stables he decided to confer with the others. For now, simply replacing Biter in the stall would be good enough.

He wandered back through the tunnel leading into the cellars, Geordie right behind him. By the time he reached the great hall it was to catch Callum and Tamhas about to leave for the night. Harcourt hoped he was not about to ruin a fine night with a bonnie lass, especially when there was a battle on the horizon. Every man deserved what could be his last night in the arms of a woman. It was how he planned to spend his.

"Found another bolt-hole," he announced and smiled at the way Callum swore.

"Where is this one?" Callum demanded. "And will it mean that I will have to wash again before going to see Peg?"

"Nay, washing will nay be required," Harcourt assured him. "'Tis a verra weel-built, surprisingly clean tunnel from the cellars to the stables and from the stables down to the burn." He handed Callum the keys. "It opens in the castle behind some old chests in the storage area opposite Geordie's cell. That is the part that leads to the stables. In the stables, Dunnie can show ye where the second part is and ye will need him. The guard o'er that part is a mean beastie of a gelding called Biter."

"Do ye wish it closed?"

"Nay as ye mean. I want it sealed against anyone entering from the outside, nay at least without sounding some alarum of some kind. Ye will understand when ye see it." He pushed Geordie toward them. "Now that I think on it, just take him. He kens the way and then settle him with Nicolas. Geordie here is our new archer."

Annys stepped into her bedchamber, her body aching from all the work she had done, but she was completely satisfied with, even proud of, all she had accomplished. Then she caught sight of the large bathing tub set near the fireplace, steam rising from the water, the soft lavender scent from her bathing herbs filling the air, and large drying clothes hung on a rack near enough to the fire to make them warm for when she was ready to use them. Someone had even set her best lace-trimmed night shift and robe at the end of the bed.

She did not think she could get her clothes off fast enough. Finally naked and a little surprised she had not torn something in her haste to shed the clothes, Annys stepped into the bathing tub, one large enough that she could submerge her body, covering it with the heated water and soothing the ache in what felt to be every muscle in her body. She rested her head against the lip of the tub, grateful to the kind person who had softened that edge with several folded-over drying clothes. A deep sigh of pleasure escaped her and she closed her eyes.

It was the scent of food that pulled her from her light sleep. Annys opened her eyes to find Harcourt kneeling by the tub, dipping a corner of the washrag into the pot of soap. When he started to wash her arm, she blushed, finally awake enough to be all too aware of her nudity, of being in her bath while a fully dressed Harcourt looked on. Then she told herself

not to be so foolish. They were lovers now. She had
no secrets from him.

"I am nay sure this is such a good idea," she said
when he nudged her forward so that he could wash
her back.

"I would love to turn this into something more
than a bath," Harcourt said, smiling faintly. "And I
suspect I will pay dearly for my good behavior, but
I mean to gently tend to my woman tonight."

"And I am your woman, am I?" She caught her
breath at the warmth in the intense look he gave her.

"Aye, and I am inclined, verra strongly inclined, to
keep ye as my woman for a verra long time."

"That wouldnae be an easy thing to accomplish."

"But one I am giving a great deal of thought to."

"I am nay sure I can be naught but a lover ye visit
now and again."

"Not my plan. I dinnae want that, either." He
tugged her arms away from her breasts to wash them.
"I want more than a lover, Annys. I want a partner, a
wife, but there are things which must be sorted out
and I am trying to give ye no promises until I ken for
certain that I can keep every single one of them."

"For now, 'tis enough to ken that ye want to." She
rose up enough to brush a kiss over his mouth. "Now,
to keep us from misbehaving and allowing that food
I smell to turn cold, tell me what ye did today."

Harcourt told her about the tunnel he, Geordie,
and Dunnie had found. Her interest and bursts of
amusement over the tale he told helped him keep
hold of his control as he finished bathing her. It was
not as easy to hang on to his control as he dried her
off and dressed her in her night shift, but he kept reminding himself that he had a plan.

Sitting down and eating eased his hunger for her a little because it kept him busy and distracted from thinking about making love to her. A hearty meal fulfilled another hunger he had gained after a full day of work as well. Each of them had done so much today that there was a lot to talk about. Harcourt knew this was what he wanted, what he needed. He had not lied to her about that; he was determined to find a way for them to be together like this for a very long time.

Annys finished her cider, set the tankard down, and decided it had been a very long time since she had felt so good. That it was on the night of a day spent preparing for an attack was certainly odd, but she could not deny the fact that she was actually happy, filled with a pleasant languor. She looked at Harcourt who was watching her with a hunger her body rapidly responded to, and smiled. For tonight, she saw no harm in thinking only of herself, her own pleasure, and to pretend that all was right in her world.

Harcourt stood, took her by the hand, and tugged her out of her seat and into his arms. His need for her strengthened immediately, but there was also a saner, calmer sense of rightness within him. This was where she belonged.

He kissed her and savored the way her body pressed against his but his control was slipping away fast. "I wanted this to be a slow, sumptuous loving," he said as he began to remove her night shift.

"Mayhap that will come later."

Despite blushing as she lay naked on the bed in front of him, she watched him shed his clothes. He was beautiful to her although she doubted he would

like her using such a word to describe him. He was
all women said a man should be, she thought, yet they
rarely found. He was strong, his muscles easy to see in
his every move as was the grace he was probably unaware of. Though he was tall, all his limbs and his
torso were of a size to appear perfectly matched. He
was neither pale nor dark but a faint golden color, his
skin looking as if it had been kissed by the sun and
inviting her to touch it. A neat, light vee of black hair
decorated his broad chest, a thin line of it began just
below his belly hole and went straight down to where
it thickened around his groin. His manhood jutted
out from his body, hard and pointing right at her, and
she smiled. Then she opened her arms to welcome
him when he joined her on the bed.

Annys lost herself in the pleasure of his kisses and
soft caresses, in the warmth of his skin beneath her
hands. By the time he slipped his hand between her
legs, she was eager for that intimate touch. A
murmur of disappointment escaped her as his back
slid out of her reach when he spread kisses over her
body and down her belly. She reached to pull him
back but then his hot mouth replaced his seductive
fingers. Shock ripped through her at such an intimacy, but she had barely acknowledged it when
passion burned it away, along with the last tenuous
scrap of her modesty.

When she felt that tight ache in her belly grow, she
opened her mouth to demand he join with her but
did not get to say a word. Harcourt reared up and
joined their bodies with a thrust strong enough to
make her slide up the bed. She grabbed his arms to
anchor herself as he bent his head to kiss her.

She gave herself over to the pleasure of being surrounded by him, his heat warming her inside and out. Despite her efforts to hold on as long as she could, to savor the rush of delight his lovemaking produced, her release mercilessly tore through her and she cried out his name, hanging on tightly as he found his own a heartbeat later.

Although it took a while before he could even move, Harcourt finally rose from her arms and cleaned them both off. He crawled back into bed when he was done and pulled her back into his arms. He sighed with contentment when she curled her body up against his. It had been fast, a little furious, but to his relief, mutually satisfying. He kissed the top of her head and decided that, after he had rested for a while, he would try again to achieve that slow, sumptuous lovemaking he kept promising her.

# Chapter Seventeen

At the first clang of the warning bell, Harcourt was immediately awake. He leapt out of the bed and yanked on his clothes. As he prepared for battle, he watched Annys wake to the continuing alarm, watched the fear come alive inside her, and wished he could chase it away. She was going to have to learn to push it aside, however. Sir Adam had caused her to feel that fear, forced her to face it and try to be strong. For that alone, Harcourt wanted the man dead.

"Sir Adam has arrived?" she asked as she slipped out of bed and began to quickly dress, pulling on her shift.

"Aye." He pulled her into his arms causing her to drop the gown she held and gave her a fierce kiss. "Keep safe."

"Ye as weel."

Annys watched him hurry out of the room and sighed. Fear was a tight knot in her belly but she was determined not to allow it to rule her. There were a lot of people inside the keep now, every one of them as afraid as she was. She needed to show them only calm and an absolute certainty of victory. That was one of the things she had been taught that the lady of a keep was expected to do. It was one of the few things that had always made complete sense to her.

Before she left the bedchamber, she looked around. The lovely hot bath she had savored was now no more than a tub of cold, soapy water, but the memory of that pleasure remained. On the table in front of the fire sat the sad scraps of the hearty meal she and Harcourt had shared, the jug of cider empty now, but she could still smile over the teasing and flirting they had indulged in as they ate. The bed was a mass of tangled covers and her body warmed at the memories that sight stirred up.

It had all been almost perfect. The only shadow was the lack of any declaration of love, from Harcourt for her, or from her for him. Harcourt had spoken of how he wanted them to stay together, even brushed over the word *marriage,* but the one thing that firmly stood between them, was where they each had to remain after the battle was over, had not been banished. The laird of Glencullaich could not leave it and, as his mother, neither could she, and Harcourt needed to return to Gormfeurach, not only out of duty to the people living there, but to his brother. A part of her was grateful that he would give her no false promises when he had no answers to their problem yet, while another part would have liked to hear them anyway.

Shaking her head, she hurried out of the room. The best thing she could do now was to bury herself in all the work that needed to be done. It would keep her from thinking too much on what had not been said between her and Harcourt as well as help her keep her fear tucked away deep inside her. First she needed Joan, or any other grown woman, to correctly braid her hair so that it was out of her way while she worked.

Passing by David's bedchamber, Annys could not resist stepping inside for just a moment. Her first thought when she entered was that Glencullaich was going to need a lot more cottages than it had now. There were ten cradles with infants in them and three more ready for the three very pregnant women there, ones due to go to the birthing room very soon. Since the children were all busy playing and running around, it was difficult to count the number of very young children but there were twenty pallets on the floor. The three women heavy with child had four older girls and three aged women plus Mary, whose new infant slept in one of the cradles, to help them.

She saw Benet being introduced to the infants by a boy who had to be close to his own age. Benet suddenly looked up, smiled, and waved at her. Annys returned the wave.

"Look at all the bairns, *Maman!*" he said.

"I see, Benet. There will have to be more cottages built soon." She grinned when he laughed and nodded. "Remember to be verra gentle with them, love," she added and turned to leave only to come face to face with Mary.

"This is a wondrous thing to do for us, m'lady. For the bairns, for us, for the old ones," Mary said.

"T'was Sir Nathan's idea, Mary," she said.

"And we have all thanked him. But, we ken weel he had the idea, aye, but ye and your ladies put it all in place. Now we willnae be underfoot, aye?"

"That was the purpose, aye. The sad thing is that 'tis also so we can move ye all, verra quickly, if the need arises." She was surprised when Mary smiled for the knowledge should have served to remind her of all the danger they were facing.

"I ken it, m'lady. 'Tis true, I am frightened but kenning that we are here, easy to gather up and move, is a comfort. Sir Nathan showed us where to go when the time comes."

"Good, but ye will have to be certain to stay together as ye go down to the ledger room."

"Oh, we dinnae have to leave here. There is a way down to the cellars right in that lovely wee privacy room." Mary pointed to the garderobe David had as part of his bedchamber. It was to the left of the huge fireplace and a room with his writing table was to the right.

Annys shook her head. "I believe my husband kept a lot of secrets, such as how this keep is fair riddled with holes."

Mary laughed. "I heard t'was from his days as a randy young lad with verra pious parents."

"It was. He did confess that. I just wish he had made some map of all the ways he found to slip away from their watchful eyes."

"M'lady!" Gavin called as he ran into the room, stumbling to a halt in front of her. "Ye are wanted at the walls."

"Why?" she asked as she followed him out only to tug him along with her so that they could use the way to the walls in her bedchamber.

"Sir Adam has demanded to speak with you." Gavin's eyes widened as she opened the way to the stairway that went up to the walls from her bedchamber. "I didnae ken about this."

"Ye would have been told when ye reached the age to take a turn at watch on these walls."

Annys moved as quickly as she dared. She knew Sir Adam was going to offer her a way to halt the battle they faced, but one that could give him all that he wanted and leave her with little or nothing. Yet, it would also halt the bloodshed that was to come. She had to force herself to be strong, to not think on saving her people from the trouble at their gates now, and think only of saving their futures. There was a part of her that desperately wanted to escape all of this but she had to keep it caged.

"Weel, that is a bigger force than I had hoped to see," said Harcourt as he looked out at the army gathered before the gates of the keep.

Bear the blacksmith paused in his self-appointed rounds of inspecting everyone's weapons, occasionally replacing a sword he thought inferior with one of the ones he had with him in a leather sack strapped to his back. "His clan has given him a lot of coin. Wagering on a big prize."

"You up on the walls," bellowed Sir Adam as he rode closer. "Where is Lady Annys?"

After winking at Harcourt, Bear stepped up closer to the wall to peer down at Sir Adam. "Inside the keep doing things the lady of the keep is supposed to do."

"Weel bring her to the walls!"

Bear looked around and then back down at Sir

Adam. "Why? She cannae wield a sword or shoot an arrow. Nay useful up here. This be men's work."

Harcourt joined the others in laughing. He knew what Sir Adam saw. A huge, shaggy-haired oaf. It was Bear's best weapon. Bear was a head taller than him, and very muscular which, for reasons Harcourt did not understand, appeared to make people believe the man had to be witless as well as if somehow having a body that big and strong stole something from the man's mind. Harcourt had been guilty of thinking the man some slow-witted overgrown fellow himself when he had first seen him, an opinion that had changed the moment he had looked into those sharp green eyes.

"I wish to parlay with her, fool. Now, fetch her."

"Nay sure she wants to speak to ye what with ye coming here with an army and threatening her and all."

"Get her!"

"As ye wish." Bear just stared at Sir Adam for a moment before saying in a low, hard voice that somehow carried down to the knight and all his men. "I am thinking ye would be wise to back away a wee bit ere one of us gives in to the temptation to end this here and now."

Sir Adam backed away as did his men and Bear nodded. "Wise lad. Now we will see if our lady is inclined to talk to you."

Harcourt signaled to a waiting Gavin and the boy scrambled off the wall to go find Annys. He had known Sir Adam would want to offer something to try to gain the keep without raising a sweat. He also knew that, no matter how badly Annys wanted to avoid a fight that could cost some of her people their lives, she would not simply hand over Glencullaich. She would refuse to do that, not just for herself or Benet but for the people. It was one of the reasons he loved her, he thought, and was startled by that realization. It was a very poor time to have it.

"She willnae give us up," said Bear.

"Nay, I ken it, although her heart will break with every drop of blood her people lose." He looked at Bear. "This is what her people want, aye? To fight?"

"Och, aye, right down to the last bairn old enough to speak its mind. It has been peaceful here so long ye cannae find anyone alive who has kenned different, but it was nay always this way. The tales are passed down and the graveyard tells the same story. Glencullaich used to be ruled by ones like that oaf down there. Ones who fought with everyone and committed near every crime ye can think of. Then the laird's twig of the clan tree took o'er and it all stopped. Pious lot but they brought peace to this place, made it prosperous, and no one here wants a return of the battles, the feuds, the raids, and the lairds who wasted the lives of their men as they did their coin."

Bear looked at the army in front of the walls again. "These are nay our people e'en if there are some MacQueens amongst them. They dinnae care about those bairns and women in the nursery, the lads too young to fight setting buckets of water and sand near anything that might catch fire. That greedy fool sitting there waiting to talk to our lady only cares that this land can fill his purse with more money to buy whores and fine clothes. Och, aye, we will all fight because we want what we have—a good life and kenning the laird cares for each and every one of us."

Harcourt nodded. He also studied the army spread out before them. There were the men with the scaling ladders just behind the archers. It would begin with a rain of arrows. In the confusion caused by that, the men on the walls and elsewhere simply trying to stay alive, the ladders would be set up against the walls. Their chance to fight back would come only when the men on the ladders began to obstruct the archers. It was going to be bloody and the fact that there was little he could do to change that enraged him. The sound of the bell announcing Annys headed up to the walls was all that stopped him from giving in to the urge to order Geordie to put an arrow through Sir Adam's black heart now.

"Oh, sweet mother of God."

It took every last shred of control Harcourt had not to pull Annys into his arms to try to comfort her. She stared out at the army, her eyes wide with shock, and her face as white as frost. Even she, with no knowledge of wars and tactics, could see that they were badly outnumbered. Bear patted her on the back and, that quickly, a thread of amusement broke his deep concern for her. A movement of her skirts told him she had braced herself the moment Bear had moved his hand toward her but she didn't flinch. It was clear to see that she had been patted by Bear before and knew it was necessary to brace herself or risk being knocked over.

"It will be fine, m'lady," Bear said. "Ne'er forget, everyone stands with ye. Every single person in Glencullaich."

"Thank ye, Bear. 'Tis good to hear. And, dinnae worry, I ken what this is about. 'Tis nay just me. Nay e'en just about Benet. 'Tis about holding fast to what we all have. 'Tis for Glencullaich." She was surprised to hear a ripple of hearty agreement go along the walls as each man there heard what was being said.

Straightening her shoulders, Annys stepped close to the wall and stared down at Sir Adam. He looked quite handsome on his horse but she knew that handsomeness truly was only skin deep. Below that covering, in his heart and soul, he was vain and greedy.

"Good morning, Cousin," she said, infusing as much cheerfulness into her voice as she could muster. "I hear ye have something ye wish to say to me."

Sir Adam rode a little closer again. "This can end here and now," he said. "There is nay a need for your people to be harmed or the property damaged in any way. Hand over Glencullaich to the rightful heir and ye can leave unharmed, as can your hired swords."

"Hired swords?" She looked around. "I have no hired swords, sir. That appears to be your way, but it isnae mine. I have merely friends who seek to aid a poor, defenseless woman against someone who wishes to take what isnae his."

"I *am* the rightful heir! Nay that boy! We all ken David wasnae the sire."

"We do? I believe ye are the only one who keeps saying that."

"Because 'tis the truth! We all ken that Sir Robert MacLeoid gelded him years ago."

Annys stared at the man, an icy chill flowing through her body. David had once said that he always wondered how Sir Robert MacLeoid and his men had come to hunt him down, that he was almost certain he had never bedded the man's wife. He had doubts only because he knew he had been a randy fool, often drank too much, and did not have the best recollection of what women he had bedded. Despite that, he had never been able to dismiss an unease about the attack. Now she knew why. Sir Adam had set MacLeoid on David. It was entirely possible that David had been brutally punished for a crime he had never committed. It was also now evident that Sir Adam had been trying to rid Glencullaich of heirs for a very long time.

"Gelded?" she asked, and tapped her chin with one finger as if considering the possibility. "Being that I am a lady and cannae use certain words, let me just assure ye of your error with the assertion that David was a mon. Fully, completely, and utterly a mon. As his wife, I believe I would be the best one to ken that fact, aye?"

"Ye have two choices, woman. Ye freely give o'er Glencullaich to me or ye watch your people die."

"Actually, there is another choice. I could say nay and watch ye and your army fall before my walls."

"Ye think ye can win this battle?"

There was no hint of her fear or uncertainty in her voice when she replied, "Aye. So I give ye two choices now, sir. Ride away home or die. Here. In a vain, foolish attempt to steal this land." She turned and started to leave only to turn back, glare down at Sir Adam, and point to the gravestone visible at the top of the hill overlooking them all. "And look there, Sir Adam, for there lies the mon ye had murdered. He will be watching, waiting to see ye pay for what ye have done and now try to do. And I mean to let him see ye die, here, on this ground while he watches over it all!"

She turned and marched away, stumbling only a

little when the men on the walls cheered and banged their swords on their shields. Just as she stepped inside the door, out of sight of the men on the walls, she felt the first tear slide down her cheek. It would begin now. There was no way every man on those walls could survive and she had to find a way to accept that, to not bury herself in blame for it all. She gave a start when a piece of linen was placed in her hand and she looked up to find Joan watching her.

"Dinnae ye dare take this on your own shoulders, Annys," Joan said as she took her by the hand and led her down the steps. "'Tis all on that bastard's head. We heard him. T'was him that got David hurt, although I would wager his plan was for David to die. I also suspicion 'tis him that prevented us from getting Nigel back or e'en kenning his fate. And it wasnae just the men on the walls cheering when ye said our laird will be watching him die. We all did."

Everyone was so fierce in the defense of Glencullaich, Annys thought. She needed to share that strength. Stopping when they reached her bedchamber, she patted her hair to make certain it was not too windblown and brushed down her skirts. Bellowed commands and a clatter against the walls of the keep made her tense but she shook aside the urge to go look.

"Best we get to work then, Joan," she said. "It has begun."

Harcourt watched Adam ride back to his men and start yelling orders. He cursed when he saw that the man had armed other men with bows, increasing the number of archers he had. The twenty hired archers were still the ones who needed to be taken down first, however. For now, their job was to stay alive until the rain of arrows about to descend upon them ended. The moment he saw the archers pull back on their bowstrings, he yelled out the command to take cover. Even as he crouched next to the wall and held his shield up to cover himself, he watched Bear get down off the walls with a grace and agility that was astonishing in a man of that size.

"Bastard needs killing," grumbled Nathan from his side. "Needed it years ago if I am guessing the full meaning of what he was yelling at your lady."

"Aye. I believe he set the jealous husband on David." He winced as a cry from farther down the walls told him someone had been injured already. "Suspicion he thought the mon would just kill him."

"Ladders up," Nathan murmured when the clatter of wood on stone echoed all around them.

"Be ready. The moment the rain stops, on your feet with sword in hand," he said to the man on his right. "Pass it down." He could hear Nathan saying the same to the man next to him.

The sound of the deadly fall of arrows faded away minutes later. Harcourt used as much speed as he dared to rise to his feet, sword in hand. He had barely adjusted his shield to cover his chest when a man began to scramble over the wall. The man swung his sword but was in too awkward a position to be a real threat. Harcourt knocked the man's sword aside and slammed him in the face with his shield. The man's scream as he lost his balance and fell to the ground brought Harcourt no joy.

Cries from the men on the walls as well as from the ones they were sending to the ground filled the air. Harcourt could not afford to check on the men who fought with him, however, as Sir Adam was sending his men to the walls without pause. Considering the number of them plummeting to the ground to die or who were dead before they got there, Harcourt had to wonder why the men did not just stop no matter how much Sir Adam yelled at them. They were not MacQueens and he doubted Sir Adam paid that well. Then he saw Clyde on a horse, riding back and forth behind the men, his sword out, and several equally armed, grim-faced men riding with him. Clyde was driving the men forward like cattle to the slaughter.

Then he saw the arrow fly over their heads, the arrow's tip a ball of flame, and cursed. "Geordie! Skewer those bastards!"

"Trying!"

Harcourt watched as the women and young boys, even some of the older girls, poured out of the keep to make sure no fire got a good start. Although he had to admire how efficiently they worked together, his heart clenched with dread. They were now in reach of the arrows. Refusing to let that prey on his mind, he turned back to the fight to keep the enemy from clearing the walls.

Annys tied off the bandage on the arm of the man who looked far too young to have been fighting on the walls, swinging a sword as he faced the enemy. Since the wound was not in his sword arm, he was already talking about getting back into the fight causing the girl who so plainly adored him to weep. Annys felt like doing the same.

Actually, what she truly wanted to do was become some great warrior, grab a sword, march out to confront Sir Adam, and start slicing off pieces of him until he was dead. Then she would put all of the pieces in a sack to send it to his father. It would be a message that man would not scorn or ignore. One he would fully understand, as would the other Mac-Queens who were helping Adam.

"Ye will rest until at least the morrow," she told the young man. "Ye lost a lot of blood and need to replenish it. Agnes," she said to the young girl, "ye will take young Auley here to the kitchens and feed him."

"Aye, m'lady." Agnes took Auley by the arm as he sat up straighter and began to cautiously stand up.

"But," Auley began only to sway and need Agnes's arm around his waist to steady him.

Annys nodded. "As I said, ye have bled a lot and need both rest and food. Off ye go and dinnae e'en think of climbing back on those walls until the morning." As she watched the couple leave, she felt Joan move to stand beside her. "How many?"

"Two dead. Could be four soon although they are doing weel enough so there is hope. Bad wounds though and bled a lot. Five who are wounded badly enough that, unless this lasts a fortnight which I pray it will not, they will nay be fighting again. Six, including Auley, who will return after they rest and eat. Except for a few wee bruises and scrapes, none of the ones who went out to fight the fires got hurt. It helped that Geordie was lessening the numbers shooting those wretched things."

"Anything burned badly?"

"Nay. Everything was too wet to catch quick and

the ones who rushed out were quick to fair drown any of those arrows that landed. Big Mary quietly picks up every arrow and takes them up to Geordie, the only truly skilled archer we have, and, I am thinking, a mon our Big Mary has decided will be hers."

"Let us pray he remains uninjured then." She looked around. "I have ne'er actually hated anyone before. Disliked, disrespected, mayhap. Just wanted to avoid, aye. But, I hate Sir Adam MacQueen. Loathe him and want him dead. Something else I have ne'er wished for anyone."

"And 'tis certain ye will ne'er feel wither way ever again so I wouldnae worry on it." Joan shook her head. "If that mon fell into the hands of the people here right now, he would be torn apart. Do ye think they would e'er do that to anyone, ever?"

"Nay!"

"Exactly. But they would do it to him in a heartbeat, so dinnae fret o'er how ye feel. Right now all these people see is that that swine out there is killing and hurting their men, their husbands, sons, and lovers." She patted Annys on the arm. "We all feel it now."

"Strangely, kenning that I am nay the only one thinking of tearing the mon apart is oddly comforting. Of course, I meant to use a sword."

"Weel, aye, of course ye did. Ye are a lady."

Annys could barely believe it when she choked on a laugh. She clapped a hand over her mouth but made the mistake of looking at Joan. Then they both started giggling.

Their brief moment of laughter ended abruptly when a badly wounded man was carried in by Bear.

# Chapter Eighteen

And so begins the third day, Harcourt thought as he made his way down from the walls. At least it was quiet for now. After a dawn attack that had come close to succeeding, even Sir Adam's men needed to rest and regroup. He spotted Geordie and Big Mary collecting up arrows and shook his head. Who would have thought the tall, broad-shouldered woman who cared for all the fowl of the keep would be attracted to someone like Geordie, a man neither handsome nor as tall as she was.

He stood by the well set in the center of the bailey and gathered the strength to pull up a bucket of water. Harcourt groaned in relief as he poured the cool water over his head. Every muscle and bone in his body ached. And he smelled, he thought crossly as he wiped the water from his face. He hated to smell bad and Harcourt decided it was yet another crime he could add to the list of ones Sir Adam deserved to die for.

"No one else will say it, so I will," said Ned as he

stepped up beside Harcourt and got some water for himself.

"Must ye? If no one else will say it, mayhap that is because no one really wants to hear it."

Ned poured the water over his head and then shook himself like a dog would, ignoring Harcourt's complaints about being splashed. "Ye are wet now. A wee bit more willnae kill ye."

"Aye, but with clean water. I dinnae think what ye just shook all over me is too clean."

"This is nay looking good for us, Harcourt." He looked at Harcourt after wiping the water from his eyes, and did not even try to hide his concern. "That bastard is wasting his men but it still looks bad for us. He throws his men at the walls and loses some but has more. We push them back and lose some of our own, but dinnae have more. Soon, nay matter how hard and weel we may fight, he will still have more and we will nay longer have enough."

"I ken it," Harcourt reluctantly admitted. "Worse, the men fighting on those walls can see it, but we have no choice."

"Mayhap nay right now, but soon."

"Ye mean for us to all flee this place."

"Aye. Ye said ye didnae believe in fighting to the last mon, woman, and bairn. I believed you."

"I meant it. But, we still have some time left us." He held up his hand when Ned opened his mouth to speak. "Nay much, but just a wee while more. I can see the time coming when we will have to leave if we mean to live, but a lot can happen between now and when it is time for us to get out, short though the time for a miracle might be."

"My thought was that we start now to get out those who cannae walk or run because of age or wounds or e'en a bairn in her belly. We ken no one is making an assault on the burn side. Too difficult to get the men there, to put the ladders up or e'en set up some archers. We put a few of our archers on the wall o'er there and begin taking out all the ones who would slow the rest of us down. Give them a head start. At night. We do it at night. After ye found that tunnel down to the banks of the burn we put a few wee boats in the cave there so that we can use them to carry some of the wounded or infirm and some could just walk until they need the help."

Harcourt slowly nodded. It was a good plan, a very good one. It was not only the aged, wounded, or infirm who needed help to escape. Women carrying a bairn in their arms, or e'en two, very small children, and, of course, the women carrying a bairn in their bellies, simply could not move as fast as others. Right now Sir Adam's full attention was on breaching the walls of the keep, or even the gates. Letting some of the people slip out now would give the slower ones more time to get out of the man's reach before the keep fell to him.

The thought that, if Sir Adam won, he would find himself the owner of a completely deserted keep and lands was a pleasant one even though he knew that deprivation would not last all that long. What would hurt Sir Adam, and his purse, would be the loss of the highly skilled people of Glencullaich whose goods not only brought people from miles around to their market but put a lot of money into the coffers of the laird.

"Do it," he said. "Start tonight as soon as the light fades ye can start. If that bastard gets in here I want him to find it empty of all but the dead, and if I could think of a way to move them, too, I would, but I think we will need what time we have left to just move the living out. Anything ye can move, do it. Be sure to take the most valuable things first."

Ned slowly grinned and nodded. "I will find a few lads too young to fight but old enough to help me and will start the minute that sun dips low enough in the sky to cast more shadow than light."

"We will keep them busy near the gates. Ye might have your brother go with ye to have a look about, see if there are any of Sir Adam's men on the banks of the burn watching for an escape. If there are, silence them. Then take two archers but leave us Geordie as we need him."

"Aye, he is the best."

Ned trotted off to the keep and Harcourt was confident everything would be well planned and efficiently carried out. If anyone could find a way to get the more vulnerable of Glencullaich's people out of Sir Adam's reach it was a MacFingal. Ned would also have a keen eye for what goods to take that would cause Sir Adam the most annoyance and the deepest cut to that fat purse the man was seeking.

The sound of geese and ducks coming from the upper floor had Annys turning around and running back up the stairs. She feared it was a sign that someone had found an opening and they would soon be attacked from inside as well as outside the walls. As she neared the ledger room she watched a line of ducks disappear inside. Cautiously she followed the birds all the way down into the cellars and found Big Mary leading her flock down the shadowed hall toward the cell Geordie had once occupied.

"Mary," she called, refusing to use the name Big Mary when there were none of the other Marys around, "what are ye doing?" She watched in amazement as Mary made a few tsking noises, then made a few odd signals with her surprisingly elegant hands, and all the birds stopped, not moving even when Mary walked away from them.

"I willnae let that bastard have my flocks to fill his evil belly," Big Mary said.

"But where can ye possibly take them?"

"Near a mile down the burn is a wee bothy. I have used it before when I wished my flock to have a time of eating something besides grain. Doing their own food hunting now and then keeps them strong, healthy for them, I think. I willnae be gone long."

"How do ye plan to get them out without being seen? Or heard?"

"No one watching the burn side. Why would they? They think 'tis naught but a cliffside what with the walls going right down to the rock which already rises out of the water a fair height. I think that fool has also wasted so many men that he doesnae have the ones needed to watch such a place he doesnae think we can escape from anyway."

"Weel, if ye are certain it is safe, then I wish ye luck with it."

"Oh, I will be back once I get this lot settled and hide this somewhere." She pointed to the heavy sack slung over her back. "Sir Ned is making verra certain that as many of the things that are worth some coin are being taken out of here. It gets a wee bit darker and they will start moving some of the people."

"Have we given up then?" Annys had known it might happen for Sir Adam had them badly outnumbered yet no one had come to wake her from her rest and even ask her about it.

"Och, nay." Big Mary frowned. "Weel, aye, in a way. It doesnae look good for us, m'lady." Big Mary stepped closer and patted Annys on the arm. "Aye, we havenae lost too many men because your mon trained them weel in how to protect themselves against arrows and fight off a mon trying to get o'er our walls, but we do have a lot of wounded, some we may yet lose. That filth kicking at our walls has a lot more men than we do and Sir Nathan said the mon could probably get e'en more if he felt he needed them."

"Even more? We will all die here," she whispered and then struggled to throw aside her fear.

"Nay we willnae because your mon doesnae believe in that. Says if we die, Sir Adam gets it all and we willnae be able to do anything about it. But, if we survive, we need but work to get it back. So, Sir Ned said we need to get the slow ones out now, start moving out the wounded, the old ones, the bairns who need carrying and anyone who cannae run and keep running. We will start as soon as the sun sets."

"And the valuables?" Annys wished someone had just taken a minute to waken her and tell her they were making such important decisions, if only because it was a little embarrassing to be told something so important from the goose girl.

"Sir Ned and our men decided they wouldnae let the mon fill his coffers with the selling of such things.

They also sent a lad to the drovers and herders watching o'er most of our livestock and Sir Harcourt sent word with the lad to tell those men where they needed to head for. Then we found ourselves a few boats and are making some litters for the wounded who cannae walk." Big Mary paused in her listings and shrugged. "Ye ken who needs more time to flee an enemy. Then if the able ones see that all is lost at the walls, they will run but, when 'tis all said and done, we will be leaving that filth with naught but empty buildings."

"'Tis really quite brilliant," Annys said. "The more I hear, the more annoyed I get that someone didnae come and awaken me so that I could have been of some help."

"Nay, m'lady, ye needed the rest."

"Aye, I ken I did, but I hate having missed something so important."

"'Tis important and people are working hard to see it all done. We were all grieving, thinking we had lost when he told us we had to leave but then your mon said we cannae just think on the lost battle. Said we will have a win now by leaving the mon naught but all these empty buildings. Said the true riches of Glencullaich were its people, that our work and skills are what make it such a fine place and that that filth can ne'er replace us. And, since we will be taking all we can that is valuable, he willnae have a quick way to get the coin to even try. Dunnie is sad that he cannae save the horses though. I am verra sad that we probably willnae be able to take our dead with us."

"That grieves me as weel. I had planned to bury them on the hill with the laird, David, so that they could look down on all they had helped to save."

She saw Big Mary grimace and her eyes turn shiny with tears.

"Their families would have been so verra proud of their men up there with their laird. I will pray that that may yet come to pass."

"So will I, Mary. Now, best get that verra weel-behaved flock of yours out of here. I will go see if I have missed anything else."

"Weel, at least ye dinnae have to fret o'er that lamb or the cat." Big Mary's lips twitched. "Your mon told Dunnie to see if he could fix up something so that those two cursed beasties could be moved fast and without the worry that they might run off."

Annys laughed. "Go. Get your work done and get back here. This lull in the fighting willnae last long."

After watching Big Mary lead her birds away, Annys shook her head and hurried back toward the great hall. The idea that they were losing the battle was indeed a hard blow to the heart, but she had always known that was a possibility. She also refused to believe the men who had died had done so for nothing. They had fought hard to try to save their homes, their loved ones, and, win or lose, their families should only have the greatest of pride in them.

And it would not be a complete defeat, either, she thought as she finally stepped into the great hall and saw Harcourt speaking with one of the wounded men. He looked exhausted and bandages circled the top of his left arm and the calf of his right leg. The way he moved told her that they were small wounds, but it took a moment to push down the intense fear roused by the sight of them.

Everyone looked exhausted, she realized. Annys knew it was not just the hard work that put that look of tight exhaustion on everyone's face. Fear did it as well, eating away at the strength everyone needed to go on. No matter how much faith one had in one's fighting men, that fear was there from the first hint of a coming battle. The sounds of battle surrounding the keep only kept adding to it. She could feel it nestled in the back of her mind and a corner of her heart.

"I hear ye have all been plotting whilst I was snoring," she said to Harcourt as she stepped up beside him.

Harcourt smiled and draped his arm around her shoulders. "Ye have discovered our plan, have ye?"

"Met Big Mary taking her flock to safety." She looked at the man on the table and was pleased to see that, although he had a serious wound on his left side, it would heal if it was taken good care of. "I didnae ken ye were anything more than a wondrously skilled weaver, Dougal."

"Weel, near every mon has had some training and Sir Harcourt gave us more. Nay as watchful as I should have been though."

"Ye will heal if ye take care of it as ye are told to," she said with such confidence she could see his fear fade away. "I dinnae think ye will be going back on the wall though."

"That was just what I was telling him," said Harcourt. "He will be going out with the others once the sun sets." He reached out and patted the man's shoulder. "Ye will make your family happy by doing so, I am thinking."

Dougal nodded. "Just wish I could have done enough to hold fast to the home they love."

"Try to think of all this as just leaving for a wee

while. For a time of healing and getting strong again. Aye, I believe we will have to retreat but then we can busy ourselves planning to come back, to take it all back, and be rid of that fool who thinks to steal from us. I will bring in my clan and some of our allies to help us do it. And, if we are lucky and nay get caught slipping out we will have a way to slip right back in." He exchanged a brief grin with Dougal. "Rest while ye can. The leaving will be hard as it isnae an easy path to follow."

Harcourt took Annys by the hand and led her out of the great hall, pausing now and then for them to speak to another one of the wounded men. He tried to find the words to tell her that it would all suddenly take a turn in their favor but his head knew he would be just giving her a false hope. He would not give her that and he knew she was strong enough to take the hard, cold truth. Harcourt also knew she would do anything that was needed to ensure the safety of as many of her people as she could.

Once inside the ledger room, the only room in the keep that was not being shared with any others, he took her into his arms and kissed her. To his relief, he could feel no tension in her lithe body and she returned the heat of his kiss without hesitation. When the kiss ended, he continued to hold her close and rested his cheek on the top of her head, enjoying the silky softness of her hair against his skin.

"Ned had the idea to get those who cannae move quickly out of reach beginning now," he said. "It means that when the time comes for the rest of us to run, we willnae be held back or, far worse, end up having to leave someone behind."

"So Big Mary told me," she said, resting her cheek against his chest, letting the strong, steady beat of his heart soothe away the lingering fear caused by seeing that he had been wounded. "'Tis a brilliant plan."

"It is, isnae it. I am glad that ye see that."

"I dinnae want my people slaughtered to save this keep. Aye, we had to fight, to try, and I grieve for the ones lost, but, if defeat is staring us in the face, I dinnae want them to keep fighting. I will confess that the plan to take all we can of what is valuable here did please me. As Big Mary said, we will leave Sir Adam with only empty buildings."

As if conjured up by hearing her name, Big Mary burst into the room through the doorway down to the cellars. The woman nearly found herself skewered by Harcourt's sword, which he had drawn even as he had pushed Annys behind him. Annys grabbed his sword arm out of fear for Big Mary but could feel the taut readiness to strike already leaving him.

"Mary," she said, speaking as calmly as she could while stepping forward, a little closer to the obviously frantic woman. "Were ye attacked?" she asked.

"Nay, 'tis nay me," Mary said. "'Tis Geordie. I need to find Geordie."

"He is on the wall," said Harcourt as he sheathed his sword.

"Aye but they have wounded him."

"Ye cannae be certain of that."

Big Mary stood straight, squaring her broad shoulders as if prepared for a blow and looked at Annys. "I will understand if ye wish me gone after I say this, but I *do* ken that Geordie has been wounded. I ken things from time to time. I was securing my flock in the bothy and kenned that I had to get back here as fast as I could, that Geordie was going to have need of me."

"Ye have the gift?" asked Harcourt.

Big Mary nodded but kept her gaze fixed on Annys.

Annys stepped over to her and patted her on the arm. "That is why your clan sent ye away, isnae it." Big Mary nodded. "I am nay certain what he means by saying ye have some gift but if ye have warnings about things, I should think ye had best heed them."

"If Geordie has been wounded then the battle has resumed." Harcourt gave Annys a brief, hard kiss. "Ye should stay back, Mary," he said as he started out the door only to sigh when the woman rushed right past him.

"How odd. Geordie and Big Mary. I best go and join the others in the hall," Annys said as she walked past him and disappeared down the hallway.

Harcourt shook his head and hurried to get to the walls, going through the door in Annys's bedchamber to save time. He had just reached the area close to where Geordie stood guard when he saw Big Mary tie a bandage on the man's upper left arm. If the wound was deep and painful, they had just lost their best archer. He was only steps away from them when Big Mary took up Geordie's bow.

"What do ye think ye are doing, woman?" demanded Geordie.

"Taking your place until ye can do it again. Quiver?"

Geordie moved his arm so that she could reach the arrows more easily. Big Mary readied the bow and Harcourt could see the strength in the woman's arms as she drew back and then sent the arrow into the advancing men. He cursed softly when a man fell, a curse echoed by Geordie. One arrow, one dead enemy. Harcourt looked at Big Mary in amazement tinged with admiration.

"It appears we have us another archer," he said and almost laughed when Geordie removed his breastplate and put it on Big Mary.

"Dinnae get your fool self killed," Geordie said as he headed down from the walls.

"Late in the day to attack," Harcourt said as he took up his post by her side.

"Then t'will be a short battle."

Harcourt kept her as shielded as he could while she efficiently took down soldier after soldier in Sir Adam's army. Twice they crouched behind the wall huddled under shields as Sir Adam's remaining archers tried to end the new, clear threat presented by Big Mary. And there was no question that she was indeed a threat. Harcourt instinctively wanted to get her off the walls and back inside the keep where it was safe, where the other women were, but the warrior inside him recognized what a useful weapon she was. It was evident Geordie did as well, or at least knew there would be no arguing with her, for he returned with his newly bandaged arm, a lighter bow, and a quiver full of arrows. Without a word, the man stood by Big Mary's side whenever she rose to her feet to end the lives of more of Sir Adam's men.

The light of day began to fade as they fought and Harcourt knew it would be their last battle. There were too many empty places on the wall, the men still able to fight now having to watch larger and larger areas. He prayed they could keep Sir Adam's men out of the keep until the dark of night drove them back to their camp. Then he would order everyone to grab what they could and leave.

Suddenly the noise on the field began to fade, starting from the back of the attacking army and moving to the front in a slow wave of silence. Harcourt looked for what had caused it and began to swear viciously. Behind the army that was already defeating them appeared even more soldiers. These were mounted men, each wearing pieces of armor and mail they had undoubtedly taken from the bodies of some defeated foe. At least twenty of them sat on their heavy warhorses behind Sir Adam's men, swords in hand. It was hard to see through the many shadows cast by a setting sun but Harcourt suspected there were more men behind the ones he could see.

Then the one mounted on a huge gray gelding gave a signal to the others and started to ride forward, his men keeping pace on his flanks. Ten more mounted men came out of the shadows to join the arc of steel and warhorse moving toward and around Sir Adam's army. The first of Sir Adam's men they reached were swiftly cut down, surprise and uncertainty making them slow to see the threat. The others immediately began to fight, or, in the case of any who were outside that arc, run.

Shock held Harcourt silent for a moment. This was all he could have hoped for yet would never have expected to get. Although it was obvious these men were not allies of Adam's, Harcourt could not be sure they would be allies of him, either.

Then the man on the gray gelding bellowed out, "For Glencullaich and Sir David!"

The battle quickly grew even more fierce and bloody. Seeing only an ally now, Harcourt ordered his men down off the walls even as Nathan ordered someone to open the gates. Once in the bailey and the gates had finished opening, Harcourt led them out to attack the enemy from behind. Their enemy was now pinned between two groups of men eager to kill them. For the first time since he had seen the army at the walls, Harcourt could taste victory and it was sweet.

# Chapter Nineteen

Covered in sweat, dirt, blood, and a few things he preferred not to look closely at, Harcourt stood and watched the man on the gray gelding dismount and walk up to Sir Adam who was encircled by men who had ridden with him. The man tore off his helmet and tossed it to the ground. Sir Adam paled and staggered back a step. Harcourt had to stiffen his legs to stop himself from doing the same. It was David, he thought, and knew that was impossible. Either Nigel was not as dead as people had thought, or David had at least one other close kinsman who was willing to avenge him and stand by his family.

"Ye were supposed to die in France, ye bastard!" screamed Sir Adam and he charged the man.

Sir Adam did not lack skill with his sword, but he was clearly allowing his emotions to control him. The man who looked so much like David was coldly enraged but was not allowing his obvious loathing and fury at Sir Adam to cloud his mind and steal any of his impressive skill. It was not long before Sir Adam was bleeding from several wounds, struggling to stay on his feet.

"Ye should have died in France," Adam repeated, his tone that of a child deprived of some sweet he wanted. "It was all planned and it was a good plan."

"I ken it. Seven years, ye bastard. Ye stole away seven years of my life. I escaped two years ago but it has taken me this long to heal and get home." The man easily knocked aside Sir Adam's attempt to cut him with his sword. "I lost two good men, two friends as close to me as brothers, in that hellpit ye had us thrown into. And when I arrive home, it is to discover that ye had the world thinking I was dead, made certain no message from me e'er reached my brother. Ye left me to doubt him, to e'en blame him for what was happening." He glanced up at the gravestone on the hill. "Then I discover that ye killed him ere I could apologize for those disloyal thoughts."

"Aye! And I saw to it that the fool would ne'er produce an heir!"

"Actually," said Harcourt, "I believe he was trying to get him killed but was probably nay so unhappy by what he got for his troubles."

The man spit at Sir Adam's feet. "Ye filthy bastard! Ye sent that crazed fool after David?"

"This should all be mine!"

When Sir Adam lunged at the man who looked so much like David, that man easily deflected his strike and ran his sword into Adam's belly. He then gripped Sir Adam by the shoulder and yanked out his sword. Harcourt could not be sure, but he strongly suspected the man had twisted it a few times as he did so. Sir Adam fell to his knees, clutching his belly in a vain attempt to hold himself together.

"It was ne'er to be yours," the man said. "David and I came before all others. Ye die here, Adam, on the land ye thought to steal and in full view of the grave of the mon ye had murdered." He stepped back, turned toward David's grave, and saluted it with his raised sword, a gesture his men repeated with an admirable precision. Then, with one graceful twist of his body and a swift swipe of his sword, he took off Adam's head.

Harcourt looked around at the once beautiful fields. They were torn up by foot and hoof. Groups of survivors from Sir Adam's army, guarded by either his men or their new allies, sat in the middle of it all. The ground was strewn with bodies, thankfully those of the enemy, and not all of them whole. He looked at the man who had killed Sir Adam only to find that man aiming his sword at him. Harcourt's companions moved to flank him as did men from Glencullaich much to his surprise. If this was Nigel or another close kinsman of David's he could be their new laird.

"Who are ye?" he asked the man.

"Sir Nigel MacQueen of Glencullaich."

"Ah, so ye are nay dead then."

The flicker of a smile touched Nigel's mouth. "Nay. Now, who are ye?"

"Sir Harcourt Murray." He indicated with a wave of his hand each of his men as he introduced them. "Lady Annys sent for us after David died and when Sir Adam began to cause her a lot of trouble, thinking she was weak and badly protected." He looked around at all the exhausted men. "Mayhap we can discuss all of this inside."

"Agreed." Nigel sheathed his sword.

Harcourt ordered the men to clear the field as best they could. Nigel informed him that a few of his men had already cleared Adam's camp and were collecting anything of value. The two of them began to walk toward the keep when one of the dead rose up from the ground and stood in their path. Soaked in blood, one eye gone, it took Harcourt a moment to recognize Clyde. The man had a knife in his hand and Harcourt could only wonder which of them would end up with that knife in their flesh even as they drew their swords. There was no way for them to stop the man from throwing that knife but the one still standing would make certain he did not throw another ever again.

Then Clyde grunted and the knife fell from his hand. Very slowly he sank to his knees. Even his subsequent fall face down on the ground was slow. An arrow stuck out of the man's back and Harcourt looked up at the wall. There stood Big Mary and Geordie and Geordie pointed at her. Harcourt saluted her with his sword.

"Ye have a woman on your walls?" asked Nigel as, after staring at Big Mary for a moment, he resumed their walk to the keep.

"Nay to my liking to have a woman on the walls instead of tucked safely inside the keep during a battle but"—he glanced down at Clyde as they walked past him—"nay fool enough to send away one with such skill when defeat was banging hard at the gates."

"Ye thought all was lost?" asked Nigel.

"Didnae just think it. Kenned it for certain. I was already getting the slowest of us out and stripping the place of all that was valuable." Harcourt turned to Callum who walked on his other side. "Best tell everyone ye can find that they dinnae have to leave and get back any who already have." After Callum ran off, he turned back to Nigel. "If I didnae have plans for taking Glencullaich back from Sir Adam later, I think I would have burned it down as weel, nay even leaving the bastard the buildings."

"I begin to think there was a great deal more going on here than just that fool deciding to kill David and take Glencullaich from my brother's widow."

"Aye, a lot happened, but it all led back to that base greed the mon suffered from."

Nigel looked around at the men who had fought so hard for Glencullaich, even glancing up at the ones on the walls. "My family worked for their whole lives to prevent this from happening here," he murmured, sadness weighting each word. "For doing this, for bringing back what had become naught but stories of the past, for that alone Adam deserved to die." He looked at Harcourt. "But, ye got the men here to fight, trained them to do it weel, too."

They entered a very crowded bailey. Harcourt almost smiled. All the people of Glencullaich who had gathered were staring at Nigel as if he was a ghost. He was certain he had looked just as stunned as they did when he had first seen the man's face. Then Joan pushed her way through the crowd, stood before Nigel, and stared at him. All the attention turned to her as people waited for her to confirm what they were seeing.

"Ye have a few new scars, Sir Nigel," she said, "but ye are looking verra hale for a dead mon."

"Ah, Joan, if I wasnae covered in filth and gore, I would hug ye," Nigel said and grinned.

"Then we shall get ye cleaned up and gather in the hall to feast and hear your tale."

As Joan was busy ordering everyone to do what was needed to get Nigel and his men clean and ready to have a meal, Annys hurried out of the keep. She looked at Harcourt and did nothing to hide her relief to see him standing. Then she saw Nigel and went so pale that Harcourt rushed toward her, thinking she was about to swoon and take a dangerous fall down the stone steps. She held up her hand and he stopped, watching as she visibly gathered her strength. By then he and Nigel stood before her.

Annys could barely believe her eyes. Nigel had the look of David with the same brown eyes and black hair, even possessing a similarity in his features. When he had ridden away he had looked enough like his younger brother to have a few thinking they were twins. Now, however, there were a few strands of silver in his thick black hair, his features had grown harsher, and there was a steeliness in his gaze that had never been there before.

"Annys?" Nigel asked cautiously when she gave him no greeting.

"I was just thinking that Sir Adam might nay have been as bad at plotting and planning as we thought," she said. "He is why we have been allowed to believe ye were dead for years, aye?"

"Aye. 'Tis a long tale and I will tell it. I am eager to hear all that has happened to ye as weel."

*"Maman!"* Benet rushed out to stop by Annys's side with Roberta trotting behind him and Roban sitting on the lamb's back. "Ye look like my fither," said Benet as he stared at Nigel.

"I am your uncle," said Nigel, glancing between

Benet and Harcourt several times and then looking closely at Annys. "I believe there is a lot your mother has to tell me about what has happened while I was gone." Smiling at Benet, he said, "'Tis a fine thing to meet ye at last, Benet. I did hear a whisper or two about David's son as I traveled here and was eager to see him."

"Sir," murmured Nigel's man who had kept his back covered every step of the way from France, "there is a cat sitting on a lamb."

"I ken it, Andrew, but I was attempting to ignore it." His lips twitched when he heard Kerr and his other men start to chuckle.

"This is Roberta," said Benet as he patted the lamb and then he added in a fierce voice, "and she is not for the pot. That is Roban on her back. He likes to ride."

"Ah, not for the pot. Understood."

Before anything else could be said, Joan hurried up to them and began to instruct them on where they could go to bathe. Harcourt watched Nigel disappear with his men and turned to speak with Annys only to find her hurrying back inside the keep with Joan, both of them discussing how to quickly ready the hall for a meal, what that meal would be, and how to sort out enough beds for Nigel and all those men with him. There would be no time to talk to her until much later, he realized. He sighed and, with his own men, headed toward the bathing house that had been prepared for Nigel, his men, and any other who fought for Glencullaich and wanted to scrub the stench of battle off himself.

* * *

"He kens who fathered Benet," Annys said to Joan as they spread a cloth over the newly scrubbed head table.

"Ye cannae be certain of that," Joan argued as she smoothed down a few wrinkles in the cloth.

"I am certain. T'was there to see in the way he looked from Harcourt to Benet. Then he looked at me and I could see that knowledge in his eyes. He kens the truth."

"Weel, I wouldnae fret o'er it. Nigel kenned what happened to David before he left, didnae he. Will ken that, with us thinking him dead, there was, and ne'er would be, an heir. Suspicion he now kens verra weel what David did and will nay give ye any trouble o'er it." Joan looked at Annys. "And, doesnae this solve the problem that ye believed would mean ye and Sir Harcourt could ne'er be together?"

"Does it? If Nigel accepts Benet then Benet remains the heir."

"Dinnae go borrowing trouble, lass. Wait. Stay calm and just wait a wee while. It will all be discussed, I am certain, and then, only then can ye truly ken what faces ye now."

Annys knew that was the sensible thing to do but it was not easy to be sensible. Although it would indeed solve a lot of problems if Nigel stepped into place as the laird and pleasantly wished her weel in whatever she chose to do, there was still a chance that it would solve nothing at all. There would also be an extremely uncomfortable confrontation to come. Even though David had been immensely pleased with his plot to get an heir, as well as the results, that did not mean that Nigel would be. Far worse would be if Nigel did not believe that it had all been David's idea, if he saw her as no more than an unfaithful wife who was trying to put her bastard child into a laird's chair he had no right to.

She pushed all her concerns aside and forced herself to think only of getting a hearty meal set out for the men who would soon fill the hall. There was also a lot of work needed in order to put the keep back to rights, from getting the returning wounded brought back and on their way home, right up to and including preparing the dead for burial. She both grieved for their loss and rejoiced over the fact that there had been so few killed.

The people who had sheltered in the keep worked hard and quickly, putting the rooms and hall back to rights with an admirable speed. Then they began to leave, eager to get back to their homes. She was pleasantly astonished to find that even David's bedchamber had been returned to what it had been before it was used as a nursery. It was now ready for Nigel who would, without question, become the laird of Glencullaich.

Assured by Joan that the meal was ready, Annys hurried to her bedchamber to clean up. Away from all the work, her worries returned, but she fought to shake free of their hold. This was a time for celebration. Sir Adam was gone, the threat to Glencullaich ended. Nigel, a man thought lost to them, had returned and Glencullaich had a laird again, one who was battle-hardened and well able to keep his people safe. Taking a deep breath to steady herself, she started back down to the hall. The one thing she refused to think about, determinedly pushed deep down inside her mind, was what Harcourt would do if she did find herself freed of all ties to Glencullaich.

\* \* \*

Harcourt sat on Nigel's left when the man asked him to. When he then turned to have a quiet word with his second, Andrew, and that man left the seat on Nigel's right empty, Harcourt knew who was going to be seated there. The head table was separated from the others enough that more private conversations could be held. Considering all that needed discussing now that Nigel was seated in the laird's chair, Harcourt had a feeling that this could prove to be a very uncomfortable meal.

Annys came in and the look on her face when Nigel stood, waving her on to take the seat at his side, told Harcourt that she, too, saw the potential for a very uncomfortable confrontation. Nigel's smile for Annys showed no hint of that possibility, however. What it did show was pure male appreciation for a beautiful woman and Harcourt abruptly experienced a new, even sharper concern. The simplest solution to the matter of Benet being named heir by David was for Nigel to claim the boy as the heir as well, but, perhaps the man would not mind claiming the heir's mother, too. She had once been promised to him.

"Nigel, how is it that Adam could keep us from kenning that ye were alive for all these years?" Annys asked as a page filled her plate with the foods she chose but doubted she would be able to eat.

"Coin and a lot of it, freely given," Nigel answered. "He paid to have me and my men tossed into a prison in a remote keep in the French hills. I believe he meant for us to die there. Two of my men did."

He paused. "Are ye certain ye wish to hear this as we eat?"

"I doubt anything ye can tell me can be too harsh for me to listen to now." She looked around. "A few more days of seeing the hall returned to this, to what it should be instead of what it was but hours ago, and, aye, I might be shocked. But now? Nay."

"Weel, the mon holding us wouldnae simply kill us and I am nay sure why," he said, "but Adam may have hesitated to actually request aloud that it be done. Howbeit, they did naught to make certain we lived. Think on the worst of dungeons, little food and that bad enough to make a mon sick, little water and often foul, and, aye, 'tis a near miracle we didnae all die. And any attempt to get away, any sort of rebellion, nay matter how small, was punished harshly."

"How did they get hold of all of you?" asked Harcourt.

"A trick. Thought we were to be hired to guard the keep. Sat down to a meal, woke up in a hole."

"How did ye finally escape?" asked Annys.

"The keep was attacked and when the ones who won came down to free their companions, they released everyone, us as weel. All they asked from us was that we go home and dinnae fight their countrymen anymore. Or e'en fight for them as many used such as us to attack their own people and nay the enemy. They didnae like all the hired swords running free about the country, nay e'en the ones who wanted to kill the English as badly as they did."

"They sent ye off sick and weak?"

"Nay. They allowed us to stay a wee while." He smiled a little. "We were a pitiful lot and the mon who had taken the keep was disgusted by the reason we had been caged, e'en more so by how it was done. Once strong enough to ride, we left. By then we were friends of a sort and he readily replaced all that had been stolen from us. Nay free, for he asked us to promise that we would return to help him if he e'er needed it. For free of course. He didnae like hired swords in France but clearly had no trouble if they came to work for him if he had need."

She looked at all the other men he had brought with him, scattered around the hall, sharing tables with the men of Glencullaich. "Ye return with more men than ye left with."

"Aye, most are the remnants of other groups that went o'er there to fight, gain some coin." He smiled at her. "And, aye, I have some. Hid it weel enough that it was ne'er found and, luck was with us in that small way at least, for the mon who caged us kept all our saddles. They held our treasure. On the long journey home we did keep our word and didnae hire out our swords, but we did have to defend ourselves a few times and collected some wealth from those we defeated. A few were prizes we ransomed for handsome sums."

He frowned. "Then I drew near home and heard the rumors of a battle at Glencullaich. So, all the way here we gathered as much information as we could. 'Tis how I kenned my brother was dead," he said, emotion making his voice unsteady. "Tell me."

Annys did but was as vague and gentle as she could be in the details about David's death. There was no need to dwell on the painful horror of it all. She could see by the grief darkening his eyes that Nigel knew it had been a hard death. It was much easier to tell him about Biddy and how she had paid for her crimes, despite the lingering sting of that betrayal.

"One of our own," he muttered, as shocked as everyone else had been. "Hard to believe."

"Aye, but e'en her sisters admit that Biddy thought of little more than of becoming a lady, someone who would have rule o'er others. I suspicion Adam and his mon Clyde recognized that greed inside her and were quick to use it. The ones who used her, killed her, and it wasnae an easy death."

Nigel nodded. "I dinnae believe in torturous punishments but cannae find any sympathy for what happened to her."

"Nor does anyone here. Ye are to stay here then?"

"Oh, aye." Nigel laughed. "My adventure in France was enough to cure me of any urge to seek another. From the moment I woke up in that French hell, all I have thought about is getting back to Glencullaich. My only regret now that I am finally back here is that I was too late to say fareweel to David." He gave her a sad smile when she briefly clasped his hand to offer comfort. "Ye chose the perfect resting place for him, Annys. He would often sit up there, enjoying the view and thinking of ways to better life for us all."

"I ken it. I was thinking to bury our dead from the battle beside him."

"Excellent idea. They, too, belong up there, overseeing the land they fought so hard for. Who died?"

Annys told him who had been lost. She discovered it eased some of her concern about whether this man she did not know all that well would be a good laird. He was saddened by each one she named, knowing more about a few of them than he did the others, and revealing a true grief over their loss. That he would recall anyone after so long a time away told her that he cared for the people as much as David had.

Nigel pushed away from the table. "Give me one hour," he said. "I wish to think and walk about. Then,"—he looked at Harcourt and then at Annys— "I believe we should meet in the ledger room and have a talk."

And there went what little appetite she had, Annys thought. She watched Nigel leave with his man Andrew and another who quickly left his seat at a signal from Nigel. Annys looked across the table at Harcourt who was frowning after the man. He did not look very concerned though and she told herself she would not be either. She also knew she was lying to herself.

"What do ye think, Andrew? Kerr?" Nigel asked as the three of them walked around the outside of the keep, idly surveying what damage had been done. "Sir Harcourt and my brother's wife?"

"Lovers," said Andrew. "Mayhap e'en in love."

"And that wee lad Benet?"

"Theirs," said Kerr. "Looks like ye just a bit, but nay so much when that mon is standing close to him."

"I think the same. I would be angry, condemn her as a whore, if I didnae ken her at all," said Nigel. "But I did ken her ere I left. True, she was little more than a child sent to learn how to be the lady of the keep before she actually married the laird, but I find it verra difficult to believe she would betray David or try to pass off a bastard child as his heir." He sighed. "I also ken poor David could ne'er have sired a child." He nodded when his companions winced at the soft reminder of what had happened to David.

"Ye think your brother got Sir Harcourt to play the stud? To breed a child he could then call his own?" asked Andrew after a few moments of thoughtful silence.

"I do and I also think that everyone here kens it," said Nigel. "I saw the way they looked when we were all together on the steps to the keep."

"It was a good plan," said Kerr. "Didnae work to keep Sir Adam away but it might have."

"Since Sir Adam kenned full weel that David couldnae sire a child since he was the one who set that mutilating bastard on my brother, I think it only made him angrier. Aye, especially when it became evident that no one here would e'er deny that Benet was David's son. Nay, nor when David's claiming the boy openly made it true by the laws of the court and the Church. But, now, I need to decide what to do about it."

"Because ye wish your own get to be the heir."

"When and if I have any, aye."

"Ah, 'tis the 'if' ye think on. Ye could breed naught but lassies."

"Or none at all. Cannae see that happening but it could."

"Then keep the lad as heir until he isnae needed any longer," said Kerr.

"But that would tie Annys here and I am thinking she would like to be with Sir Harcourt. I had thought, for a moment, that I would just get a dispensation from the Church and wed her myself, but I dinnae want a lass whose heart is given elsewhere. She would ne'er leave that boy, though."

"Ye dinnae need the lad here for him to remain your heir until ye can have one of your own," said Andrew.

Nigel looked at Andrew and slowly nodded. "Nay, I dinnae, do I. Do ye ken? As Annys's brother, I believe it is my duty to make certain she isnae shamed."

"Shamed?"

"Aye, used by some rogue of a Murray and left behind, her good name ground into the mud, her tender heart broken." He smiled faintly when his companions laughed. "He should be offered the chance to do what is right and honorable for our lady. Aye, that is what a good brother would do. Kerr, go see if we still have a priest in Glencullaich and bring him to the keep."

"Ye mean to put his back hard up against the wall, dinnae ye?" Andrew asked as soon as Kerr left.

"I do. I also think those two need someone to do just that." He turned back toward the doorway into the keep. "Time to go and sort out the last of the tangles my brother left behind. Mayhap we will e'en be guests at a wedding."

# Chapter Twenty

"Benet isnae David's son."

Annys stared at Nigel. She could see no anger in him but her heart pounded with fear. If he thought she had betrayed David or was trying to falsely sit her child in the laird's seat, Annys was certain he would be furious. Yet he just studied her and Harcourt as if he was looking for something.

She carefully sat in the chair facing the table he sat behind. Harcourt sat next to her and she could feel the tension in him. Then she decided to just tell the truth. David would have told Nigel himself if he had been able to. Annys was certain of that. So, she could do no less.

"David claimed Benet as his son before all," she said. "The Church and the court consider him David's son because of that claim and the fact that he was born while David and I were husband and wife. Everyone here at Glencullaich accepts him as David's son."

"But he isnae."

"Nay, not by blood. David could nay sire his own child but ye kenned that."

Nigel looked at Harcourt. "How did my brother get ye to agree to give him a child? Your child?"

"I owed David my life," Harcourt replied. "He also told me what would be the fate of the people here if he didnae have one, people who had been naught but good to me. And, I dinnae think I tell ye anything ye havenae already guessed when I say I found it easy enough because I already coveted his wife." He almost smiled at the deep blush that covered Annys's soft cheeks.

"But then ye left both behind, the wife and the bairn."

"I did. T'was what was agreed to. A mon's honor demands he keeps a promise made. And that is what I told myself, repeatedly, for five long years. That, and that it was the right thing to do, the best thing to do, for all concerned."

Nigel sighed and rubbed the back of his neck. "David could be both cunning and convincing, nay doubt about it. And, aye, an heir might have settled things if he had been dealing with a mon who wasnae half insane with greed and envy. And one who kenned full weel that David couldnae sire a child. It didnae work and, in the end, my brother still lost his life. I suspicion he didnae realize that it was Adam who had been the cause of his maiming for David wasnae a fool and would have kenned that his plan would ne'er work then."

Annys shook her head. "I think David suspected but then he couldnae recall if he had bedded that woman or nay. At times, I wondered if he thought it had been some punishment for his sins as he saw them."

"My parents' teachings," Nigel said, his tone making it very clear he disdained such teachings, "but mayhap David found an odd sense of peace in thinking that." He tapped a finger against a small ledger on the table in front of him. "It appears he also tried to bribe Adam and the other MacQueens to leave Glencullaich alone."

"Oh, ye found it!" Annys glanced at Harcourt. "I forgot that Biddy had stolen it that day I followed her to her meeting with Clyde." She looked at Nigel. "'Tis where David noted what little we could discover about you and a precise accounting of all he gave to the MacQueens."

"It will be useful in ending their aspirations," said Nigel. "David preferred to use bribery. I prefer to use threats. They let Adam do all the work but supplied coin and men to help him. Adam also had a wee ledger in which he noted who gave him what help and how much. I suspicion it was so he would ken how to divide up his gains when he won Glencullaich."

"Ye actually mean to confront them over all of this?"

"Only if they push me to do so. And that brings us back to the matter of David's heir."

Annys inwardly sighed. "Ye wish to keep him as *your* heir, too?"

Nigel nodded. "Until I have my own. I dinnae e'en have a choice of a bride yet so not even the promise of an heir. I did think to just step into David's place, fulfill the original betrothal agreement. A Church dispensation would settle any questions about its legality." He grinned at Harcourt who had growled softly. "Dinnae think that would be appreciated by one and all though."

"Nay," said Harcourt. "Have lived through that for five years. Dinnae feel inclined to do so again."

"Didnae think so." Nigel looked at Annys. "And I would prefer that any wife I take be one who hasnae already given her heart away to another." He nodded when she blushed. "So, here is what I have decided. For now I will keep Benet as my heir. To do anything else will mark him and ye, Annys, with a stain that isnae easily washed away. Benet doesnae need to live with me but he must remain David's child and my heir. There needs to be an unwavering acceptance of that by all concerned."

"Aye, there does." Harcourt could not hide all the disappointment he felt over still being unable to claim his child but he understood why he could not.

"When I have a son or, even better, when I have two, then it can change, at least amongst ourselves and those closest to us. Since Benet was born and bred whilst Annys was legally wed to him, and David openly claimed Benet as his son, by all the laws I can think of, Benet *is* the heir. This secrecy just saves us all a great deal of trouble and ugly talk. So, aye, Benet remains my heir to all who might speak of it outside of the family."

"But he doesnae have to stay here," said Harcourt.

"Nay, but he does need to stay with a mon who can train him to be a warrior and a laird."

"I think I can do that."

"As do I or I would ne'er let the child go. So, the goodly priest Kerr found for me is waiting in the great hall and—"

"Wait!" ordered Annys, jumping to her feet. "Am I hearing this correctly? Have the two of ye just decided my entire future for me? Without e'en asking one wee question before ye did?"

It pleased her to see the wary looks both men gave her. As she had listened to Nigel and realized that all that kept her and Harcourt from planning a future together was being pushed aside, her heart had filled with a joyous burst of hope. Then they had continued speaking, neatly sorting out what would happen next without once asking her opinion. Twice she had had a husband chosen for her. She had dutifully accepted Nigel as a future husband because her parents had chosen him. When that did not come about, she had accepted David, again with her parents' approval and because it was the best thing to do for all concerned. This time she would be properly asked and she *would* be offered more than a man who had no true feeling for her but would be a good husband.

Even as she prepared a speech to make that very clear to these two men, Harcourt leapt up, grabbed her by the arm, and dragged her over to the far corner of the room. She caught sight of a grinning Nigel putting his feet up on the table, picking up the small ledger Biddy had stolen, and beginning to look through it. Then she looked at Harcourt and struggled not to be swayed in her determination by how much she wanted him.

"This solves all of our problems, Annys. It sweeps away the verra thing that meant we couldnae be together, would have to part all over again," he said.

She sighed. He was right. It almost made her smile to realize how much she wanted to kick him for that.

They had both wrestled with the barriers keeping them apart and been repeatedly defeated by the tight restraints of duty. Now Nigel offered them an answer, yanking away the barrier her duty to David and Glencullaich had erected. It was rather foolish to balk now.

Yet, she wanted more now that she could actually choose. She wanted more than passion. She wanted love. It was rare in marriage but she was almost certain it was just within her reach. What she was not certain of was how to let Harcourt know without bluntly asking for what she needed, something that would expose her own weaknesses. Annys shied away from such boldness and was terrified of baring her heart to a man who had never actually said he loved her.

"No one asked me," she said, inwardly cursing her cowardice.

"Ah, nay, we didnae, did we." Keeping his back to Nigel, Harcourt pulled her into his arms and rested his chin on the top of her head. "Then I shall ask. Wed with me, Annys. Come home with me to Gormfeurach so we can begin the life I believe we have both wanted for five long years."

It was so tempting. The fact that he claimed to have wanted it for five years, just as she had, warmed her heart. It was not the words of love she needed or craved, but she wanted to believe that they held the promise of it. He had already told her once that she was his woman. Most women would think that more than enough. Perhaps she was being greedy, impractical, she thought.

"So? I have asked. Wed with me, Annys. Let us seal the bonds between us, ones formed all those years ago in our river bower. Seal them now so that no one can sunder us again."

"Aye," she heard herself say and silently cursed her own weakness.

Harcourt kissed her. He could sense a lingering uncertainty inside her but would deal with that later. Now he had the chance to tie her to him and he had no intention of letting that chance slip through his fingers. The sound of Nigel clearing his throat broke into his thoughts and Harcourt ended the kiss. He took Annys by the hand and went back to where Nigel sat.

"Then let us be about it," Harcourt said.

Nigel stood up. "Just remember that Benet remains, in the eyes of the world, David's son and my heir. I will think hard on it if, at some time, I nay longer care if the truth slips out, but for now I want it held secret. Ye can still be a father to him," he said to Harcourt as he started toward the door. "He can e'en call ye *Father* if he chooses. Since ye will be wed to his mother no one will care."

"And ye dinnae think anyone will be suspicious since ye will nay be raising the boy yourself."

"Nay, he is verra young and most would believe that he should be with his mother. I suspect none will find any reason to think ye a poor choice to raise my heir, either. Mayhap, if I have my own heir and enough time passes that people no longer think on David or the child he claimed, ye can be more open since ye dinnae live here. Mayhap when my own grief o'er David's death eases, I willnae be so deeply concerned o'er keeping that particular secret. I cannae say."

"I understand."

The moment they stepped into the great hall, Joan took over. She insisted Annys needed to ready herself and, ignoring Nigel and Harcourt, hurried Annys up to her bedchamber. One look at the gown spread out on the bed told her that Joan had not done this in order to talk her out of marrying Harcourt.

"Are ye being forced into this marriage?" asked Joan.

"Nay."

"It just seemed that Nigel and Sir Harcourt's mon Callum were busy deciding it all for ye. I kenned Nigel saw just whose laddie our Benet was and when the priest toddled into the hall, I kenned what was happening. Aye, and Callum assured me that Harcourt wanted this as did his other men. 'Tis why they so readily helped Nigel."

"They did?"

"Oh, aye, quite firmly. I thought it was what ye wanted, too."

"It is. Yet, he speaks of beginning a life we have both wanted for five years, and there have been a lot of sweet words born of need, but he has ne'er said that he loves me."

"Ah, I see."

When Joan said no more, just started to undress her, Annys demanded, "Ah what? What do ye see?"

"That he is being an idiot mon and ye are allowing it to trouble you."

"And I shouldnae worry that the mon I am about to marry doesnae love me?"

"Ye wed David and he didnae love ye, nay then and certainly nay as ye mean. Nor did Nigel and ye

were going to marry him first. This man is at least
nay bound by contract to wed ye for some dower
purse or land."

That was true, she thought as Joan fixed her hair.
She had nothing. Harcourt gained nothing by marrying her, neither land nor coin. Annys doubted
Nigel would argue if she chose a few cherished things
to take with her, but she would be going to Harcourt
with only her clothing, towing a child who possessed
only a lamb, and bringing a cat. She smiled.

"Is that smile because your mind wandered off to
something funny or because ye have ceased fretting
and will now go down and wed the mon ye want?"
asked Joan.

"A little of both," Annys replied. "But, ye are right.
There is no contract forcing Harcourt to the altar.
There is no gain in this for him. Only me and Benet."
She grinned. "And Roberta and Roban."

Joan laughed. "Och, aye. I wager he hasnae thought
much on that yet." She suddenly grew serious and
stood up straight. "And me and my two lads."

"Joan?" Annys was speechless for a moment, only
able to croak out her friend's name.

"That is, if ye will have me."

"Of course, I will, but this is your home."

"Nay, this was my husband's home. He and all his
kin are gone now. Aye, I love it here but I suspicion
I can love it at Gormfeurach. My lads will miss
Dunnie but they have stables at Gormfeurach."

"Ye have already talked to some of Harcourt's
men, havenae ye."

"Aye, because as badly as I wish ye to stay with me,
I need to be what I was here or near to. I cannae step
down, if ye ken my meaning. Weel, Sir Gybbon said I

would be as they dinnae yet have any woman with my skills. Seems it was a rough place with a bad laird ere Sir Harcourt stepped in. Always work in the stables, too. Dunnie will miss the lads but he says there are a lot of others who will run to take their places as his helpers. So, I will go with ye."

"Listening to all ye just said, I begin to think I do have a dower. 'Tis you." Annys laughed and hugged her friend. "Then, welcome. I hope ye dinnae regret your decision." She frowned. "That may leave Nigel lacking a woman to run his keep, however."

"Nay, there are several women capable of stepping into my place. I gave him their names and he will choose the one who fits him best. I will wager a part of him welcomes this clearing out of some of the old, of David's time as laird."

"Ye have been busy. And, aye, mayhap he will find he appreciates making this wholly his keep now."

"There. Ye look bonnie enough." Joan hooked her arm through Annys's. "Let us go and get ye wed to that fine mon."

Harcourt pinned on his finest silver brooch, liking the way it shone against his plaid. It had been a gift from his whole family to celebrate his knighthood. He was nervous and he did not know why. This was what he wanted, what he had wanted for a very long time. Nothing he had done in the years since riding away from Annys had pushed her from his mind and, he now admitted, from his heart. He was happy, eager even, and yet that nervousness lurked beneath all those other feelings.

"Now why are ye frowning?" asked Gybbon, handing Harcourt a tankard of cider.

"Just realized I am, weel, nervous. Cannae understand why. This is what I want."

"Ye are about to tie yourself to one lass for the rest of your days. Ye would be an idiot if ye were nay at least a wee bit nervous. And, considering the family we come from, the bond ye are about to make will indeed be tight for all the rest of your days. 'Tis nay a small step for any mon to take, even one who badly wants to take it."

Harcourt nodded and started for the door. Gybbon was right. It was a natural, understandable feeling concerning the step he was about to take. Unlike anything else he had done in his life, this was forever. This woman would be at his side until the day he breathed his last.

He stepped into the great hall, took one look at Annys, her blood-red hair hanging free, falling in thick waves to her slender hips and looking glorious against her dark blue gown, and immediately lost any hint of nervousness. This was the woman he wanted. He might not have her love yet, although he suspected he did, but he had her passion. Without hesitation he walked up to her, took her by the hand, and faced the priest.

Annys sipped her wine and looked yet again at the marriage band on the finger of her left hand. She wondered where Harcourt had gotten it. Nigel now had the one David had given her, a family heirloom, and would save it for the day he found a wife.

She swallowed a sigh, not wishing Harcourt to hear it and question her about it.

Married again. This time she could look forward to a passionate marriage bed. That was good. What she still did not know was whether or not she had love to go with it. It is something to work for, she told herself firmly. Many married couples found it later in their marriage.

Harcourt took her by the hand and gently tugged her to her feet as he stood up and thanked everyone for being there and witnessing their marriage. Annys struggled not to blush as he led her out of the hall to a chorus of ribald remarks, but knew she failed. She was concentrating so hard on keeping her blushes to a minimum that she was startled when they confronted Benet outside the doors to the great hall.

"Are ye my father now?" Benet asked Harcourt.

"Aye," said Harcourt and Annys could hear the emotion behind the word, that need to say so to everyone, to let the truth be known.

"We will be leaving here now, aye?" Benet's voice trembled a little as he spoke and Annys had to fight the urge to hug him.

"Aye, lad. I will be taking ye and your mother to my keep. Joan and her two sons will be coming along with us."

Benet visibly cheered up at that news. "I best go say fareweel to people and get Roberta's and Roban's things all packed." He ran off.

Harcourt looked at Annys. "Those animals have enough things that they need to be packed?" He grinned when she laughed, picked her up in his arms, and ran up the stairs.

Annys got a brief glimpse of flowers set in pots all

around her room before Harcourt kicked the door shut behind them. He set her on her feet and kissed her. Her passion roared to life, the sudden ferocity of it fed by the fact that the battle with Adam had interrupted their time together and the knowledge that this man was now all hers.

Harcourt skillfully removed her gown as he kept her drugged with kisses. When she wore only her shift, he carried her to the bed, smiling faintly at the rose petals sprinkled over the clean linen. The way she watched him as he shed his clothes fired his blood until he feared he would begin panting like a dog on a hot summer day. There was a glint of possessiveness in that look and he welcomed it. For the first time in his life he liked the fact that a woman saw him as *hers*.

Joining her in bed, he kissed her again as he tugged off her shift. When they were finally skin to skin, he groaned with pleasure. The way she trembled faintly at the same time delighted him. The passion they shared was fierce and he wanted that to lead to a love that was just as fierce.

Annys stroked the smooth, warm skin on his broad back. As he kissed his way to her breasts, she noticed that something was different. The desire she felt for him had always been hot but now she realized that there were no tethers on it. Deep inside, where she had been able to ignore it, had lingered a shame over how much she had craved and enjoyed lovemaking with a man who had not been her husband. She had obviously not been disregarding the rules as completely as she had believed.

Desire stole her ability to think as he made love to her. He left no part of her untouched or untasted.

Annys was trembling with the need to feel him inside her. She clutched at his broad shoulders and tugged, urging him back into her arms. The way he made love to her with his mouth, his intimate kisses, made her ache, but she wanted them to find their releases as one, joined in body as they were now joined by vows.

"Harcourt," she cried, barely recognizing her own voice, which was thick and husky with desire, "I want ye with me."

He stroked her one last time with his tongue, intoxicated by the taste of her, before slowly kissing his way back up her body. The way her eyes were darkened by passion's heat only added to his need for her. He, too, wanted them to find their joy as one. It would be the perfect seal to their wedding night, to the vows they had just exchanged.

Annys cried out with pleasure as he thrust himself inside her. She slid her hands down his sides until she could clutch his taut backside as he moved. When her release came it shook her to her core. The way Harcourt's thrusts grew fierce told her he was close and then she felt the warmth of his seed spill inside her, telling her he was with her as she fell. That knowledge sent yet another wave of intense pleasure through her. A small, sane fragment of her desire-fogged mind heard him say something and clung to the words.

Harcourt had already cleaned them both off, settled at her side in bed, and pulled her close to his side before that desperately grasped memory spread through her mind. At first Annys doubted what her mind was telling her. She had not been clearheaded and her need to hear those words was so fierce she could easily have imagined it. She sighed. It was time to grow a backbone.

"Did ye say ye love me?" she asked, her heart beating so fast she was surprised he did not feel it.

"Aye. Wondered if ye had heard me." He kissed the top of her head and lightly stroked her back. "I can wait until ye feel the same. I think 'tis near. Ye just need a wee bit more time. I understand that. Matters have moved fast and there was a lot that needed doing."

Annys propped herself up on one elbow and stared at him. "I think Joan is right. Men can be idiots." She bit back a smile when he looked both confused and a little insulted. "Do ye truly believe I would yet again marry a mon I didnae love?" The glint of hope in his eyes made her brave. "I think I loved ye five years ago. 'Tis why it hurt so badly when ye rode away without a word, without a backward glance."

He pulled her into his arms. "That was the hardest thing I have e'er done but ye were married."

"I ken it and I finally let that heal the wound. Ye had no choice. I had no choice."

"So, ye love me."

"Aye, fool."

He laughed. "Aye, I think I might be. Then again, men dinnae often think marriage or passion need love."

"I ken it. 'Tis why I didnae dare hope that it was what inspired you."

"I think there is a lesson here."

"Aye? What would that be?" She began to stroke his belly, smiling to herself when she felt him harden against her leg.

"The lesson here is that we must nay just think we

ken what the other feels or thinks. We must say it. Just say it."

"A verra good plan, Sir Harcourt." She lifted her head from his chest and kissed him. "I love you."

"And I love you, m'lady."

"I am actually thinking something now if ye care to hear it."

"What would that be?"

She slid her hand down his belly and clasped him in her hand. "I am thinking 'tis my wedding night and ye are nay paying the proper homage to your new wife."

He laughed and rolled until she was beneath him. "I will pay ye homage until ye scream my name, m'lady."

"We shall see, my boastful knight."

She did. Annys just prayed everyone at Glencullaich was asleep or she would never hear the end of it.

Harcourt looked at the woman asleep in his arms and sighed. He should tell her about his concerns after all that fine talk about just speaking up. Yet, it had just been a small worry. It had begun to grow as they spoke of love though. Gormfeurach was no Glencullaich. It was a warrior's home with good defenses but little else. He could not help but wonder what she was going to think about her new home. He did not fear one look at the place would kill her love, but he did dread the fact that she could be sorely disappointed in the home he was offering her.

# Chapter Twenty-One

Annys stared at the keep as their cart rolled through the gates of Gormfeurach. It was big, but much the same as the one at Glencullaich and she found some comfort in that. There was none of the softness of Glencullaich, however. The place was certainly defensible but it did not appear all that livable. She and Joan would have their work cut out for them.

As Harcourt helped her and Joan out of the cart, Benet and Joan's two sons scrambled down and cautiously looked around. Benet tugged Roberta down and Roban quickly leapt onto the lamb's back. Annys tried to ignore the interested and amused looks the pair drew. Her attention was fixed on the couple that had just stepped out of the keep and waited for them on the steps.

The man bore a strong resemblance to Harcourt with his black hair and strong features but, as Harcourt led her closer to the couple, she could see that the man's eyes were a deep, rich green. The woman was pretty but her one truly memorable feature was her eyes as they were an odd mixture of gray and blue. Annys tried not to be nervous as Harcourt introduced her to his brother Sir Brett Murray and his wife, Lady Triona. To her surprise, Harcourt introduced Joan to them as well, immediately placing Joan in a position of importance in this new household.

"Oh! My dear friend is also called Joan," said Lady Triona. "'Tis a good thing ye are at different keeps or we should have to add some silly second name like Tall Joan or Old Joan, or Round Joan, which my friend now is for she is carrying another child."

"Just as long as I dinnae end up being *Old* Joan," said Joan and laughed along with Triona and Annys. "Sir Harcourt said I would be the one to run the household for her ladyship," she added, standing straighter, her pride clear to hear in her voice.

"Oh, and ye are sorely needed. Come, let us leave the men to their talk and I will show ye around your new domain."

Harcourt sighed with relief when Triona, Joan, and Annys disappeared into the keep. He had not feared that Triona would not sweetly welcome any wife he brought back but knew Annys worried. She had, in many ways, lived a cloistered life, and meeting new people, especially ones whose good opinion she craved, made her very nervous. He then looked at Brett and sighed again for his brother was staring hard at Benet.

"There is a cat sitting on that lamb," Brett said.

"Lamb is called Roberta, who is not for the pot, and the cat is called Roban," Harcourt said. "It seems the cursed cat really likes to ride around on that lamb." He waited patiently for Brett to stop laughing.

"And, aye, Benet is just who ye think but to the world he is the only son and heir of Sir David MacQueen of Glencullaich and now the heir to David's brother Sir Nigel."

"And why should your blood be claimed by another mon?"

"Because David saved my life. I had been attacked and was close to dying. Couldnae move, couldnae e'en do anything to stop myself from bleeding. David found me and took me in. He didnae ken who I was and I was in no state to tell him until later. I had been robbed so there was no sign of what place I held in this world. I was also just tossed on the side of a drover's path. It took a verra long time and lots of work to get me back to my fine, handsome self.

"Naturally I wanted to repay him. He said I could give him a child and told me something we thought no one outside of Glencullaich kenned—he had been gelded by a jealous husband. He could have no children. Couldnae really bed his wife, although I think that problem came from more than the gelding. He asked me to bed his wife until she was with child. He had seen how I looked at her and, though it sounds vain, how she looked at me. The reasons he gave me, the mon who sought to take hold of Glencullaich being all David said he was, made me agree. I also thought it would nay matter to me. That I could ride away from it and ne'er think of it again."

"But ye couldnae."

"I did but heart and mind ne'er did. This may nay have to stand forever. Nigel is young and may find a wife, breed his own son. Then we dinnae need to be so secretive. He just wouldnae want David's name, weel, stained in any way. Right now I can act the father just as many men do when they marry a lass with a child." He cocked one brow at Brett who then nodded. "It will do and when the boy is old enough, I will explain it all to him."

"We will hold faith with your promise to David. After all, we owe the mon your life. 'Tis just a verra high price the mon asked for your life but I am nay sure I would have done differently."

"David loved the lad, treated him as if he truly was his own get. The lad could someday be a laird." Harcourt shrugged. At that time I certainly couldnae have offered a child a future like that. But, 'tis done and I will live with it. 'Tis comforting that I can now have the raising of him and he already calls me Papa."

"'Tis good." He glanced toward the keep. "Think they are done with whate'er it is they were doing?"

"Only one way to find out."

"There is ale in the great hall."

"Then we will wait for them there." He looked back at Benet and Joan's two boys. "We are going inside. If ye stay out here, be careful. If ye can find one of those MacFingals they would show ye around if ye like."

"We will be careful, Papa," said Benet, "and we have Roban to protect us."

Harcourt nodded and, as he and Brett walked into the great hall he had to explain why his son would think a cat that liked to ride around on a lamb would be protection. He had to pour Brett's ale for him because he was laughing so hard.

* * *

"Weel," said Annys as she, Joan, and Triona walked through the kitchens heading for the kitchen gardens, "'tis clean enough but verra bare, isnae it."

"Aye," agreed Triona. "'Tis a household of men. Be grateful for the cleanliness."

"'Tis untouched," said Joan as they stepped outside. "Ye dinnae need to take away anything or change anything. Just decide what ye want."

"Verra true," said Annys. "I can actually plan what I want and just do it without much rearrangement. Oh sweet Mary's cow," she muttered as she looked at what she supposed was supposed to be a garden.

"Aye." Triona nodded and scowled at the weed-choked area. "Men. Aye, I ken there are some women about but no one who appears to ken what chores need to be done. They clean and they cook and then they go home. Only a verra few stay here." She looked at Joan. "It wasnae safe for a lass under the last laird. I fear it will take time for the women to believe it is safe now."

"Nay that long," Joan said. "After all, there is a lady here now. The laird is wed and brought her home. I will get some of them to come here. Start with the ones who would verra much like to be away from home."

"Clever."

Joan looked at the garden and quickly grabbed Annys by the arm when she started to bend down. "Ye can tend it later. We both will. We will get my lads to help or find a few lassies from the village."

"Aye. It can wait. What hasnae been choked to death by now will last a few more days." Annys looked around. "I would wager there is nay a place with any flowers."

"I think there used to be. Over here," said Triona as she led them around the corner and to an area near the rear wall.

It took Annys a while to look through the growth that had been left to go wild to find traces of some order. "Aye, once there was a nice wee spot here. I will add reviving that to my list."

"This is nay what ye were expecting, is it?"

"Weel, nay, but it is solid and it is defensible. I have learned the importance of that just lately. And, as Joan has said, I start anew with little in my way."

"Just dinnae try to do it all at once."

"Wheesht, nay. I cannae." She slid her hand down and rubbed her belly. "I am fair sure that would be a verra bad idea." She grinned when both women cried out in delight. "Hush! I havenae told Harcourt yet."

"But ye are certain?" asked Joan.

"Aye. I had begun to wonder for I was late with my woman's time. Then, yesterday, when Harcourt offered to take me for a wee walk"—she ignored Joan's snort of laughter for they all knew what he had intended, and succeeded at, when he had suggested a walk—"we went by where all the horses were tethered and it was, weel, a wee bit ripe, and my stomach roiled so much, I grew so pale, and began to sweat, that Harcourt was quite worried. I assured him it was just being in the cart all day and then smelling so much *horse*. We went a wee bit further away and he gave me some cider from his drinking horn and I revived."

"And that is when ye kenned for certain?"

"Aye. Dinnae ye recall? I couldnae e'en bear to

be around a mon who had been in the stables or riding for a long time when I carried Benet."

Triona nodded. "There is always a smell that hits hard. I couldnae abide eggs with my Ella and it was mutton when I carried Geordan."

Joan nodded. "Eggs with me as weel and then leeks."

"Weel, I will let the knowledge settle in my own mind and heart for a wee bit and then tell Harcourt," said Annys as they all headed back to the kitchens.

"He will be happy," said Triona.

"Aye, I ken it. Especially because he can at least claim this one openly." The look on Triona's face told her that Harcourt had not told his family everything and so, carefully she explained.

"Weel, that was an odd price to ask of a mon," Triona said after a moment, "but at least he didnae pick someone ye didnae like." She winked at Annys.

"Ye took that verra weel."

"Your husband couldnae be a husband to ye and he kenned it. He couldnae give ye a child or e'en get his heir if he wanted to and he kenned that, too. Aye, I am a wee bit surprised a Murray agreed to such a thing but Harcourt was young. Still, ye got a bairn and I suspicion ye are verra glad of that and that the making of that bairn was nay a chore. Also, it didnae hurt your husband to have ye do it so no hurt feelings. Save mayhap yours when Harcourt left."

"Aye, I was hurt and that was stupid." As they stepped inside the kitchens, Annys looked around again. "This place definitely needs a staff. And, I think that needs seeing to immediately."

"Then we must go to the village as these cold meats and bread willnae do for a hearty meal. Ye will now meet some of your people, Lady Annys," Triona said as she led them out of the keep, slipping around the great hall where they could hear the men talking.


Harcourt sniffed. "Is that a roast I smell?"

Brett did the same. "Aye. There wasnae anything but cold meat and bread in the kitchens when I looked earlier."

Callum, Gybbon, Tamhas, Nicolas, and the Mac-Fingals wandered in and Ned said, "Suspect the ladies from the village are cooking up some of those supplies they brought with them."

Harcourt looked toward the kitchens but the heavy doors were shut. "I have ladies cooking in the kitchens?"

Brett poured himself another ale. "The ladies must have had a good look at how bare your larder was and went to do something about it."

"Oh. That is one of those things I should have seen to, had ready before I brought Annys here, isnae it." He dragged a hand through his hair, silently cursing how quickly she had seen the poor state of the keep.

"Dinnae look so morose," said Callum. "We will eat a fine meal soon."

"I ken it and I do look forward to that but I was concerned about what she would find here. 'Tis why I sent word for it to be cleaned. I kenned this would nay be what she was accustomed to. I think it may have been worse than I kenned." He sat up straight as he suddenly recalled what the garden looked like, something he had glanced at once, decided it was too much trouble, and walked away from. "There isnae even a garden."

"Oh, there is one," said Annys as she and the other two women walked into the great hall. "'Tis just buried beneath weeds and there is e'en a little bonnie garden spot but it will need work as weel."

Joan looked toward the kitchen and straightened her shoulders. "I will go see that I am kenned by the lassies in there and be certain all we asked for arrived and is as good as promised."

"That woman is going to be a pure gift," said Callum.

"Aye," agreed Harcourt and started in surprise when Joan's two boys came scurrying out with cheese and bread plus the plates for it. "Thank ye, lads," he said.

"I will get ye more ale, aye?" asked the taller one.

"Aye and cider, if ye will."

"My mother will ken what is needed," said the small one and then they both trotted back to the kitchens.

Before long, food was brought out, and the other men from the garrison began to slip in and fill the other tables. Harcourt watched in astonishment as his hall became something close to what the great hall at Glencullaich had been. Good food, servants keeping the platters and jugs filled, and the men all talking, made content by that food. Even a few of the young maids had cautiously come out of the kitchens to help serve the food.

"They havenae done that since I have been here," he said. "Some men did it for a wee while and then the women from the village would come with food, bake a few things, and leave before the sun set."

Annys nodded as she helped herself to a warm

chunk of bread and slathered it with honey. "Joan did a lot of talking when we were in the village, which is a verra pleasant place, although it could use some trees and flowers. She told everyone who would pause long enough to listen that there is now a lady in the keep and that she has come to put the house in order." She shrugged. "It seemed to help."

"Just make certain the garrison understands that the lassies are here to work and all flirting has to be consensual," said Triona from her seat next to Brett, "and the fear that Sir John and his men put in them will fade away."

Harcourt nodded and turned his attention to his meal. He kept glancing at Annys as she spoke with Triona about work that needed doing. He saw no disgust or disappointment, not a hint of anger, but he grew more and more uneasy. She was well trained in hiding such things before company so he could not put his faith in her apparent calm.

By the time the meal was done, he was ready to talk to her about the state of the home he had brought her to. He had even composed his apology for the sad state of it. Unfortunately, Triona and Brett took their leave and Annys was caught up in that. Then Joan called for her and she ran off to see what the woman needed. He sat down on the steps to the keep and watched the dust fade from his brother's leave-taking. A moment later Gybbon sat down next to him.

"That was the best meal I have ever eaten here," Gybbon said, rubbing his belly in appreciation.

"I ken it. The great hall actually looked like one should for a wee while."

"And every man in the garrison is madly in love

with your wee wife as weel as Joan." Gybbon watched Harcourt for a moment. "Strangely, this does nay seem to please you."

"I have brought her to a keep that will bring her naught but hard work."

"Ah."

Harcourt looked at his brother. "Ah? That is all ye have to say? Ah?"

"Weel, wasnae sure I ought to call my older brother an idiot."

"Ye were at Glencullaich. Ye saw what a fine place that is." Harcourt waved his hands around to indicate the stark keep and bailey of Gormfeurach. "Look at this."

"A good sturdy place. A lot cleaner than it was with all the cracks and crumbling parts cleared up and strong again. What has nay been done is what women do. Aye, if we had thought about it we could have done it, but, right or wrong, we dinnae think about it. Have ne'er been trained to, have we? We saw clean and safe. 'Tis the women who make it comfortable, mayhap even pretty or whate'er ye wish to call it. Ye have brought her to a good home. It just needs a touch of softness. And, if that meal tonight is any in-dication, it also needed a woman here to get the maids back."

Harcourt nodded, agreeing with everything his brother said but not feeling all that much better about what he had brought Annys to. He was not such an idiot as to think she would fall out of love with him just because his home for her did not match what she had left. What he was terrified to see, however, was her disappointment. Stiffening his backbone, he stood up and went looking for her.

* * *

Annys was just about to explain to a young kitchen maid how she needed to keep a close watch on the supplies when Harcourt strode into the kitchen. He hesitated when all the women gathered there gaped at him but then took her by the arm and gently led her out of the kitchens. Harcourt said nothing until he had led her all the way up onto the walls surrounding the keep.

She looked out at the land surrounding the keep and smiled. The land was not as good as the land at Glencullaich but it had its charm. There were enough fields and grazing lands to supply them all and that was all that mattered. And there was water, she thought, looking at the winding burn that wriggled over the land and curved around one side of the keep.

"I am sorry this keep is in such poor repair," Harcourt said. "I should have warned you."

She frowned and looked around. "It isnae in poor repair. 'Tis just, weel, bare. Stark."

He frowned at her. "But that is what is nay right here, what I should have warned ye about."

Annys shrugged and rested her forearms on the wall. "I couldnae see what was needed until I got here, could I. Ye have linens enough for the beds. The kitchen has all the tools it needs." She grinned. "And now it has cooks."

"And that is just because ye are here."

She began to get a sense of what troubled him. The man was clearly thinking of Glencullaich and seeing the home he offered her as so much less. At the moment, she supposed it was, but that was fixable. It was actually work she looked forward to doing because it meant this place would have only her touch showing here. At Glencullaich she had been able to add just a few things to make it more hers and that had mostly been in her bedchamber. This place just waited patiently for her touch and only her touch. She was not sure he would understand how that actually pleased her.

"Aye, having a lady wife at the keep eased a lot of fears, but ye didnae put the fears there. And kenning that Joan will be the one ruling the household also helped. They could see she was a strong woman who kens what she is about and will stand for them. Now ye can truly shake off the last taint of Sir John."

"It doesnae change that much. 'Tis still a verra stark place."

She moved closer and hugged him. "It willnae be for long. I have plans." She was pleased to hear him chuckle.

"So, ye are nay disappointed?"

"Was that what ye feared? Nay. I am nay disappointed. In truth, I shall enjoy making this all mine. There are no other woman's touches here. I just pray ye can endure my attempts to put my touch all over this place."

Harcourt put a hand under her chin, tilted her face up to his, and kissed her. "I believe I can endure. And, aye, I was afraid ye were severely disappointed. I couldnae abide the thought of disappointing you, of seeing that look in your eyes. Truth is, I began fretting on it from just before we left. I kept looking around Glencullaich and then recalling what Gormfeurach looked like and would wince. I did send word to make sure it was cleaned but there was a lot I realized I hadnae thought of when we got here. Like a meal."

"We had a good one. Ye did have a good cook ready to work but she wasnae sure if any of the old men were still here and none had the courage to come and actually see that things had changed."

"Weel, it was a fine enough meal that I have been told every man in my garrison now loves ye and Joan." He smiled when she laughed. "Are ye certain, Annys? Ye can abide this place?"

"Aye. I can abide this place. After all, 'tis where ye are, aye? And where ye are is where I wish to be."

"Is that so? Weel, right now I am thinking I wish to be in my bedchamber."

"We will go there soon. I need to tell ye something."

"Is it bad news?"

"I dinnae think so." She took a deep breath and blurted out, "I am fair sure I am with child."

"Truly?"

"Remember how I got sick in the woods?" He nodded and he stroked her cheek. "It was the strong scent of the horses. That bothered me when I was carrying Benet as weel."

Harcourt held her close and struggled to control the wild pleasure running through him. Another child, one he could openly claim as his own. One he could watch grow in her belly, be with her when the bairn was born, and help raise into a good man or woman.

"Thank ye," he finally managed to say.

"I think I should thank ye," she said and eased out of his grasp. "So? Nay more concern about whether I like your home or nay?"

He gently kissed her cheek. "None. I think we'll do."

"Oh I think we will do verra fine indeed. Now, didnae ye say ye had a wish to be in your bedchamber?"

"Are ye sure we should?" he asked, gazing at her still-flat belly.

"Nothing ye can do in the bedchamber is going to shake this bairn out." She could see him start to frown as he considered her assurances and began to reject them. "Weel, I shall go to your bedchamber and ye can join me there as ye will." She started to walk away. "Of course it will be verra hard for me to carry out my plans if ye are nay there."

"Ye had plans for me?" Harcourt was torn between interest in those plans and concern for indulging in them with a woman carrying his child.

"Aye," she replied as she started down the wall. "I was thinking it might be verra nice to see how ye taste for a change."

Harcourt took just a minute to think that over. She was carrying his child and he should be gentle with her. Then a memory of his parents slipping off to their bedchamber with that look on their faces came to him. His mother had been with child. That he could recall clearly because, although he knew what went where, he had still been a virgin and he had wondered just how his father was going to manage it when his mother had such a huge belly. Obviously his own parents had never stopped just because his mother had gotten with child.

He hurried down the wall and ran up behind

Annys who was slowly, very slowly, making her way back to the keep. Harcourt grabbed her from behind and swung her up into his arms. She laughed, flung her arms around his neck, and kissed him. As he hurried her up to their bedchamber he smiled. She was right, they were going to do very fine indeed.